Praise for
THE PERFECT SCORE

"Buyea confidently mixes humor and heart."
—*Publishers Weekly*

"Readers will be drawn in by the lively voices and eventful lives of these likable and engaging students."
—*Kirkus Reviews*

"A heartfelt look at social interactions in middle school, a pointed commentary on standardized testing, and an entertaining read." —*Booklist*

"Readers will . . . enjoy watching the Recruits fight back against scholastic tyranny." —*The Bulletin*

"Kids will gobble it up because it is pure literary joy."
—*HuffPost*

Praise for the
MR. TERUPT books

Because of Mr. Terupt
"Compelling. . . . Readers will find much to ponder on the power of forgiveness." —*Booklist*

Mr. Terupt Falls Again
"The student voices are spot-on. Moving and real."
—*Kirkus Reviews*

Saving Mr. Terupt
"Warm, wise, and packed with hope."
—JOAN BAUER, Newbery Honor Winner

ALSO BY ROB BUYEA

The Perfect Secret

The **MR. TERUPT** Series

Because of Mr. Terupt

Mr. Terupt Falls Again

Saving Mr. Terupt

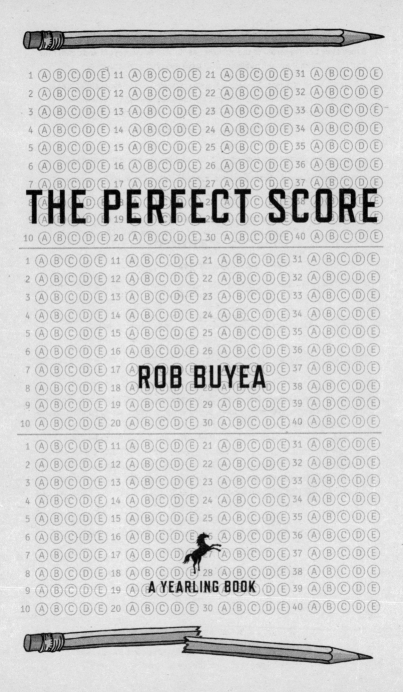

THE PERFECT SCORE

ROB BUYEA

A YEARLING BOOK

Text copyright © 2017 by Rob Buyea
Cover art copyright © 2017 by Will Staehle
Interior illustrations copyright © 2017 by Penguin Random House LLC

All rights reserved. Published in the United States by Yearling, an imprint of Random House Children's Books, a division of Penguin Random House LLC, New York. Originally published in hardcover in the United States by Delacorte Press, an imprint of Random House Children's Books, a division of Penguin Random House LLC, New York, in 2017.

Yearling and the jumping horse design are registered trademarks of Penguin Random House LLC.

"The Guy in the Glass" by Dale Wimbrow. Copyright © 1934 by Dale Wimbrow.

Visit us on the Web! rhcbooks.com

Educators and librarians, for a variety of teaching tools, visit us at RHTeachersLibrarians.com

The Library of Congress has cataloged the hardcover edition of this work as follows:
Names: Buyea, Rob, author.
Title: The perfect score / Rob Buyea.
Description: First edition. | New York : Delacorte Press, [2017] | Summary: Told from different viewpoints, five sixth-graders, facing various challenges and under pressure to do well on statewide assessment tests, agree to a plan for acing the tests.
Identifiers: LCCN 2017017571 | ISBN 978-1-101-93825-6 (hardcover) |
ISBN 978-1-101-93827-0 (library binding) | ISBN 978-1-101-93826-3 (ebook)
Subjects: | CYAC: Interpersonal relations—Fiction. | Middle schools—Fiction. |
Schools—Fiction. | Examinations—Fiction. | Cheating—Fiction. | BISAC:
JUVENILE FICTION / School & Education. | JUVENILE FICTION / Social Issues /
Friendship. | JUVENILE FICTION / Family / General
(see also headings under Social Issues).
Classification: LCC PZ7.B98316 Per 2017 | DDC [Fic]—dc23

ISBN 978-1-101-93828-7 (pbk.)

Interior illustrations created by Leslie Mechanic

Printed in the United States of America

10 9 8 7 6 5 4 3

First Yearling Edition 2018

For Mom and Dad

THE PLAYERS

GAVIN

Things need to get ugly before they can get better. It's that simple. It's a fact of life. Think of a good bruise you got from a football game. That bruise is a nice black-and-blue to start. Then it turns into a nasty green-and-yellow mix before finally getting better. Think of a leaky pipe in your ceiling. My old man would tell ya you've gotta cut a big, gaping hole up there in order to fix it. It's gonna be ugly before he can make it any better. And think of babies. A lot of people think babies are adorable, but I happen to disagree. When my little sister, Meggie, came home from the hospital, I took one look at her and said, "Wow, she's ugly." She was all round and pudgy like a snowman, with a floppy and misshapen head.

"*Niño!* Don't say that!" Mom scolded.

"Well, she is," I mumbled. Her dented head reminded me of someone who had just taken his football helmet off.

The good news is, after a while things straighten out and we don't look so bad—usually. That's not the case for everyone, though. There were definitely a few kids in school that hadn't happened for yet—and might never—like Trevor and Mark and definitely like Scott Mason. That boy was a mess. He mighta been one of the smartest kids in the whole darn school, but that didn't keep him from showing up every day with his shoes untied, his backpack half zipped, and scarecrow hair. He woulda looked better behind a face mask. Meggie, on the other hand, wasn't all that ugly anymore, but I didn't dare tell her that. Good looks aside, my little sister was still a royal pain in the you-know-what. Dad liked to say she was fortunate to have his good looks, but I think he meant Mom's.

My old man said lots of things, and I made sure most of them went in one ear and out the other. He didn't know what he was talking about half the time, but that truth about things needing to get ugly before getting better . . . I got that from him.

Except that bruise and leaky pipe and baby stuff is simple compared to the kind of ugly that went down this year.

Randi

I've been doing gymnastics since I was five. I've got a natural talent and body for it, but to be great, it takes more than that. It takes lots of hard work and commitment. So when I turned seven, Jane had me join the traveling team and I began practicing five days a week and it was fun.

By the time sixth grade rolled around, I was practicing six days a week. My sessions went for three hours—sometimes longer. Every so often I missed a Friday in school, because that's when Jane and I were putting on the miles to get to the next meet, but it was worth it. Jane was always reminding me that if I managed to win at some big competitions and kept getting all As, then I'd get a college scholarship.

This year Jane had me scheduled for a few smaller warm-up meets in preparation for my big run at the end of the season—first the state championships and then Regionals. The top gymnasts in the state qualify for Regionals. I made it last year but didn't do much at the meet. This year Jane's plan had me winning States and making noise at Regionals. I was already picking at my calluses. Jane kept telling me if I placed high at Regionals, then I'd put my name on the map. She said that needed to happen so college coaches would start paying attention to my results.

Of course, I also needed to make sure I kept doing what I was supposed to in school. Jane said school and grades came first, but she didn't seem to get nearly as worked up over my tests as she did my gymnastics. School was more like the thing I did in between my practices. That's just the way it was.

I used to love gymnastics.

BRIEF #1
Summer

I know the difference between right and wrong—always have. It amazes me how people can actually goof that up. I mean, it's not terribly complicated. When in doubt, stop and deliberate with your conscience. I do it all the time.

Natalie, should you do this?

I know that if I have to ask myself this question, chances are I shouldn't do it, because something is wrong. So you see, it's really very simple. That's why I plan to follow in my parents' footsteps and be a lawyer when I grow up. (This is also why I document everything.) I know the rules and I follow them. I like rules. It's also true that lawyers are generously compensated for their services, and naturally I want a job where I'll make money—I won't deny that—but not because I'm greedy and want to be rich and famous; that would be wrong. Rather, I hope to do something brave and important. What? I don't know yet. Ambitious, certainly.

Now, two things happen when one's always doing what one is supposed to in school. Being well-behaved and following the rules makes one perfect in the eyes of adults but repulsive in the eyes of one's peers. As a result, one develops the reputation of being a know-it-all. And you might assume that since I'm a know-it-all, I must also be the teacher's pet.

Objection! That's speculation.

However, in this case, you'd be correct. I am the teacher's pet—every year. I could let that upset me—kids saying those things about me—but that would be foolish. So what if I don't have any friends; I don't need them. My conscience keeps me company, and our conversations are far more important for my lawyer training than the meaningless gossip that would transpire with any immature kid my age. So what if everyone wants to call me a know-it-all? They can tell me how sorry they are when they come knocking, begging me to be their lawyer because they've done something wrong. Lucky for them, if that happens, I'll do what's right.

But, Natalie, not everything in life is so black-and-white.

Yes, I've heard that before. When it comes to right versus wrong, I don't believe it.

I should've listened more to my conscience. Things got blurry this year. It wasn't so easy to see clearly.

SCOTT

I might be messy, but I like to help, and I always mean well. It says that right on my old report cards.

Scott is a nice boy. He likes to help out,
and he always means well.

They also say I need to work on self-control, because sometimes I say and do things without thinking. And I need to work on completing my assignments, especially in writing, because I hate to write. I love math and reading—but I hate to write! I also need to improve my organization. (Mom swears I'd lose my head if it weren't attached.) But my report cards have said those things ever since kindergarten.

Something else I'm good at is coming up with ideas, but things don't always turn out the way I hope or plan—even though I try hard. That's been noted on my report cards, too.

Scott has no shortage of ideas,
but things don't always turn out as he envisions.

Those are the exact words Mrs. Hollerbeck wrote back in first grade after I caught a snake at recess and brought it inside so we could have a class pet. Lightning—that's what I named him—snuck out of my pocket, and I didn't know it until he slithered across Mrs. Hollerbeck's foot. Boy, did she holler then. I scrambled after my snake, but Lightning didn't want to cooperate. I chased him this way and that way, zig-zagging around desks. It took my fastest hustling, but I finally got him cornered and grabbed him.

By then a bunch of kids were standing on their chairs, screaming and yelling. Trevor and Mark, too, only they were hooting with laughter. And Hollerbeck was still hollering.

I didn't have to go see Principal Allen that time because there was so much noise coming from our classroom that he came and found me. We walked outside and released Lightning back into the wild before going to his office.

None of this changed in sixth grade. It only got worse. Way worse. I really made a mess of things this year.

Trevor

I couldn't wait for school to start—and I didn't like school. But I liked summer even less. I'd had enough of summer.

2

A LETTER ARRIVES
AND SCHOOL BEGINS

GAVIN

It was our last summer weekend before the start of school, and me and Randi were hanging out in my yard, throwing the football back and forth.

Randi'd been my best friend since we were little. No, we weren't boyfriend-girlfriend, even though my snot-nosed sister liked to say that. We happened to live near each other, out in the hills, where there weren't any other kids around, so we'd been playing together our whole lives. We mostly hung out at my place, 'cause I was always busy watching Meggie. Maybe some people found it weird that a boy and girl could be best friends, but we didn't. Randi's name wasn't very girly, and neither was she. She had a short haircut and was often mistaken for a boy 'cause of it, but that didn't bother her. No kids made fun of her, 'cause she was tough and she was nasty at football. She was even nastier at gymnastics.

Anyway, we were looking forward to sixth grade. It would be our first year at Lake View Middle School, and we'd both been assigned to Mr. Mitchell's class.

"Do you really think he'll be as awesome as everybody says?" Randi asked, passing me the pigskin.

"Are you kidding? He rewards his students with extra recess, and he plays football with them, too. He's gonna be way awesome!"

"Must be it's our destiny to have an unforgettable year," Randi said. She was a big believer in destiny.

"Whatever," I said. I was a believer in luck—all kinds, even though my family had never known the good sort.

I tossed her a spiral and then jogged out to the mailbox to grab the stuff our mailman had just delivered. There was never anything for me, but I always looked through the stack of envelopes. It was a good thing I did, 'cause this time something caught my attention. There was an envelope for Mom and Dad from school. I opened it.

"Read it," I told Randi, handing her the paper.

That was when me and Randi first learned that Mr. Mitchell wasn't gonna be our teacher anymore. According to that letter, Mr. Mitchell had had a family emergency and was moving away for personal reasons. In a scramble, the school had pulled Pearl Woods—an old lady!—out of retirement for a one-year stint teaching our class.

This wasn't destiny. It was rotten luck.

Randi

"I can't believe it—we've been Brett Favred!" Gav said after I finished reading the letter.

"What're you talking about?"

"Brett Favre? He was only one of the all-time greatest quarterbacks in the history of the NFL."

"Yeah, so?"

"Don't you know anything?" He looked at me like I had three heads. "Brett Favre retired after an amazing career, but he came back to play again. He sort of retired a second time, only to come back and play some more, before finally retiring for real. We've been Brett Favred!" Gav exclaimed again, grabbing the letter from me. "We've got some old-lady teacher who they've yanked out of retirement to play again."

Gavin's one of those boys who love sports. He's a football nut, so I was used to him talking like this. I felt bad, because he had really been looking forward to playing with Mr. Mitchell this year. Gav did all his football playing during recess and with me in his backyard. He never got to play on a team outside school. He told all the guys that was because his mom was worried about concussions, but really it was because his family wasn't in a good spot. His parents were always working because they needed the money, so Gav was forever stuck babysitting Meggie. His mom cleaned houses during the day and bartended at night—she'd been doing that ever since coming to the United States—and his dad was a plumber with as many evening calls as he had daytime ones. That's actually how his parents met. His father went to a house to fix a leaky toilet, and Carla happened to be there cleaning that bathroom. Imagine falling in love over a toilet! That's how it happened.

Call me crazy, but I wished my parents had a love story like that. The only thing they were good at was fighting. Really good at it. They'd only had me to try to save their marriage. I guess a lot of people make that mistake. Turns out I just gave them more to fight about—even before I was born. Dad wanted to name me Brandy, but Jane wasn't having that. She wanted to name me Destiny, claiming I had an important one, but Dad refused. Jane did her best to compromise by settling on Randi for my first name and Destiny for my middle name, but that's where their compromising ended. They finally called it quits when I was one. The story goes that when Dad split town, he told Jane she could have her Destiny, because we weren't part of his. I really wish he hadn't said that to her.

Gavin's father pulled into the driveway, just getting home from one of his jobs. "What's wrong?" he asked when he saw the way Gav was sulking.

"Mr. Mitchell isn't gonna be our teacher anymore," Gavin complained, handing the letter to his dad. "He had to move away for personal reasons, so now I've got some old lady named Pearl Woods."

"Pearl Woods?" his father repeated. "I didn't know she was still alive. She's one tough old bird."

"You know her?" Gavin said.

"Sure do. She'll straighten you out," his father said, taking the mail and laughing.

Come to find out, Mrs. Woods had taught Gavin's dad back in the day—before he quit school. He knew exactly what we were in for, but Gav and I had no idea. The only thing I knew was that I could kiss the handsome male teacher I'd been dreaming about all summer goodbye. Instead, I was destined to have a wrinkly old woman. Or maybe Gav was right. Maybe this wasn't destiny, just rotten luck.

NATALIE KURTSMAN
ASPIRING LAWYER
Kurtsman Law Offices

BRIEF #2
September: Firsts

The first day of school is of the utmost importance, much like the opening of a trial. In court you need to meet and feel out the judge, jury, defendant, and other legal counsel. Similarly, the first day of school is all about finding out who your classmates are and determining what kind of teacher you've inherited.

I made certain to arrive early on day one to ensure that I made my best first impression. (First impressions are hugely important; you only get one chance.) I wanted my new teacher to see right away that I was her most serious student, though I highly doubted she could ever miss that about me, because I dressed the part. Today I was wearing my new khaki skirt with my Converse sneakers. I had a white polo with a navy-blue short-sleeved cardigan on top, and my hair was pulled back in a tight braid. I looked good. Very professional. My peers, on the other hand, usually looked like slobs with no interest in learning. They knew nothing about proper attire, which was precisely why I was strongly in favor of school uniforms and had written an essay on the topic in fourth grade and again in fifth. If things don't change, I intended to pen an editorial for the town newspaper.

I stepped into my classroom, eager to meet my new teacher—I even had an apple for her—but she was nowhere to be found. Not what I was expecting, and not a good start. Disappointed, I placed the apple on her desk and turned around to inspect my surroundings. I had to suppress a smile when I noticed that our desks were lined up in rows and not arranged in groups of four. Finally, a teacher who wasn't going to make me help these immature, and often dim-witted, classmates of mine.

I found the desk with my name on it—first and last—and sat down. In addition to the name tags, Mrs. Woods had also distributed sharpened number-two pencils and sheets of loose-leaf paper. Stacks of textbooks rested next to the windows. The place smelled of work, so I was feeling hopeful, but that changed the instant my colleagues began spilling into the classroom and I learned who I was going to be stuck with for the year.

I'd been in class with many of these individuals at least once before. Unfortunately, I couldn't say I was particularly excited about any of them. There'd be no shortage of surprises and head-shaking moments with the likes of Scott Mason, Mark Kassler, and Trevor Joseph in my class—that I knew for certain—and Gavin Davids was the last, last person I wanted in my company. The feeling was mutual. Gavin wanted nothing to do with me. He actually hated me—hated me more than he loved his football—but I didn't care. I couldn't fault him for his shortcomings and poor judgment. After all, he was just a dumb jock.

Nevertheless, these concerns were quickly brushed aside, because next to arrive—finally—was Mrs. Woods. Suffice it to say that first impressions were not her strength.

She was old. Gray-hair-and-wrinkly old. Her skirt and blouse were from forever ago, and she had on knee-high compression stockings with Velcro shoes. Velcro! Her glasses were fastened to a chain around her neck. I suspected that was so she wouldn't misplace them.

Let the record show: I could tolerate some absentmindedness, but I did not have the time or the patience for any loonytune business. If Mrs. Woods was unable to keep these boys in line, then I would be going straight to the principal and demanding a transfer.

I simply had no idea how tricky and complicated things would wind up getting.

Trevor

Woodchuck was the name I came up with for Mrs. Woods. She was plump in the middle like one, dumb like one, and I was ready for her to crawl back in her hole.

"Sit up straight and pay attention." She rapped my desktop with the yardstick she was holding, and I jumped and banged the underside with my knees. I wanted to rap her one. "We've got a lot to do this year, Mr. Joseph. I don't have time to keep repeating myself."

If that old lady thought she could scare me, she was wrong. I'd seen a lot worse than she could dish out. But I still didn't like the way she was trying to intimidate me. That wasn't cool. She'd find out soon enough there was no way I was going to back down from her. I didn't back down from anybody.

"If we're going to become a supportive community, then we need to know a little something about each other," Woodchuck babbled. "Knowing your neighbor is important—" Blah blah blah. This sounded stupid already. "You'll be making collages that represent you," she continued. "I have a pile of magazines up here on the front table, along with some card stock. I'd like you to go through the magazines and cut out pictures and words that tell us about you. When you're done, we'll share our collages and I'll hang them up."

The only thing stupider than this activity was the magazines Woodchuck had for us to use. Where were the *Sports Illustrated*s and car magazines? There was nothing but woman stuff, like gardening, fashion, sewing, and cooking. I didn't have any choice, so I flipped through some of the pages, and that was when I discovered there's more than just makeup and beauty advertisements in those things. These pictures weren't exactly like the ones in the magazines my brother kept hidden under his bed, but they weren't bad. It was time to spice up this stupid activity and get even with Woodchuck. It was time to show her who was really in charge.

GAVIN

Let me tell you, the ugly started with Mrs. Woods. One look at my teacher and I knew she wasn't headed for the Pro Football Hall of Fame in Canton, Ohio, but for the graveyard over on Nelson Road. This was gonna be awful. I was already looking at the clock, wondering how long till the end of the day—till the end of sixth grade.

I didn't get much time to sit around feeling sorry for myself, though, 'cause as soon as morning announcements were over, Woods got started. Making the collage was okay, but I couldn't find any football pictures. I was struggling to find anything I wanted to cut out, and I wasn't the only one.

"She doesn't have any good magazines here," Mark complained.

"How am I supposed to make a collage out of this junk?" Trevor griped.

Well, let me just say, he figured it out. A few minutes later he suddenly got excited. That's when I knew he was up to something. Trevor kept his work hidden from us until it was time to share, so I didn't know exactly what was coming, but I knew it was trouble. When it was his turn, he stood up with a big grin on his face.

"This represents me because I'm a lady's man and these women could all be my wife someday," Trevor said, holding his poster up high so everyone could see it. He'd covered the entire thing with pictures of half-naked women! Pictures of women modeling bras and underwear!

"Ugh!" Natalie Kurtsman groaned. I coulda done without her being in my class, that was for sure. She was the worst. I hated that girl.

"Mr. Joseph, perhaps that poster represents you because you have big dreams," Woods said. "And that's good for a boy your age. You should have aspirations. The good news is, I'm here to make sure you work to achieve them. So you'll spend your recess writing an essay for me about your goals."

"What? Why? What did I do?" Trevor whined, acting like he didn't know.

"Way to go, moron," Mark whispered. "First day of school and you're missing recess."

"Mr. Kassler, I advise you to leave Mr. Joseph alone or else you'll be joining him," Woods warned.

That was the end of that. Trevor had tested Woods, and now he was paying the price. I was starting to see what my old man meant when he said she would straighten us out. This old lady wasn't fooling around. I came in thinking Woods was the has-been quarterback long past her prime, but she was still very much at the top of her game.

After Trevor's poster-of-babes presentation, I listened to Lenny, Rachel, Connor, and Corey give theirs, and then it was

Scott's turn. He was the last to finish his, 'cause he spent most of the time reading the magazines instead of cutting them, and he had more paste on his shirt than he did on his paper, but he got it done.

"I like cats and dogs," he told us, pointing to his wrinkled pictures. "I hope to get one someday, but my mom says life's too crazy right now. I also have the best grandpa, and we like playing chess." He pointed to a different spot on his collage. "And I love cookies and brownies and reading, but I hate writing." He showed off a pencil picture that had a big X drawn through it.

"Thank you, Mr. Mason," Woods said, taking his poster. "You might not believe me when I tell you this, but there'll come a day when you want to write because of something that's important to you."

"Not happening," he said.

Woods had me go next. I'd given up trying to find something in those magazines and decided to draw a couple pictures instead. I had a sketch of Meggie standing in her overalls, and I'd drawn a football.

"I have a little sister, and I like football," I said.

"Isn't there anything else you enjoy or you'd like to tell us, Mr. Davids?" Woods asked.

"No."

"Well, it certainly looks like you've got a talent for drawing," she said.

I shrugged. I sorta liked art, but I kept that to myself. Randi was the only one who knew that about me.

"Wish I could draw like that," Scott said. "Then I'd never have to write. Those pictures say more than all the sentences I could ever come up with. They're really good, Gavin."

I shrugged again. Scott Mason was a goofball. That kid woulda thought a stick figure was something great.

Woods took my collage and hung it with the others. Then her next move surprised me. She held up one last collage and said, "I thought you might like to know a bit about me, other than my being old. I enjoy reading and rocking chairs, paintings—especially those with flowers—and though I can't run anymore, I still like to watch a good game of football."

I sat up straight as an arrow when I heard Woods say that. Maybe there was hope? She hung her collage with the rest of ours, but then she ruined everything with her fairy-tale teacher talk.

"I want you to notice how our posters make a beautiful quilt when brought together," she said. "Each of us is unique and has interests and talents—as our collages show—and we can accomplish much on our own, but when we bring our individual strengths together, we have the potential to achieve something truly special."

This was the kinda nonsense I let go in one ear and out the other, like I did with my old man. Us coming together to do something special was never gonna happen. Tell you the truth, I was shocked that Woods even bothered pretending it could. An old lady like her shoulda known by now that the real world doesn't work that way.

NATALIE KURTSMAN
ASPIRING LAWYER
Kurtsman Law Offices

BRIEF #3
September: Mrs. Magenta

For many, recess was a highlight of the day. I could've done without it. The obnoxious boys played football in the field, while the non-athletes either goofed off on the playground equipment or stood in their groups talking. I tended to either visit with the adults on duty or stand by myself, silently conversing with my conscience. In my professional opinion, the entire recess concept is a waste of valuable teaching time.

Needless to say, I was delighted when recess finally ended and we got to return to the classroom. I was eager for the next thing on our agenda, which had us meeting Mrs. Magenta, the other teacher on our team, with whom we would be learning math and science this year. It was a favorable schedule, studying reading and writing in the mornings with Mrs. Woods and then exploring math and science in the afternoons with Mrs. Magenta.

"Ladies and gentlemen, clear off your desks and sit up straight," Mrs. Woods ordered. "Mrs. Magenta will be coming in to introduce herself and talk to you for a few minutes while I go across the hall to do the same with her students."

"Who's Mrs. Magenta?" Scott asked. He must've left his brain outside on the playground.

"I am," a sweet voice answered.

No offense, but Mrs. Magenta wasn't exactly great at first impressions, either. She had a mountain of curls stacked on top of her head and sported pink pointy glasses, a long breezy skirt, and bare feet. Bare feet! I had some eccentric free-spirit hippie for a teacher. I know it's not fair to judge people by their attire or before hearing their entire testimony, but this lady was not playing with a full deck.

Despite her alarming appearance, the conversation inside my brain was quickly quieted by what I observed next. Typically, when teachers see each other throughout the building, they are cordial and exchange pleasantries, especially if they happen to work on the same grade level. Mrs. Woods and Mrs. Magenta were anything but typical. They were about as warm and fuzzy as opposing lawyers arguing a case in court. They avoided making eye contact and never said a word to one another. I attributed this to their difference in age, Mrs. Magenta being a much younger woman, only in her second year of teaching, but I still had plenty to learn—about both of my teachers.

"Hello, young apprentices. I'm Mrs. Magenta, your math and science teacher."

"Young apprentices?" And people say I'm *weird. Puh-lease. This woman is nuts.*

"Do you have a collage to share with us so we can get to know more about you?" Scott asked. "We made collages this morning. They're over there. Mine's the one with the X through the pencil." He pointed. "Trevor's is the one—"

"Scott," I hissed, cutting him off. Honestly, the boy didn't know when to stop.

Mrs. Magenta stared at our posters longer than I expected. I wondered if it was Trevor's that she couldn't stop looking at or someone else's. "No, I'm afraid I don't have one, Scott, but I will make one to share with you tomorrow when you come to my classroom."

"How did you know my name?" Scott asked.

"It's on your desk, genius," Trevor remarked.

"Ha ha!" came the laughs from my classmates. Why did they have to egg him on by making him think everything he said was so funny when it wasn't? I was already sick and tired of him—and it was only the first day!

"We will be doing a variety of activities and projects this year as we explore the beauty of math and science," Mrs. Magenta explained, "so please come to class prepared to do some thinking and investigating."

"Math is boring," Trevor said.

"You can say that again," Mark added.

"It doesn't have to be," Mrs. Magenta remarked. "Not on my watch. You'll see. After this year your views will have changed.

"I'll see all of you tomorrow. Please remember to bring your notebooks and pencils. I'll have everything else you'll need. Toodle-oo."

I still had her listed as slightly nuts in my book, but Mrs. Magenta had me curious and looking forward to our first class.

SCOTT

Mrs. Woods knew something about saving the best for last, because she waited until the end of the day to dim the lights and sit on the front table. "Ladies and gentlemen, there's one thing I can promise you this year," she said. "You will get to enjoy a number of wonderful books. You're growing up in a fast-paced world driven by tests and more tests, and sadly, because of that, the magic of a read-aloud is being lost. But not in here. And not on my watch. We're going to settle in and get lost in stories together."

"What is this, preschool?" Trevor mumbled.

Mrs. Woods ignored his comment. "The first book I've decided to read is *Wonder*." She held it up for us to see. "It was written by R. J. Palacio." She held the book under her nose and smelled it. "When you love books and learn to appreciate the written word, you can smell the beauty of a good story." She took another big whiff. Tommy and Lenny thought she was crazy, but I was going to smell all my books when I got home.

I'd already read this one, but it was different when Mrs. Woods started reading it. For one thing, it mentions a farting nurse in the first few pages, but that didn't stop Mrs. Woods. She read that part and all that followed with the best read-aloud voice in the whole wide world. Her voice was so good I had to get closer, so I got out of my seat and went and sat on the floor by her feet. I settled in and got lost in that story just like she said I would. When we ran out of time, she closed the book and looked up.

"Don't stop," Gavin blurted out, just like I blurt out sometimes. He'd been lost in the story, too.

"I'll read more tomorrow, Mr. Davids." Mrs. Woods said this to Gavin, but her gaze was elsewhere. She was eyeing Trevor. "Mr. Joseph, I'll take whatever it is you and Mr. Kassler seem to find so funny back there."

"It's nothing," Trevor said.

"I'll take nothing, then. Please bring it up here."

Trevor scuffed his angry feet to the front and handed Mrs. Woods his paper. Then he went and sat back down, all the while huffing and puffing like the big bad wolf.

Mrs. Woods studied his paper and then walked over and stuck it on top of his collage. He'd drawn a horrible picture of her. It had her name on the top, and on the bottom he'd written the words "Farting Teacher."

"I'm glad you were listening to the story," Mrs. Woods said, "but you just bought yourself another day of no recess."

Trevor had lost two recesses in one day! I didn't even know you could do that. It's safe to say that after our first day of sixth grade I knew this for a fact: Mrs. Woods was tougher than Dolores Umbridge, that nasty teacher from Harry Potter.

Randi

I was supposed to give the note to Mrs. Woods as soon as I made it to my classroom this morning. That was the plan, but the first day of school is scary when you don't know all the rules and procedures—or your teacher. So I still had my note at the end of the day. I had to give it to Mrs. Woods before going home, though, because the thought of telling Jane I hadn't handed it in was even scarier.

I got my things packed, and then I took a deep breath to steady myself, same as I did before my gymnastics events, but instead of sprinting toward the vault this time, I eased over to my teacher's desk. I was hoping to slip the envelope in her basket and quietly leave, but Mrs. Woods noticed me before I was able to do that. The old woman didn't miss much. I'd learned that about her in just our first day. I'd learn a lot more about her before our year was up.

"May I help you, Miss Cunningham?" she asked.

"I was just dropping this in your basket," I said, showing her the envelope.

"I'll take it."

I didn't expect Mrs. Woods to open it right in front of me, but that's exactly what she did. I wanted to run, but I stood there picking at my calluses and staring at the floor.

"You'll be missing school next Thursday and Friday for a gymnastics competition," she said, raising her eyebrow. "And it's all the way in South Carolina?"

"Yes," I answered. *What did Jane write on that paper?* I wondered.

Mrs. Woods put the note down. "It must be a big meet to go that far—and to miss school for it."

I nodded. *That's what Jane says,* I thought. Originally, the plan had been to stick with only a few smaller competitions leading up to the state championships, but once Jane saw this South Carolina meet advertised, that all went out the window. Coach Andrea, my real coach, tried telling her this wasn't a must-do, but Jane wasn't the best listener, especially after she had her mind made up.

"Must be important, too," Mrs. Woods said, bending her neck so she could look me in the eye. "I'm surprised there was no mention of gymnastics in your collage. You must really love it."

I didn't say anything.

"Well, that's exciting," Mrs. Woods said. "Good luck to you, Miss Cunningham. You can tell your mother I'll have all the work you need ready for you to take."

I gave her my best weak smile, and then I left to catch my bus.

I didn't like talking about gymnastics, because if I didn't do well, then I'd have to explain that to everybody, and there was no way to explain it so people would understand. But Mrs. Woods was different. It seemed silly, but I felt like she was asking me questions she already knew the answers to, and she was only asking to see how I'd respond. But how in the world could my teacher understand anything about gymnastics or my feelings?

I wanted to ask Mrs. Woods if we could study rocks again this year, like we had in fifth grade. I liked learning about them. I like how they're formed, the result of years and years of extreme pressure. Sometimes I wished I could be one of those igneous types with the crystals. I'd like to have my own crystal ball so I could be a fortune-teller and see my future. I wanted to know my destiny, and not the one Jane had mapped out for me.

3

A SECOND DAY FOR
THE RECORD BOOKS

SCOTT

I made my way around Grandpa's towers of newspapers and junk mail, careful not to knock anything over, and found him where I always found him, sitting in his green recliner and staring out the window.

"Hi, Grandpa."

"Huh? What? What're you doing here?"

Mom and my little brother, Mickey, check in on Grandpa every morning after dropping me off at school, but I came along to get him early that day because he had a doctor's appointment.

"You've got a doctor's appointment, remember? Mom and Mickey are out in the car."

"Oh, jeez. The dumb doctor. That's right. Give me a minute."

"Okay," I said.

While Grandpa went to get ready, I crammed a bunch of his junk mail in my backpack. There was no way I'd ever get rid of all of it, but if I didn't keep taking as much as I could every time I came over, Grandpa was going to be buried alive. Once he had his shoes on, we walked outside. I slid in the backseat next to Mickey, and Grandpa got shotgun.

"Doctors," Grandpa grumbled, buckling his seat belt. "I swear they just make all these appointments so they can keep taking my money. There's nothing wrong with me."

"Dad, you don't go to the doctor only when you're sick," Mom reminded him, backing out of his driveway.

"Then what're we going for?"

"I told you yesterday. Today is a physical."

"A physical! What for?"

"So you don't get sick," I said. "Today is routine service, like you do to your car. We're keeping you in tip-top shape, Grandpa."

"Tip-top shape, all right. For what?"

"For Cheerios!" Mickey yelled. He lifted his plastic bag high in the air for everyone to see before shoveling another handful of cereal into his mouth.

"For Cheerios. Now, that's a good reason," Grandpa said, and chuckled.

I was glad we had Mickey, because even though I was good at blurting stuff out, I never knew what to say when Grandpa started talking like that. If I'd been the doctor seeing him that morning, my diagnosis would've been loneliness. Grandpa had been suffering from loneliness ever since Grandma died two years ago. He'd aged more since then than he had in all my life before that. I never used to think Grandpa was old, but he was old now. Mom said the best medicine was family, which was why she and Mickey checked in on Grandpa every morning and why they'd pick me up after school so we could all go back again.

With no other family around and my dad busy with his job, Mom is the one left to take care of Grandpa while also making sure we're okay. Luckily, Mom works from home, so she's able to do that. She takes on those extra responsibilities without complaint, but it's a lot. My mom is a superwoman, but she gets tired.

"I don't know if I'm coming or going anymore," she sometimes says.

I don't like to see Mom exhausted, so I do my best to stay out of trouble and help whenever I can. I'm good at helping.

We pulled up in the drop-off lane in front of Lake View Middle. I had to hurry so I wouldn't be late.

"Hey, there's my teacher," I said, spotting Mrs. Woods on her way into the building.

"Well, I guess you can't be late if she's just getting here," Mom said.

"That old woman is your teacher?" Grandpa asked, pointing.

"Yup."

"Yup, that's her," Mickey said. "Her is old."

"Old and mean," I mumbled.

"Give her a chance, Scott," Mom said. "And don't get on her bad side."

"Hit her with your charm and she'll warm up to you," Grandpa suggested.

"Stay out trouble and be good boy, Scott," Mickey said, repeating what he heard Mom tell me every morning.

"That's right. And don't do anything I wouldn't do," Grandpa added.

"Dad, I'm not sure that's great advice," Mom said.

"I'll tell you all about my day when I see you this afternoon, Grandpa," I said.

"I want to hear a good story, so you better make it a special day."

"I will," I promised.

I hopped out of the car and booked it into school.

NATALIE KURTSMAN
ASPIRING LAWYER
Kurtsman Law Offices

BRIEF #4
September: Rules and Expectations

Every good teacher knows that day one is when the ground-work is laid; rules and expectations need to be established from the beginning. Unfortunately, Mrs. Woods never got around to that yesterday. Apparently, she felt that attempting to build community was more important. To my amazement (and delight), she did manage to keep Trevor in check, but without something more formal and significant in place, I was doubtful she could keep it up. Trevor Joseph was sure to continue testing her, because he was a Class A jerk, as was his sidekick, Mark Kassler. Honestly, why did I have to get stuck with those two in my class? Needless to say, I was concerned. Very. If Mrs. Woods didn't put some concrete rules in place by the end of the day, I was resigned to going to Principal Allen.

*   *   *

As was the case yesterday, Mrs. Woods didn't arrive early, but the moment morning announcements ended, she began. Mrs. Woods may have moved slowly because of her age, but she did not waste time. From the back of the room she wheeled out an overhead projector. I didn't even know what it was until she told us.

"Whoa! Mrs. Woods, that thing might be older than you," Scott said. "You know we use computers now."

Clearly, summer had not rectified this boy's issue with blurting things out. There was plenty of giggling on the heels of his remark, but I did not participate.

"Actually, Mr. Mason, I've got a few years on this projector," Mrs. Woods responded, "but like me, you can count on this trusty piece of equipment to get the job done. Wish I could say the same about computers, but those things seem to work only half the time—not so different from today's youth. But don't you worry. We're going to fix that."

Was that a warning or a promise? Either way, her words put an end to the giggling. Mrs. Woods flipped a switch, and her trusty overhead came to life. "Who can tell me what this is?" she asked.

I read the words that were illuminated on the front board:

We the People of the United States,
in Order to form a more perfect Union,
establish Justice, insure domestic Tranquility,
provide for the common defence,
promote the general Welfare,
and secure the Blessings of Liberty to ourselves and our Posterity,

do ordain and establish this Constitution
for the United States of America.

I raised my hand.

"It's the Constitution," Scott yelled out.

"Ugh!" I groaned. I was ready to stuff a sock in that boy's mouth. I appreciated it when Mrs. Woods didn't bother with him but called on me—the person practicing classroom etiquette—instead. "Yes, Miss Kurtsman."

"More specifically, it's the Preamble to our United States Constitution," I answered.

"That is correct," Mrs. Woods said, "and it dates back to 1787. Now, that's old." She smiled at Scott but never said anything to him about needing to raise your hand before speaking. In my opinion, that was a mistake. If she didn't keep him in line, she would lose control. "The Preamble is over two hundred years old, and yet our country still operates by these principles," she continued. "And so will our classroom," she added. "Because sometimes old is the best."

"Sometimes old is stupid," Trevor wisecracked under his breath, but not under his breath enough.

"Indeed, there are days when I feel that getting old *is* stupid," Mrs. Woods remarked. "But being old does not make one stupid—or necessarily hard of hearing. I trust that's what you meant, Mr. Joseph."

Trevor glowered and turned pink under her glare. Despite her outdated clothes and knee-high stockings, Mrs. Woods was still quick on her feet. Maybe she hadn't said anything to Scott about raising his hand, but she'd put Trevor in his place—again. No stupid boy was going to get the best of her.

For her next move, Mrs. Woods took the dust-covered box she had sitting under the projector and plopped it on Scott's desk. "Mr. Mason, please pass these out."

Always excited to help, Scott jumped up from his desk and raced around the room, tossing paperback dictionaries with thesauruses to each of us. The books were torn and yellowed and looked older than the projector, but no one complained.

"The dictionary is another example of something that has been around for many years and is still reliable," Mrs. Woods remarked.

Trevor decided not to offer any wisecracks this time. Perhaps he wasn't quite as dumb as he looked.

"I want you to look up definitions and synonyms for the words I've highlighted in the Preamble so that we may begin to talk about what the fancy language truly means," Mrs. Woods explained. "I want to see you taking notes. Now get going."

I didn't need to consult the dictionary or thesaurus—I knew what these terms meant—but I did what my teacher asked. It didn't take me long. I was done before Scott Mason had anything written down.

After discussing the highlighted terms, we then created our very own Classroom Doctrine:

We the citizens of Classroom 613 do create
this official document in order to establish and maintain
a Safe and Hard-working Community,
where we will Listen and show Respect, use Common Sense,
and Think of Each Other before ourselves.

Without a doubt, this was the best and most interesting activity any teacher of mine had ever used for developing a set of classroom rules. It was simple yet perfect. All that stuff about taking turns and not running with scissors, yada yada, was summed up in our concise document. To make it official, Mrs. Woods had each of us sign the Classroom Doctrine. It wasn't until we were done adding our names that she mentioned the word "consequence."

"When rules are broken, there needs to be a consequence," Mrs. Woods said. "Unlike with our doctrine, there will be no discussion about consequences. If someone or something disrupts our community, then I will deal with it as I see fit. I am the judge and the jury in this classroom."

Mrs. Woods talked like a lawyer! I didn't need to wait any longer. I already had my verdict. Mrs. Woods wasn't only old; she was old-school. She was a no-nonsense lady who'd been around the block, and she was going to be an excellent teacher.

Trevor

As promised, Woodchuck kept me in from recess today. Her old brain didn't forget, like I was hoping. And she didn't let me sit there doing nothing, either. She handed me a piece of paper.

"What do you want to achieve? Who do you want to be? These are important questions for a young man to consider, Mr. Joseph. Think it over and then write a page about your goals."

My paper was still blank when she collected it from me at the end of recess.

"I don't have any goals," I said.

"Let's hope we can change that this year, Mr. Joseph."

She didn't say anything more. That was the first smart thing the dumb old woman had done.

SCOTT

Recess was my favorite part of the day. I never got invited to playdates outside of school, so this was my chance to have fun with other kids. The only person I knew who wasn't crazy about recess was Natalie Kurtsman, but that was probably because she never did anything but walk around by herself.

I spent my recess running all over the place. I wasn't allowed to play football, because I wasn't good at it like the other boys, but I was good at running, and I was a monkey on the playground equipment. Lucky for us, Lake View Middle used to be an elementary school, so we had an awesome playground left over from those early days. I loved swinging across the bars and rings and zinging down the zip line, but my favorite was still the twisty slide—even after what had happened.

A few years ago the teachers at my old school made a special rule that if you climbed the stairs to the twisty slide, then you had to go down it. There were no turn-arounds allowed. Trust me, it was a dumb rule.

There was a day last year when I raced to the top and flew down the slide without knowing there were puddles of water on its surface. Everyone laughed at my wet butt. They had fun pointing and calling me Wet-butt. They had more fun saying I'd peed my pants, even though they knew that wasn't true. I was glad everyone was happy and smiling—but I wasn't. Try spending the afternoon with wet underwear rubbing you raw and you'll know why. It was no fun, and it was all because of that dumb rule.

After that terrible mistake I made sure to inspect the slide first. But the only way to inspect it was from the top. A few times I climbed the stairs and discovered puddles and had no choice but to break that rule about no turn-arounds. I told everyone to stay off the slide whenever that happened, because I didn't want anyone else to end up with a wet butt. That was the worst—or so I thought. What happened today was one for the record books.

When I scurried to the top of the twisty slide this afternoon, I discovered something other than puddles of water on its surface. I found bird poop. White splotches were littered all over it, like the bird had aimed and dropped his bombs there on purpose. And it wasn't the white chalky kind that you could brush off, but fresh, wet bird poop. There was no way I was going down that slide, but I also couldn't leave it like that, because the unlucky kid who did go down would end up with white bird doo smeared on his behind. That was way worse than a wet butt. I had to do something, and I had to do it fast. So I did the only thing I could think of. I hid under the top part, where it's covered and no one could see me, and I peed down the slide to wash off the poop. I have good aim, so I hit all the white spots. The way I saw it, I was doing everyone a favor. My pee stream did the trick. It worked like magic. When I finished, I hurried back down the steps.

"No turn-arounds!" the recess aide yelled.

We had the same dumb rule at Lake View Middle. I didn't stop. I jumped from the stairs and joined the game of tag that had started.

We always played with two taggers and two safeties, which were the tire swing and the large oak at the other end of the playground. Our rule was that you had to stay in the wood-chip area that surrounded the playground campus.

I didn't like the game as much when I wasn't "it," because no one ever chased me. But then Tommy yelled out, "Scott's it!" For some reason, I was the only tagger when it was my turn. I chased kids everywhere, but I wasn't able to get any-one, and then I saw Natalie standing nearby. She was all by herself. I knew what that felt like, so I took off after her. I just wanted her to have some fun. I don't know if she ran from me because she was playing or because it was me, but I didn't expect her to run to the top of the twisty slide.

"Natalie, don't go down," I warned her.

"You're just trying to trick me, Scott Mason. Besides, the rule says if you go up the steps, you must slide down." She stuck her tongue out at me and then disappeared.

Poor Natalie was wearing an all-natural pee-fume after that. I felt bad for her. It would've been better if she'd broken the twisty-slide rule, but Natalie never broke the rules.

NATALIE KURTSMAN
ASPIRING LAWYER
Kurtsman Law Offices

BRIEF #5
September: The Twisty-Slide Aftermath

I knew it was urine I had gone through the moment I got off the slide, but I didn't freak out. That would've only drawn attention to the situation, and the last thing I wanted was for everyone to know that I was soaked in pee. I simply walked off the playground and went directly to the nurse. I explained everything to Nurse Wilcox, informing her about the game of tag and the urine that was trickling down the twisty slide—but I never mentioned Scott's name. I might be a know-it-all, but if there's one thing I'm not, it's a tattletale.

Scott knew there was pee on the slide, and I suspected it was his, but still, I couldn't ignore the fact that he had warned me not to go down it. Did he really mean for me not to go down, or was he egging me on? I imagined what his trial would look like.

From the Case of Scott Mason versus the State

DEFENDANT: SCOTT MASON
PLAINTIFF: THE STATE
The Jury: Natalie Kurtsman

EXCERPT FROM THE DEFENDANT'S TESTIMONY:

> I didn't mean for it to happen. . . . I warned her not to go down the slide. . . . Afterward I didn't run around telling everyone what happened. . . . I didn't want anyone to laugh and make fun of her. . . . I kept my mouth shut.

EXCERPT FROM THE PLAINTIFF'S ARGUMENT:

> Scott knew the condition of the slide, and he deliberately chased Natalie toward it. This was all part of his plan; he's not that stupid. He knew she'd go down the slide, because she never breaks the rules. He chose not to run around telling everyone about the incident so that he would have an alibi.

THE JURY'S DECISION:

> Was Scott truly innocent or guilty? In the court of law it doesn't matter; he was innocent because of reasonable doubt. For a person to be found guilty there must be rock-hard proof. Therefore, the jury had no choice but to find Scott not guilty—but let the record show: I knew he was the pee-er.

* * *

Nurse Wilcox gave me some clothes to change into, and I put my gross ones in a plastic bag to take home. Mother left the office and picked me up early. Once we got in the car, my hands started shaking. I bit my bottom lip to keep it from trembling, but that didn't stop the knot from forming in my throat. I was deeply upset. I'd put on a good face for Nurse Wilcox, but what had happened to me wasn't only disgusting, it was humiliating. Still, I never shed a tear. If there's one thing I'll never be, it's a crybaby. I'd be a tattletale before I was any sort of crybaby.

Mother leaned over and put her arm around me. "I'm sorry about what happened today, Natalie." She touched her head to mine and gave me a squeeze.

I pushed her away. "Can we get going?"

Mother didn't say anything. She started the car and pulled out of the school lot. We rode in silence, but my brain kept going over everything that had happened. I felt myself getting angrier and angrier until I could hold it in no longer. "Do you realize I'm missing an entire afternoon of school because of this? Everyone's going to find out why." I kicked my bag. "And when I return to school tomorrow, they'll all be whispering and calling me names behind my back."

Mother handed me her water bottle. "Try to calm down," she said. "Getting upset isn't going to do you any good."

"That's what kids do, you know."

"Yes, I know," she said. "And many of those same kids who are immature and mean and do that whispering-behind-backs stuff today will still be doing it when they're so-called adults. I know because they're the same ones getting in other kinds of trouble and then coming to your father and me for help. It isn't easy, Natalie, but you've got to be bigger than that."

I took a drink. "I know," I said, "but it's hard to always ignore it."

"If you think you want to be a lawyer, this is good preparation. People love to say mean things about lawyers."

"Why?"

"Oh, people pass judgment all the time when they don't know the whole story. It's unfortunate, but it's true."

"I still wish I could skip being a kid and just be a lawyer now. Being a lawyer seems easier than being a kid."

Mother sighed. "Not always," she said. "Not always." She pulled into her parking spot at the office and turned the car off.

"What's wrong?" Something I'd said had hit a sore spot.

"Not now, Natalie. It's been a long day for me, too. Some other time."

"Okay," I said, respecting Mother's wishes. I unfastened my seat belt.

"You know, you don't need to be perfect, Natalie, but make sure you're a good person. That's what's most important."

This time I was the one to lean over and wrap my arm around Mother—and she didn't push me away. She hugged me tight. "I'm still sorry about what happened to you today, honey."

"It's okay. I'll survive," I said. "I'm sorry I got upset with you."

"Apology accepted." She brushed the hair out of my face. "Now c'mon. Let's go inside and see what your father is up to."

Randi

I walked into Mrs. Magenta's classroom and sat at a table with Gavin, but not for long.

"Okay, you smart thinkers," Mrs. Magenta began, "I want you to stand up and sit with the people whose birthdays are closest to yours—and you need to figure that out without talking. Ready? Go."

We looked at each other with puzzled expressions, but then Scott got us started. He hopped out of his seat and held up six fingers. After that Lenny held out three and then Tommy stuck up two. Eventually we understood they were telling us their birthday months, and we got busy arranging ourselves. When I heard Mark laughing, I glanced over and saw how Trevor was using sign language—by giving everyone the middle finger! I was glad not to be a January birthday.

After we got settled, Mrs. Magenta asked, "Any idea why we did that?"

"Because it was fun!" Scott exclaimed.

"Fun for a weirdo," Trevor grumbled.

I was not liking him very much.

"I'm glad you enjoyed the activity," Mrs. Magenta said. "We did it because both problem-solving and communicating were needed in order for you to succeed, and problem-solving and communication are essential in math and science."

Little did we know how important silent communication would be in our not-so-distant future.

"We will spend the rest of today with a different problem-solving challenge," Mrs. Magenta continued. "If you look at the easel, you will notice a piece of chart paper with a series of pictures. Each of you will be given a set of Chinese puzzles called tangrams, which consist of seven shapes: five triangles, one square, and one parallelogram. Using all seven of these shapes, you are to create as many of the pictures as possible and draw the solutions in your notebook. You may begin when you have your materials. Good luck."

This was fun. Even Trevor and Mark got into trying to solve the puzzles. Mrs. Magenta walked around checking on our progress and giving us small hints, but she didn't tell us how to do any of the puzzles. We worked right up till the end, and I still didn't get all the pictures done. Gav did, but that was no surprise to me. His artistic brain was good with shapes, just not letters.

"Okay, problem-solvers," Mrs. Magenta called, "you've all done a wonderful job with this challenge, but now I need you to pack up your tangrams and get ready to return to your classroom."

"Aww," my classmates moaned.

"Before you go, I do have a couple last items to share with you. The first is the collage I promised you." Mrs. Magenta held up her poster.

"Whoa!" we gasped.

Her entire collage was made out of tangrams. She had flowers, a person reading, a few animal shapes, and another person, who she said was a teacher. "These are all things I enjoy. I also love art, so I had fun creating this collage."

"How come you're not teaching art, then?" Scott asked. He could go on and on with questions, but this was the exact thing I was wondering.

"It's complicated," she said. "But the next thing I have to share with you gives me a chance to do more with art—and you too."

Mrs. Magenta passed out a flyer while she continued talking. "I'm excited to tell you about my new after-school program, which will be starting in just a few short weeks—Art and Community Service. This is an opportunity for you to do more art-related projects while also doing good. I hope you'll consider joining."

It looked like Trevor was already done considering it, because when we were leaving, I glanced back and saw the flyer still sitting on his desk. I liked Mrs. Magenta and thought her program sounded interesting, but none of that mattered, because there was no way I could fit it in with my gymnastics schedule. Coach Jane needed my after-school hours to be spent perfecting the artistic element in my routines, and then I could do good by winning.

GAVIN

"So how's school goin' with Mrs. Woods?" Dad asked when I got home after the second day.

"It's fine," I told him.

"Is your teacher nice?" Meggie asked, not knowing anything about Mrs. Woods.

"She's okay," I said.

"'Fine' and 'okay,' huh?" Dad said, making it sound like there was more to it than I was letting on. Truth was, I couldn't stop thinking about Woods and her reading to us, but I wasn't gonna try explaining that to my old man. Reading wasn't something that happened in our house. He wouldn't get it. "All right, then," he said. "I'm off to my next job. You listen to your brother, Meggie. He's in charge. Your mother will be home later."

"Okay. Bye, Daddy." Meggie ran over and hugged him before he hopped into his truck and drove away.

I grabbed my football and headed out back to throw some passes and do some thinking.

Reading definitely wasn't anything I was good at. I could read football defenses but not words. I didn't know why, but when I tried, the letters would run around on the page like players on the field. Those "b's" and "d's" were always pulling trick plays on me. I couldn't keep them straight. It was my bad luck that I had two "d's" in my last name—Davids. You might say it was good luck that I didn't have any "b's" or "d's" to worry about in my first name, and that would be true, but I'm a last-name sorta guy. My last name was the one going on my jersey. The big "d" in Davids didn't give me fits, but the little one gave me more trouble than a blitzing linebacker. Davids came out right half the time, and it came out as Davibs the other half. I was probably the only sixth grader in the world who still goofed up spelling his name. If it were up to me, I woulda kicked "b" and "d" off the alphabet team.

It's safe to say I didn't like reading all that much, which was why I was struggling to understand how my favorite thing about sixth grade so far was the way Woods read to us. Maybe she wasn't a champion football player, but she deserved a trophy for reading aloud. She had a way of making the words come to life so I could see the whole story in my head. I'd never had anyone read to me like that, and I couldn't believe how much I'd started looking forward to it.

When Woods closed that book, *Wonder,* today, the only sound in our room was breathing. Nobody was quick to say anything, not even Trevor or Mark. I sat there thinking.

"What's going through your head, Mr. Davids?" Woods asked.

"Nothing."

"I'm sure it's a lot more than nothing. Tell us."

"Well . . . I guess I was wondering about that Julian kid in the story."

"He's awful!" Rachel Livingsten exclaimed.

"I don't know," I said, "maybe we should give him the benefit of the doubt. He might not be all bad."

"No, he's all bad," Rachel insisted.

"Or maybe not," Trevor said.

No one added anything more after that, and I didn't know if it was 'cause everyone was thinking about Julian—or about Trevor. I can tell you one thing, it was nice having this talk without snobby Kurtsman around. She woulda ruined it with her know-it-all attitude. Maybe Julian wasn't all bad, but that girl was—no question about it. She was just like her mother. Good thing she disappeared after recess.

"Gavvy, can you get us snack?" Meggie called from the porch.

"Only if you catch my pass."

Meggie held her arms out, knowing I'd get her snack even if she didn't catch it. A perfect throw would be near impossible for her to drop, so this was a fun challenge. I scrambled around, pretending I was being chased by ugly defensemen, and then I lofted a soft spiral that fell into her basketed arms like a feather.

"Touchdown!" I yelled.

"Touchdown!" she squealed.

Her excitement made me smile. Deep down, I wished I

could be throwing my touchdown passes on the football team, but that was a wish I quickly pushed out of my brain. That was never gonna happen. I had responsibilities.

"C'mon, Megs. Let's get that snack." I wrapped my arm around her shoulders, and we headed inside.

4

GETTING DOWN
TO BUSINESS

SCOTT

"Ladies and gentlemen, your honeymoon is over. This morning we start getting down to business," Mrs. Woods announced.

"What does that mean?" I asked.

"Mr. Mason, it means we start doing some real work—and lots of it."

Mrs. Woods wasn't joking. She peppered us with one worksheet after another. I tried, but after a while enough was enough. I'd hit my limit. "These worksheets are horrible," I blurted out.

"Watch it, Mr. Mason," she warned me. "I'm not a huge fan of them myself, but the school wants us using them to get you ready for those CSAs you'll be taking in the spring, so we'll be doing lots of them. Get used to it."

"You want to know what CSA stands for?" I was on a roll.

"I know what it stands for, Mr. Mason."

"It's not Comprehensive Student Assessments, like they say. It's Complex Student Abuse. Those tests stink worse than these worksheets."

"Those tests suck," Trevor added.

"Mr. Joseph, you will now spend your recess writing an essay for me on the appropriate use of the word 'suck.'" (Poor Trevor was making a habit of losing his recess.) "You will also compile a list of its synonyms so you don't make the same mistake twice.

"As for you, Mr. Mason." Mrs. Woods was the one on a roll now. "Sometimes we have to do things we don't like. Not everything in life is fun and games. But if you want your fun at recess this afternoon, you won't have anything more to say, or else you'll be joining Mr. Joseph."

Mrs. Woods had a way of getting me to do the impossible. I zipped my lips. The last thing I wanted was to spend my recess writing! After a morning of torturous CSA worksheets, I'd need my recess more than ever. It was my one and only chance to burn off some energy.

Somehow I made it through those worksheets. Then Mrs. Woods decided to give us silent reading time, and I let out a ginormous sigh of relief. I couldn't find my book, so I had to get something from our reading corner, but that was okay, because we had a good one. Mrs. Woods had chapter books, nonfiction books, and even picture books for us to choose from. I still liked picture books. They weren't only for little kids, like a lot of people thought. The one called *Grandpa Green* caught my attention.

I'd like to know why Mrs. Woods chose that book to put on display. Was it because it had a medal or for some other reason? Did she know about my grandpa? I picked it up and held it under my nose. It didn't smell bad, so I started reading it.

Just like the grandpa in Mrs. Woods's book, my grandpa

had lots of important memories. His were of Grandma. That's all he had left of her, and they were his treasure. Grandpa didn't dare throw anything out for fear of losing one of those memories forever.

Over time, refusing to get rid of anything had turned into keeping everything. And I mean everything. Every piece of junk mail, newspaper, you name it, Grandpa kept it. And that was how his house had become a maze of papers stacked into towers. Mom said Grandpa was sick—not like cough-and-cold sick but brain sick—which is why he wouldn't throw anything out. I told Mom it wasn't Grandpa's brain but that he was broken-heart sick.

The bad news was, that dumb doctor gave Grandpa a clean bill of health after his physical. The good news was, if they couldn't help him get better, then I would. I wished Mrs. Woods's book told me how, but it didn't. I needed to come up with something on my own. I would. I loved my grandpa.

Trevor

This time when I missed recess, Woodchuck wanted me to write about the appropriate use of the word "suck." And she warned me not to give her a blank paper again. I had three synonyms for her when I got done: Brian, Chris, and Garrett.

"And who might these people be?" she asked.

"My older brother and his goons."

"I see." She didn't say anything more. That was a smart move.

NATALIE KURTSMAN
ASPIRING LAWYER
Kurtsman Law Offices

BRIEF #6
September: Flowers and Flyers

Although the CSA material was easy for me, I enjoyed my morning of "real work," as Mrs. Woods called it, and I was looking forward to my afternoon in Mrs. Magenta's classroom. I'd missed the previous day's class for reasons that do not need repeating.

As Mrs. Magenta's wardrobe suggested, she had a very different teaching style. While Mrs. Woods conducted business like a lawyer and had a black-and-white approach, Mrs. Magenta was unpredictable. Her classroom resembled a mad scientist's laboratory, with stuff everywhere.

"Hey, Mrs. Woods loves flowers, too!" Scott exclaimed when he saw the oodles of tiger lilies Mrs. Magenta had perched on her front table.

"Oh boy! Oh boy!" Trevor cried, bouncing in his seat and clapping his hands like a doofus.

Honestly, the fact that Scott never realized Trevor was making fun of him infuriated me, but at the same time I also recognized the blessing in disguise.

"Lots of people love flowers, Scott," Mrs. Magenta said. "It's hard not to appreciate something full of beauty. That's why we're going to spend today exploring and experimenting with these wonderful creations."

Our first activity was a flower dissection. Using special guide-books that Mrs. Magenta passed out, we had to create a diagram by taping the various flower pieces in our notebooks and labeling them. I found it fascinating, but Trevor and Mark seemed to be missing the beauty in it.

"Hey, Scott. You've got something on your cheek," Trevor said.

I looked. There was nothing on Scott's cheek, but he did have orange pollen all over his fingers, and he started rubbing the spot under his eye with those hands.

"No, it's the other side," Mark said.

Scott rubbed his other cheek.

"Actually, it's on your forehead," Trevor said.

Scott rubbed. He had streaks of orange covering his face when they got done with him.

"Check out Scott," Trevor called. "He's a flower boy with war paint."

Of course, everyone laughed. I was disgusted. I couldn't stand Trevor or Mark, and Scott was no better. Why did he have to be so clueless? Mrs. Magenta was busy elsewhere, so she missed all this. If Mrs. Woods had been around, she would've collared those two jerks and sentenced them to another day of no recess, but without her there was no one to look out for Scott. Fortunately, Mrs. Magenta got a phone call in the middle of class and Scott was asked to go to the office, so he was spared any additional torture.

Following the dissection, Mrs. Magenta attempted to lead a discussion about pollination and flower reproduction, but as soon as she mentioned the male and female parts, things fell to pieces. Did she really think she could say those words in front of these boys? It was disappointing.

After our conversation was cut short, we moved on to the last thing, which involved setting up mini-experiments with colored water and various colored lights. We would analyze our results at the start of tomorrow's class. Once I had my equipment situated, I gathered my belongings and went to line up at the door.

"Natalie." Mrs. Magenta called my name. I walked back to her desk, wondering what she wanted. "Natalie, you weren't here yesterday when I passed out this flyer, so I wanted to make sure you got one today. It's about an after-school program I have starting in a few weeks. You're a great candidate, so I hope you'll consider it. I'd love to have you join."

"Thank you," I said. "I'll look into the possibility."

"Wonderful."

SCOTT

I was sitting in Mr. Allen's office. It was so awesome that he'd moved from the elementary school to Lake View Middle the same year that I did. He'd been my principal there, and now he was the guy here. Mr. Allen and I went way back, so he didn't scare me, but I didn't like the thought of Mom finding out I had to pay him a visit, because then she'd worry, and she already had enough on her plate with Grandpa.

"Scott, it's been less than a week of school, and you've already landed yourself in my office. How's that even possible?" Mr. Allen asked.

"You invited me here," I said. "How's the new job?"

Mr. Allen cracked a smile and chuckled. We'd had many conversations over the years, and he almost always ended up laughing and putting his face in his hands and shaking his head before we got done.

"Invited. Now, that's an interesting way of looking at it," he said. "I invited you down here because Nurse Wilcox told me about yesterday's recess. I was hoping you could tell me what happened."

"You just said Nurse Wilcox already told you about it."

"Yes, but I'd like to hear the story from you."

Mr. Allen used to ask me to write about my mishaps whenever they happened, but he gave up on that tactic once he saw it was hopeless. Dad used to get all kinds of frustrated about me not writing, too, but even he gave up the fight when he saw it was getting us nowhere. Grandpa tells me I better make sure I have a good secretary when I'm older to keep me organized and transcribe my dictations.

Maybe it was because of our collage activity and my pencil with a big X drawn through it, but, whatever the reason, it didn't take Mrs. Woods nearly as long as everyone else to figure out I wasn't writing, and she left me alone. She told me all my reading was helping me more as a writer than our arguing about it ever could. I wished everyone had been as smart as her from the get-go.

"You'll write when it's important to you," she tried telling me again. "I'm not worried."

"Don't hold your breath," I said.

"Don't get wise," she replied.

I zipped my lips.

So Mr. Allen sat and listened while I told him the story about recess. There was no writing involved. I was careful not to leave any parts out, and sure enough, he had his face in his hands and was shaking his head when I finished.

"Mr. Allen, do you need to tell my mother about this?" I asked.

"Scott, you and I have had many conversations over the

years, and they always seem to come back to you trying to be helpful but then somehow things go wrong along the way. I know your teachers have had the same talks with you."

I nodded.

"I'm not sure if Mrs. Magenta has shared this with you yet, but she was awarded a grant for an after-school program this year. It's called Art and Community Service. Since you like helping people so much, I think this sounds like a good fit for you and an appropriate consequence for what happened at recess."

I nodded again. "Mrs. Magenta told us about it, and I wanted to show my mom the flyer, but I lost it."

"Tell you what, as long as you agree to attend Mrs. Magenta's program, I don't see the need to tell your mother about this recess mishap. What do you think?"

"You've got a deal!" I said. I jumped from my chair and shook his hand. Mr. Allen and I were good at making deals. This wouldn't be the last one we made. "Thanks, Mr. Allen. I've got to go now, before I miss read-aloud with Mrs. Woods. She's the best in the whole wide world."

"See ya, kiddo. And don't run in the halls."

Too late.

NATALIE KURTSMAN
ASPIRING LAWYER
Kurtsman Law Offices

BRIEF #7
September: Mrs. Magenta's Program

The moment I climbed in the car after school, I started my interrogation. "Mother, did you talk to Mr. Allen about what happened at recess?"

"How about 'Hi, Mom. How was your day?'"

"Sorry," I said. "Hi. And how was your day?"

"Busy but good. How was yours?"

"Scott was called down to the office during science class this afternoon. Did you talk to Mr. Allen?"

"No, I did not. I know you prefer to handle these things on your own, so I'm staying out of it."

I sighed. "Thank you."

"You know, you don't always have to be so grown-up, Natalie."

"Or perfect. You keep reminding me of that."

Now Mother sighed.

"You also told me to make sure I'm being a good person, because that's what's most important."

"Yes, and I hope you don't forget that."

"Well, today I found out about this new after-school program. Even though it might mean more time with individuals I don't particularly care for, I think I want to try it. It's about being a good person."

"Really? What is it?" Mother asked, brightening.

I waited until she parked the car, and then I pulled the information sheet out of my backpack and handed it to her. "It's called Art and Community Service," I said. "I know it's the right thing to do, but if I join, I won't be able to help you and Father in the office on the afternoons when it meets. Is that going to be okay?"

"Are you kidding? This is wonderful. I'm signing you up as soon as we get inside. Let's go and tell your father this exciting news."

Had I known then what I was getting myself into, I'm not so certain I would've joined—even if it was the right thing to do.

Randi

"So whaddaya think of Woods?" Gav asked me. We were in his backyard playing catch. I got to hang out with Gav (and Meggie) for about thirty minutes after school. Then Jane would pick me up, and we were off to gymnastics. We had an hour drive to get to practice, which lasted three hours, and the hour drive back home, so there wasn't any time for friends after that.

"I think she's pretty good at taking Trevor's recess away," I said. Gav laughed. I gripped the laces and threw the ball to him.

"For real, though," he said. "She's pretty good at reading aloud, don'tcha think?"

I almost dropped his pass. "Reading" and "Gavin" didn't even belong in the same sentence together. Sure, I'd seen the way he fell into a deep trance every time Mrs. Woods opened her book and read to us, but to hear Gav bringing it up while we were playing catch was a whole different story.

"Yeah, she's the best," I said, "but she's even better at piling on the homework." I lofted a pass his way.

"At least it's easy for you," he said. He hit me in the numbers with another perfect throw.

I didn't say anything more, because school wasn't easy for Gav—especially reading—but the truth was, this amount of homework was new for me, and I was struggling to get it all done around gymnastics. It wasn't as simple as it used to be. I complained to Jane, but she didn't listen. She couldn't even begin to think about something possibly interfering with my gymnastics. "Just do what you're supposed to," she told me. She didn't care, as long as I kept getting all As. And to make matters worse, she'd gone and found another thing to plug into my schedule.

"Jane signed me up for Mrs. Magenta's after-school program," I said, squeezing the football. "She thinks it will look good for colleges, and it happens to meet on the one day when I don't have gymnastics." I let a deep pass fly.

"Touchdown!" Gavin yelled, catching it over his shoulder and making it look easy. He spun around, planted his feet, and threw another perfect spiral. "Why is your mother so crazy about college?" he said. "It's not all it's cracked up to be, you know."

"Don't call my mother crazy," I said. I gunned the ball at him.

"Take it easy. I didn't call her crazy. I asked why she was so crazy about you going to college, that's all. It's not like it's happening tomorrow." He tossed a soft pass.

"Jane says it'll be here before we know it. She's just looking out for my future. She wants me to do well in life." I threw an easy one back.

"Oh, and that means you have to go to college?" Gav said. "You know, my old man's always talking about the college-educated people he meets on the job who don't know their right from their left."

"And you listen to your father all of a sudden? Maybe he only says those things because he's jealous."

"Yeah, maybe," Gav mumbled. He tucked the football under his arm and went and sat on their rusty and tired swing set.

I walked over and plopped down next to him. "Sorry. I didn't mean that."

"No, it's true. And I'll probably follow in his footsteps. I'll grow up to be some dumb plumber."

I knew that was the last thing Gav wanted, but there was a good chance that was his destiny. "At least you know you'll get a job," I said, trying to sound optimistic. "Your dad's right when he says that no matter how fancy the world gets, people will always need plumbers."

"I think Jane's right. It's better to go to college."

"Yeah, well, that's only going to happen if I manage to get a free ride."

"You can do that easy," Gav said, looking at me. "Randi, you're awesome at gymnastics and school. You've got it. No sweat."

I smiled. He meant what he said. Gavin was the best best friend. We never stayed upset with each other, and we always knew how to make the other feel better.

A car horn honked out in the front driveway. It was time for gymnastics. I hopped off my swing and pulled the folded paper out of my pocket. "Sign up for Mrs. Magenta's program with me, please." I handed him the flyer.

"I'll ask."

I knew he would. Gav was the most honest person in the

world. "See you tomorrow," I said. I turned and took off running. Jane didn't like to wait.

"Aren'tcha gonna give her a kiss?" Meggie yelled from the porch.

"Be quiet or I won't getcha snack," Gav warned her.

"Have fun at gymnastics, Randi!" Meggie called.

Yeah, I thought, waving over my shoulder. Sometimes I wished it was me with the little sister to babysit, but that wasn't part of my destiny.

GAVIN

I waited till Mom got home from bartending that night to ask her and Dad about Magenta's after-school program. I didn't think they'd go for it, but I had told Randi I'd ask, and I always keep my word. That's one thing I'm good for.

I found my parents cuddling on the couch, watching TV together. "Can I ask you guys something?" I said.

"Gavin! My *niño*. You're still awake?" Mom sat up. "It's late. You've got school tomorrow."

"I know. I'll make it quick."

"What is it?" Dad said.

I did my best to explain about Magenta's program. Mom and Dad didn't say anything until I was done, and then they told me I could do it.

"What?" I said.

"You can do it," they repeated.

Talk about being shocked. Their answer made me wish I had asked if I could sign up for football. That was what I really wanted, but that was never gonna happen. It cost to join Pop

73

Warner, and what money Mom and Dad made had to go to other places. Starting in seventh grade, there was a modified school team that you didn't need to pay for, but Mom and Dad both worked such long hours that I knew there'd be no time for me to play 'cause I'd still have to watch Meggie.

"Your mother won't be bartendin' quite as much anymore," Dad explained, "so she'll be around to watch your sister, which means you can start doin' some of these after-school things."

"But don't we need the money?"

"Things are finally startin' to look better for us, Gavin. Come next fall, you should be able to go out for the modified football team."

"Really?"

"*Sí,*" Mom said, and sighed. "I'm still not crazy about all the concussion stuff I keep hearing in the news, but I can't keep you from playing. Not when it's your passion."

There was no hiding my excitement. This was the best news I'd heard in forever.

"It's like I told you," Dad said. "Good things happen to people who work hard." He leaned over and kissed Mom.

So do bad things, I thought. Had he forgotten about what happened? One thing was for sure: a high school dropout wasn't smart. I shouldn't talk like that about my old man, 'cause he didn't have a choice and had to quit school when his dad got sick so he could run the family plumbing business. He saved the business but not his father. Still, you don't run around bragging about your old man when that's his story. I didn't want to end up a nobody like him, but my brain wasn't very good at school. So I was gonna shine on the football field when I got my chance. Football was gonna take me places.

I said good night to my parents and gave my mother a hug. "The future is bright," she whispered. I squeezed her, hoping she was right, then headed off to bed, but I struggled to fall asleep. All I could think about was throwing game-winning touchdown passes. I couldn't wait to tell Randi I was gonna be able to play, and then I remembered the other news I had for her.

Tell you the truth, I never wanted to join Magenta's program. I only asked about it for Randi. I never expected that I'd end up doing it. Don't get me wrong, it was gonna be nice having the day free from Meggie duty, and the art part sounded okay—but that wasn't enough to get me excited. I left that to Randi.

The next day, when I told her my news about football, she was really happy for me, but she was pumped when she found out I could do Magenta's program. "Really? That's awesome!" she cried.

"You owe me one," I said.

"It won't be that bad," she promised.

That's what I kept telling myself, but then I found out who else was gonna be doing this thing with us. She definitely owed me now.

"Hey, I'm joining that program, too!" Scott said. He'd heard me and Randi talking in the hall. You woulda thought he'd just scored a touchdown, the way he was celebrating. "Mr. Allen's making me do it, because I'm good at helping people," he said.

I choked. Good at helping?! Good at messing up, was more like it.

"I'll see you guys there," he said, holding out his hand for me to slap him five.

This was typical Scott, acting like we were best buddies or something. I'd only ever hung out with him once, and that wasn't 'cause I wanted to, but 'cause I had to after we got in trouble thanks to one of his brilliant stupid ideas back in kindergarten. Brilliant stupid ideas had been Scott's talent for as long as I'd known him. And this year was no different. He really came up with a whopper this time around. One that changed everything.

5

A GROUP IS FORMED, BUT NOT A TEAM

Trevor

Woodchuck wasn't fooling when she told us she'd be the judge and the jury in our classroom. She was a straight shooter who never hesitated to tell us exactly what she thought. Make no mistake about it, she was a mean, crotchety old lady.

"I'm appalled," she said after taking one look at our papers. "It's October and your spelling is still atrocious. By the looks of these, we should be studying diphthongs, never mind open-response questions and CSAs. You children probably don't even know what a diphthong is, do you?"

Natalie Kurtsman's hand shot up in the air. I swear, sometimes I didn't know if I hated her or Woodchuck more.

Good ol' Mark didn't give her a chance to answer. "Diphthongs!" he crowed. "I know what those are! They're a type of underwear!"

"Ha!" I busted out laughing. "Yeah, they give Natalie constant wedgies. That's why she's always so uptight."

Gavin liked that one. He was snickering now, too.

"Ugh!" Natalie gasped. "How dare you!" She glared at us.

I don't know what she thought she was going to do, but it didn't matter. Woodchuck came to her pet's rescue.

"I'm glad you find that so funny, Mr. Joseph. You can spend your recess writing an essay on diphthongs along with your buddy Mr. Kassler."

"What? That's not fair!"

"Life's not fair, Mr. Joseph. It's best you learn that now."

"Wait till my father hears about this," Mark whispered. "She'll be kissing our butts after that."

"And, Mr. Kassler, I know your father is on the school board," Mrs. Woods said. "That doesn't concern me. I happen to know him. He was my student once, too."

At least Mark was missing recess with me today, so I wasn't stuck alone with Woodchuck again. We had our desks pushed together, and I was flipping through one of the books Woodchuck had given us while Mark wrote out a few sentences on the paper he was going to hand in. This was all his fault, so I told him he could do the writing for me, too, and I'd put my name at the end.

"Dude, my dad signed me up for Mrs. Magenta's after-school program," he said. "It starts this afternoon."

"What? You didn't tell me that."

"I just found out this morning, and I haven't had a chance to tell you until now."

"Why'd he do that?" I asked.

"You know how it always looks good for him if I get involved in this stuff. I guess it helps his image as a school board member or something."

"Wow. That sucks. Have fun with that, bro."

"I told him I didn't want to do it."

I put my book down and sat up straight. "Really? What'd he say?"

"He said he'd pay me to join. He wants me to be his spy and give him insider information. That way he knows the real story and not the sugarcoated version that he gets at his board meetings."

"Whoa. So what're you going to do?"

"I'm in if you come, too," he said.

"*Pff!* Yeah, right! Sorry, bro. I'm not doing any flower-power thing after school. Your dad's not paying me."

"So what you're telling me is you'd rather spend the afternoon with your brother and his goons?"

I leaned forward. "I'm not doing your stupid program," I said.

"Gentlemen, I'll take your papers now," Woodchuck announced, startling us from behind.

What! I wasn't ready. I hadn't signed my name. That idiot Mark had done so much blabbing about this after-school thing that I'd forgotten—and he hadn't even written a word on my paper!

"I see you've managed to produce the same thing again, Mr. Joseph—nothing."

"I lost track of time," I said, searching for an excuse. "I was going to write something. Honest. It was a mistake."

"A mistake, huh? I see. Well, we can talk about mistakes some other time. The good news is I'm going to let you off the hook for today, but only because I overheard you two talking. Your friend is right, Mr. Joseph. You should join that after-school program. I'm sure Mr. Kassler's father knows it will be good for you boys, which is the real reason he's pushing it. Besides, I don't recall seeing Mrs. Magenta's name listed as one of the synonyms on your last paper, but I do seem to remember a few others. Consider the program, Mr. Joseph."

I didn't say anything because Woodchuck was letting me off easy, but there was no way I was doing that program, especially if she was suggesting it. No way. No how. Not ever.

SCOTT

With October came Rachel Livingsten's birthday—our first one of the year! Birthday celebrations were my favorite. I didn't get to have a party in school, because my birthday was on June twenty-ninth, right after school was out. The one time I tried having my party at home, no one could make it. Everyone said they were already too busy with summer plans. And since I wasn't ever asked to any of the other parties, I always looked forward to the ones in the classroom. The moms never failed to bring in cookies or brownies for everyone to share. Rachel's mom showed up with these ginormous vanilla and chocolate frosted cupcakes. They were awesome!

"Remember your manners and make sure you clean up after yourselves," Mrs. Woods reminded us.

Using our manners meant we waited for Rachel to pass out all the cupcakes before touching ours. Then we sang "Happy Birthday," and then we ate our treats. I devoured mine. They were so yummy I licked all the crumbs off my desk and chair and the rug under me so Mrs. Woods didn't need to worry about any messes. I thanked Rachel's mom a bunch and told her she made the best cupcakes in the universe. She liked that. The only people who didn't eat one were Mrs. Woods and Randi. I tried, but Mrs. Woods wouldn't let me have hers.

After we were done and had cleaned up, Rachel's mom left and Mrs. Woods moved on with things, but she did that by making an announcement none of us were expecting. "When you get to be my age, you're not much for celebrating birthdays," she said, "so I happen to think you should take advantage of the opportunity when you're young. So how about it, Miss Livingsten—what would you like for your birthday? Free time? No homework?"

I ran up and hugged Mrs. Woods.

"Sit down, Mr. Mason. It's not your birthday."

"I'd like it if you read extra to us," Rachel said.

I jumped up and ran over to hug Rachel, but she held out stop-sign hands.

"Sit down, Mr. Mason. It's still not your birthday," Mrs. Woods said.

"It sure feels like it!" I exclaimed.

Besides birthday parties and recess, Mrs. Woods reading aloud was the other thing I loved about school. We were almost done with our third book already. After finishing *Wonder,* Mrs. Woods smelled and read *Ungifted* by Gordon Korman so we could hear another story with multiple perspectives, and now we were reading *Shiloh* by Phyllis Reynolds Naylor. Not only was Mrs. Woods the best at reading with expression and different voices, but she knew that the way to enjoy a story was not to open the book once a week or to make kids do a gazillion reader-response questions or activities, but just to read it.

When we ran out of time and she closed *Shiloh* today, I was sad, but then I remembered the second thing October brought with it—Mrs. Magenta's program!—and that was next! I'd been waiting for this day ever since Mr. Allen and I had made our deal. I jumped up and rushed to get my stuff jammed into my backpack. Not even Mrs. Woods could've slowed me down.

Trevor

It really bugged me that Scott was so excited about this stupid flower-power program, so I crammed one of Rachel's extra cupcakes into his backpack when he wasn't looking. I hated Woodchuck and I hated that she was going to think I was listening to her, because I wasn't, but I hated going home after school even more. I forged the stupid permission slip, grabbed my stuff, and headed to the art room instead of to the bus. I'd get a lift home with Mark after we were done.

I was doing this for Mark. Let's leave it at that.

NATALIE KURTSMAN
ASPIRING LAWYER
Kurtsman Law Offices

BRIEF #8
October: Mrs. Magenta's Program Commences

Even though the art room wasn't Mrs. Magenta's regular classroom, we assembled there for our first after-school meeting. It was a lovely space with beautiful paintings hanging everywhere, yet despite the inviting atmosphere, I was already concerned—on account of two reasons. First, I got stuck sitting next to Scott Mason. The boy was a colossal mess, so naturally, packing up took him forever; hence, he was the last one to arrive.

"Better late than never," Trevor remarked when Scott finally spilled into the art room.

"I couldn't get my bag to zip," he said.

"Dude, you're going to be late for your own funeral," Mark jabbed.

Dude, like what're you two even doing here? I felt like saying. But it was true; Scott was late for just about everything. By the time he showed up, the only stool left open was the one next to me. Nobody had bothered to sit in it, and up to that point I didn't care. *Nobody* would've been better than Scott. If I weren't mature, I would've made a fuss and told him to move away from me, but that wasn't my style. I simply turned my back to him.

The second item that had me concerned was the obvious absence of any art materials. I thought I'd signed up for an art and community service program, but it appeared we wouldn't be doing any art—at least, not today.

"Welcome, caring souls and creative spirits," Mrs. Magenta began.

"How do you know we have caring souls?" Scott asked, already interrupting her.

"Because you've chosen to join this program."

"I didn't choose. I'm here as a consequence," he clarified.

"Oh" was all Mrs. Magenta managed in response.

"But I don't mind being here," Scott said. "I like helping people. This is my consequence because it's a perfect fit for me."

His comment prompted a chorus of laughs. We all knew that was a joke.

"Good one," Mark said.

Mrs. Magenta sighed. I understood. Our spirits couldn't very well fly if this was turned into an after-school prison. I began to wonder if there were any other prisoners in our midst we didn't know about. Seriously, what were Trevor and Mark doing here?

"Young apprentices," Mrs. Magenta continued, "it's a crying shame that we do not have a library here at Lake View Middle School. Libraries and books are vital necessities for creativity, dreams, hope, and so much more. This is why we'll be visiting the public library for our first community service project. We're going to help make it a place where everyone wants to go, young people especially. Every child needs to get lost in stories. Every child should be reading all the time."

"You sound like Mrs. Woods," Scott said. "She reads to us every day after we do those boring CSA worksheets all morning long."

Mrs. Magenta smiled. Not a big, toothy smile, but one that I would categorize as sheepish. It was one that said "I'm happy for you" but that hid something on the inside. Peculiar.

"Her read-alouds are way better than those worksheets," Scott continued. "Those worksheets—"

"Okay, Scott," I said, cutting him off. "We've got it. Let Mrs. Magenta finish."

My classmates laughed. They were always laughing at Scott.

"Okay, then," Mrs. Magenta continued. "We'll be walking to the public library in just a few minutes, once I've taken attendance and have everything organized. Scott, I will need your permission slip before we go. The rest of you are all set."

Scott unzipped his backpack and started rummaging through it. No wonder it took him forever to pack up. The thing was crammed full of all kinds of stuff: crumpled papers, a half-eaten bag of chips (which could've been from fourth grade), several battered books, a glove with two fingers missing, a couple of rocks, an action figure, and a huge pile of junk mail. And smooshed around among everything else was one of Rachel's cupcakes! Gross! All that but no permission slip. Or at least, not one that he could find.

"Mrs. Magenta, I can't find it," he said, clearly upset.

Maybe it would help if you cleaned out your backpack, I thought.

"Don't worry," Mrs. Magenta said. "Go down to the office and have them call your mother. She can give permission over the phone for today. In the meantime, I'll get you a new slip that you can take home and have filled out before our next meeting."

I huffed in disgust. Because of Scott's extreme disorganization, we had to wait. I was more than a little annoyed.

"Natalie, please accompany Scott to the office. I never like to send students alone."

I suspect Mrs. Magenta recognized that Scott could be unpredictable, and sending somebody to help keep him on track was certainly a good idea—but why me? Honestly.

The moment we stepped into the hallway, I started speed-walking ahead of him. I was not interested in taking a stroll with this boy. And I did not care that I was acting bratty.

I pushed open the door to the office. Mrs. Lane, our school secretary, looked up from her desk. I stepped back out of the way. This was Scott's problem, not mine. He could do the talking.

"Hi, Mrs. Lane. I lost my permission slip, so Mrs. Magenta sent me down here to call my mother."

"Sure thing, sweetie." She handed Scott the phone, and I watched his fingers push the buttons.

"Hi, Mom. I'm really sorry, but . . . um . . . I can't find my permission slip."

I could hear her exasperation through the phone. Scott cringed. So did I.

"It's okay, Mom. You don't need to drive over," Scott said,

his shoulders sagging. He looked defeated. "I know you're busy. You just need—"

That was when Mr. Allen came out of his office. He must've overheard the conversation. He gave me a quick smile, and he took the phone from Scott.

"Hello, Mrs. Mason? Hi, it's Mr. Allen. I understand Scott has misplaced his permission slip. . . . Yes, I know. It's okay to give permission over the phone for today. We can get that slip filled out for next time. . . . No problem. . . . Have a good day, Mrs. Mason."

Mr. Allen hung up the phone.

"Thanks," Scott said.

"Hey, we had a deal. I wanted to make sure you were going to keep up your end of the bargain." Mr. Allen squeezed Scott's shoulder and winked at me.

What deal? I wondered. Was Mr. Allen the one who had decided Scott should attend this program?

"It's nice to see you, Natalie," Mr. Allen said.

"Likewise."

"You two have fun this afternoon."

"We will," Scott promised.

"Thank you, Mr. Allen," I said.

We left the office and started back to the art room—but this time I didn't speed-walk ahead of Scott.

GAVIN

When I found out that Natalie Kurtsman was also doing this after-school thing with Magenta, I was ready to wring Randi's neck. She owed me big-time! A good football player knows how to channel his anger and keep control, though, so I took a deep breath, gripped the laces on my football, and ignored the girl on the opposite side of the room. Besides, when Magenta announced that our first project would take place at the public library, I suddenly had more to worry about than snobby Natalie Kurtsman.

I knew where that building was and what it looked like on the outside, but I'd never been inside before. All my life teachers had talked about how important reading was and how fun it could be when you found the right book, but I couldn't see how I was ever gonna enjoy it when I was always stuck in the groups using the baby books. And there was no way around that. I needed the baby books, 'cause then I could figure out most of the words, but those stories were for little kids.

My teachers in elementary school never wanted to label

my group the dumb bunch, so they tried creating sneaky code names. Calling us by different colors or animals didn't make one bitta difference. Everyone knew who the best reader was—and the worst. Maybe I struggled to sound out words, but that didn't mean I was stupid. A good football play had a much more complicated system than reading groups.

I gotta say, reading with Woods had been different so far, though. She didn't have us in any groups. We mostly read to ourselves, and then we'd go over it as a class, but she also gave us time to read whatever we wanted. I usually faked the silent reading, but I liked the whole-class stuff, 'cause even though I wasn't great at making out the words, once I knew what they said, I was pretty good at understanding what it was all about. My journal was full of different sketches that came to me while listening. I never raised my hand to read, but every once in a while I raised my hand to answer a question.

Our newest read-aloud was my favorite so far. *Shiloh* was an older book, but it had me doing a lot of thinking. The story takes place in the olden days out in the West Virginia hills. Being old herself, Woods knew how to make those back-woods words sound. I liked that it was a boy character, Marty, who had to deal with his twerp little sisters, but it was Marty's struggle with right versus wrong that was really tricky and interesting. I felt for him. I know that was 'cause the author did a good job writing it, but it was also 'cause of the way Woods read those pages. Her reading was about the only thing that could make Scott sit still.

"What's on your mind, Mr. Davids?" Woods asked.

I swallowed. "I guess I was wondering what I'd do if I was in Marty's shoes," I said.

"You've got a smart brain in that head of yours, Mr. Davids. The world could use more people asking themselves questions like that.

"I want all of you to think about Mr. Davids's question," Woods said. "We'll discuss it tomorrow."

I knew what she wanted, but all I could think about was how that was the first time any teacher had ever told me I was smart. I wouldn't forget that.

After Scott got back from the office with Kurtsman, we were finally able to get going to the library. Magenta had us leave our things behind, 'cause we'd be coming back before getting picked up. I tossed my backpack in the corner, but I carried my lucky football with me. I never left that behind.

It wasn't a long walk to the library, so we made it in only a few minutes, but sure enough, once we got there, things started going downhill pretty fast.

Randi

"Okay, my eager helpers, I need you to arrange yourselves into groups of four," Mrs. Magenta announced when she had us gathered in the library lobby.

That was all we needed to hear, and suddenly we turned into a bunch of owls. Heads spun in all directions as we tried to find the right people.

"Who do you want in our group?" Gav asked.

Maybe I was feeling sorry for Scott, I don't know, but for some reason he's who I suggested. It was better Scott than Trevor or Mark. You didn't need to be a geologist to know those two had rocks in their heads. Gav shrugged. Maybe part of Gav was feeling sorry for Scott, too. Being best friends, we often had the same thoughts.

"Scott, you can come with us," I said.

"Really?! Awesome!" he squealed, throwing his arms around me in a hug. It was like he'd just nailed a high-flying vault at the national championships. Gav and I should've tried to settle him down, but we didn't, and then Scott lost his head.

He went and picked our fourth person before we even realized what was happening.

"Natalie, c'mon," he said. "You can join our team."

I wasn't expecting that, and by the look on her face, I'd say Natalie had been caught off guard, too. Gavin was fuming. The last thing he wanted was for this girl to be in our group, but it was too late. Once Scott opened his mouth, Mrs. Magenta stuck Natalie with us and that was that. She had to put her somewhere. It wasn't like anyone else was asking her. If Natalie was one of those cliquey girls, then she was in a clique of one. I wasn't thrilled with her addition. If Gavin didn't like her, that was reason enough for me.

After Mrs. Magenta had us organized in groups, she sent us to different areas in the library. Trevor and Mark went upstairs to the study center with their bunch, another group went to the lounge, and a third went to the young adult section. We were assigned to the children's room. It reminded me of gymnastics, with girls going to the bars, vault, beams, and floor. I wondered if we'd rotate stations, like at practice, or if we'd spend our entire time in the children's room. At gymnastics I would've spent my entire practice on the bars if given the chance. I loved everything about the bars, except when it came time for my dismount. If I didn't stick my landing, Jane got mad at me.

But it wasn't Jane or gymnastics that I had to worry about in the children's room that afternoon. Scott was far from done for the day. He still had an unforgettable floor routine up his sleeve.

NATALIE KURTSMAN
ASPIRING LAWYER
Kurtsman Law Offices

```
BRIEF #9
October: The Public Library
```

The four of us walked down the stairs leading to the children's room. At this juncture, it's safe to say I was feeling slightly unsure about my chosen after-school program, but at least we got assigned to the children's room, a familiar spot for me—a place where I was comfortable, even in my uncomfortable group. Honestly, why did Scott have to choose me? Just because I went to the office with him, that didn't suddenly make me his friend. Gross.

"Now what?" Gavin asked after we arrived at our destination.

The room was dark and no one seemed to be around.

"Welcome to the children's room," Mrs. Magenta said, flipping the lights on.

"There's no one down here," Randi said.

"I know. The longtime librarian, Mrs. Kylie, passed away

several months ago, and they haven't found a replacement for her yet, though I have heard that her ghost likes to visit from time to time."

"Really? Her ghost?" Scott croaked.

"That's what I hear, but don't be scared. Mrs. Kylie was an angel even before she died. She loved this place, which is why it's sad to see it being neglected. It's beginning to feel like a dungeon down here. Well, I say this room has been left to the spiders and cobwebs long enough. It's time we give it a makeover."

"A makeover?" Gavin repeated.

"Yes," Mrs. Magenta answered. "I've volunteered to get this room back in shape and fill in as librarian while they search for a replacement. This place needs to be bright and inviting, not dark and dreary."

"Mrs. Magenta, you do it all!" Scott exclaimed. "You teach math and science, you're doing an art program, and you're a librarian. That's a lot."

For once, I agreed with the boy. It was a lot, especially for a hippie lady.

"That's why I have the four of you to help me," Mrs. Magenta said. "You're my special recruits. I have all the paint and supplies you'll need sitting right over there." She pointed to the reading nook. "There are two gallons of a happy yellow for the walls. After you get them painted, we'll talk about what to do next, but that will be for another day."

"Had I known we'd be painting, I would've worn different clothes," I said.

"Don't worry, Natalie. I have smocks with the rest of the materials. Let me show you." Mrs. Magenta led us over to the supplies and went through our instructions, taking time to give us a few pointers. Then she stopped to see if we had any questions. Of course, Scott did.

"What's our team name?" he asked her.

"I don't know, Scott. You'll have to come up with one."

"What's our team called?" he asked us.

"We're *not* a team," Gavin snapped.

"Yes, we are. We're the Recruits." The name just popped out of Scott's mouth, like things sometimes do. I saw Randi crack a smile. And so did Mrs. Magenta.

"So how about it, Recruits, any other questions?" she asked us.

My smile masked the thoughts swirling in my head. *Mrs. Magenta has everything we could possibly need, except someone to keep an eye on Scott.* I should've said something, but I bit my tongue.

"Great. I'm going to check on the other groups while you get started. I'll be back in a bit."

By the time I donned my smock and commenced with the paint, Scott was already distracted. He'd found a picture book on the shelf and started reading. I let him be. What harm could come if he was out of the way?

GAVIN

I was good with this job. We'd finally been given a school-related project that didn't have anything to do with book smarts. We were doing some manual labor, and I was no rookie when it came to that. When your old man is a laborer, you might not spend your afternoons discussing poetry, but you definitely learn a thing or two about swinging a hammer and changing the oil in a machine. If there was one thing Dad wasn't gonna let me become, it was one of those ignorant educated people, which was exactly what I was dealing with right now. I had two people in my group with only book smarts, and asking them to do manual labor was just another way of asking for trouble.

I glanced at that stuck-up brat Natalie Kurtsman and snickered. She was all high and mighty. I bet she'd never done anything like this. I hoped our next community service project had us using rakes and shovels so her princess hands would end up raw with blisters.

Me and Randi covered the floor as best we could with

Magenta's tarp while Kurtsman managed to drape a couple bedsheets over the nearby bookcases. Scott was busy reading, so Kurtsman was on her own. Me and Randi got started on one side while Stuck-Up Girl worked on the wall behind us. Magenta wasn't kidding, that yellow paint was super bright, but I liked it. It was a heckuva lot better than the original puke green.

After a while I saw we were making pretty good progress. Stuck-Up Girl was holding her own. I couldn't decide if it was beginner's luck or dumb luck. Either way, I knew it wouldn't last—and it didn't.

First came the funny noises. Then books started falling off shelves. And then "Boo!"

"Ahh!" Scott screamed. "It's Mrs. Kylie's ghost!" He dropped his book and took off running.

"Watch out!" I shouted. But it was too late.

Two strides later Scott's left foot came down smack-dab in the center of Kurtsman's paint tray.

"Oh no!" he cried.

He started hopping around with his bright yellow foot in the air. If there's one thing Scott's not, it's coordinated. The doofus lost his balance and collided with the bookcase—the same one that had my gallon of paint resting on it, where I thought it was safely out of the way. I tried to catch it, but I make a better quarterback than I do a wide receiver. The paint can flipped and crashed to the ground. Some of the paint fell on our tarp—but not all of it. We stood there with our mouths hung open, gaping at the massive yellow splat that had landed in middle of the carpet.

SPLAT!

Trevor and Mark came out of hiding. They took one look at us and busted out laughing.

"Mrs. Kylie's ghost, huh?" Trevor teased. "You sissy."

"This isn't funny," Kurtsman said. "Look at this mess."

"Don't worry. We'll get it cleaned up," Mrs. Magenta said, coming back into the room.

"Mrs. Magenta, I'm so sorry," Scott said. "I didn't mean it."

"I know you didn't, honey. It's okay. Accidents happen. Besides, I have just the thing to fix that. Follow me.

"The rest of you can take the paper towels and get started soaking up the spill. Trevor and Mark will help. Many hands make light work."

We were supposed to make the place look better, but thanks to Trevor and Mark, Scott had just made it worse by ruining the carpet—and Magenta wasn't mad. How was that possible?

I can tell you this: after two minutes of crawling around on my hands and knees sopping up Scott's mess with paper towels, I wasn't too happy.

"There's never a dull moment with that kid around," Randi joked.

"You can say that again," me and Kurtsman said together.

Sometimes me and Randi say the same thing at the same time, and then we always go, "Great minds think alike." That sorta stuff happens with your best friend, but it's not supposed to happen with your worst enemy. What was Kurtsman playing at? Was she trying to get under my skin? I'da paid money to line up across from her on the football field. Randi knew it, too. She could see my veins popping. That's why she went ahead and started telling that story about Scott in the pool. She was hoping I'd calm down.

"A couple summers ago, on a scorching-hot day, I was at swim lessons," she began. "As destiny would have it, Scott was in my class."

"You shoulda drowned him," I said.

"Yeah," Trevor agreed.

"Believe me, I wanted to after what happened. We were just finishing up our lesson and had a little bit of free time when Scott swam over to me. He got right next to me—right next to me!—and he whispered, 'There's no red stuff like the legend says.'

"I said, 'What're you talking about?'

"Then he goes, 'Legend says there's a mysterious red substance that will surround you if you pee in the pool. I'm peeing right now—and look! There's no red! You can pee, too, and no one will ever know! We can all pee!'"

"Eww! That's disgusting!" Kurtsman cried.

Randi started laughing and then Kurtsman was laughing with her.

"Gross," Trevor said. Mark and him were laughing now, too.

"You shoulda drowned him," I said again. Then I went back to sopping up the paint.

Magenta came trudging back with Scott right about that time. She had a tray of cookies in one hand and some sort of throw rug in her other. Scott was carrying the juice.

"I've been waiting to find the right place for this thing," Magenta said. "Guess I know where it belongs now." She laid the rug down, and it completely covered the paint splat. "Perfect," she said. "The only ones who will ever know that spot is even under there are you—the Recruits."

Great! Now *she* was calling us that. We weren't a team!

"Before we cover it, I think you should add your names

next to the spot," Magenta said. "Artists always put their name next to their work."

"That's a great idea!" Scott exclaimed. "Then we'll be immortal, like all the people who wrote these books."

Scott Mason and Natalie Kurtsman were the last people I wanted my name tied to for eternity. My name wasn't going under some rug but in Canton, Ohio, in the Pro Football Hall of Fame. I grabbed my roller and went back to the wall. Randi hesitated, but she followed me.

Me and Randi finished the section we'd been working on and got our stuff cleaned up while Scott signed his autograph and enjoyed his juice and cookies. Trevor and Mark got to stick around for snack, but then Magenta sent them back upstairs. I wasn't sure if they signed the splat or if Kurtsman added her name—and I didn't care.

Everything worked out fine and dandy for Scott that afternoon, but we'd find out soon enough that not all messes could be so easily covered up.

NATALIE KURTSMAN
ASPIRING LAWYER
Kurtsman Law Offices

BRIEF #10
October: Dirtbags and Cheats

We returned to school to find many parents already parked along the front curb, waiting. We were running late. This, of course, was no surprise to me. Free spirits often have carefree attitudes about time. Unfortunately, the same was not true for all the parents.

Our organized bunch quickly disintegrated into kids on mad dashes to get their belongings before hurrying out to their cars. Scott was among them, and with good reason. His mother was likely to be upset when she saw his paint-splattered sneakers and pants, so making her wait was not advisable—even Scott recognized that. Unfortunately, in his haste, he completely forgot the new permission slip that Mrs. Magenta had given him. I saw it sitting in plain sight the moment I walked into the art room. Add that goof to his ruined clothes and his mother probably wasn't going to be very pleased.

"Oh boy. Scott's going to need a lawyer if he's going to have any chance with his mother today," I said, picking up the piece of paper. I was talking out loud but to myself. I do that sometimes when I'm all alone. I certainly didn't think anyone was listening.

"Lawyers are dirtbags!" Gavin exploded. "Dirtbags and cheats!"

My mouth fell open. For the first time in my life, I was rendered speechless. Astonished, actually. But once the initial shock subsided, I rallied and became royally ticked off! "You have no basis for that accusation. Take it back!" I demanded.

"I've got every right," he said. "Ask your mother."

He stormed away, leaving me red hot and with no opportunity for a rebuttal. I was beyond mad at this point. I was ready to take him to court for defamation of character, but more than that, I was determined to prove that lawyers are, in fact, decent people. And not just decent people but great people who uphold justice and make our world a better place. I didn't need to ask my mother anything. I took off after Scott. If I hurried, I might still catch him.

SCOTT

"What is all over your pants? And look at your sneakers!" Mom cried when she saw me. I wasn't even in the car yet.

"Ello. Ello!" Mickey shouted from the backseat.

"Sorry, Mom. It was an accident," I said.

"I can see that. A big one!" she exclaimed.

"Ello!" Mickey yelled.

"Excuse me . . . Mrs. Mason?"

I spun around. It was Natalie.

"Hi, I'm Natalie Kurtsman. Mrs. Magenta asked me to bring this out to you."

It was my permission slip. The one Mrs. Magenta had given to me. I'd forgotten it in the art room.

"Thank you, Natalie," Mom said, taking the paper. "Scott often needs help keeping track of his things."

"Actually, it was my responsibility to give him the slip when we got back from the library and I forgot. I'm sorry, ma'am. I'm sorry about the yellow paint, too. I moved our tray and neglected to tell Scott, and then he stepped in it by accident. It was my fault."

Mom paused and eyed her carefully. "Natalie, are you Scott's friend?" she asked.

"He's in my after-school group, ma'am."

"But is he your friend?" Mom asked again.

"We're on the same team."

"Well, thank you, Natalie." Mom smiled and then looked at me. "C'mon, Scott. We've gotta get going."

I climbed in the passenger seat, and Mom eased away from the curb.

"Yes, he's my friend!" Natalie yelled.

Mom sighed and waved in the rearview mirror. She'd heard her. I twisted in my seat and saw Natalie waving back. Today was the best day of my life. I couldn't wait to tell Grandpa all about it. I was on a team, my name had become immortal, and Natalie was my friend. Nothing could ruin that, not even all the homework Mrs. Woods had given us.

NATALIE KURTSMAN
ASPIRING LAWYER
Kurtsman Law Offices

BRIEF #11
October: Friends

You can't call someone your friend and then not be it. That would be a dirtbag move, and I'm not a dirtbag. I know the difference between right and wrong.

6

TOUGH LOVE

Randi

Math is about memorizing facts and doing calculations, and I'm very good at that, but Mrs. Magenta had different ideas. She was all about these wild and complicated problem-solving challenges. I liked them—we all did—but her problems took time, and that was what I didn't have.

"Okay, you royal knights," she greeted us at the start of class today. "King Arthur is ready to pass his crown. You're all invited to sit at his round table, where he will determine his successor. Who will it be?

"He points at the first chair and says, 'You live.' He points at the second chair and says, 'You die.' The third chair lives and the fourth dies. Round and round he goes until only one of you remains. Who will it be?"

"Told you she was nuts, bro. She's got us killing people today," Trevor whispered to Mark.

"Can you tell me where to sit no matter how many knights are in attendance?" Mrs. Magenta asked. "That is today's challenge. Good luck, and may the wisest wear the crown."

This was her craziest problem yet. She let us work alone or with partners, whichever we preferred. Scott and Natalie were math wizards, but they worked alone, because no one wanted to work with them. Besides, it was impossible to make sense of Scott's scribbles, and Natalie was a perfectionist. Trevor and Mark worked together, which was no surprise, but the fact that they actually worked was surprising. They got into Mrs. Magenta's challenge, even if they did think she was nuts. Gav and I teamed up and managed to get a decent amount of tables and lucky numbers figured out, but we were far from done when class came to an end.

"Okay, royal knights, I'd like you to keep working on this for homework," Mrs. Magenta said. "We will continue to devote some time to this problem for the next week or more. It's not easy to solve. Remember, you need to discover a formula so we know where to sit no matter how many knights are present. Toodle-oo."

Class went fast because the problem had been fun, but I was not looking forward to working on it for homework. Forget King Arthur; Gav was the one I was still wondering about. I'd heard what he said to Natalie before storming off the other afternoon, and I saw what Natalie did to help Scott, so I wanted to ask Gav what that was all about. But school was not the place for that conversation. As soon as I was over at his house again, I tried bringing it up. We were outside, passing his football back and forth, waiting for Jane to come and take me to practice.

"So what's the story with Natalie Kurtsman?" I asked him.

"Just don't like her," he said, throwing the ball to me.

"Why?" I passed it back.

"'Cause." The ball came at me harder this time.

"Why?" I asked again. I wanted to know.

"I don't want to talk about it," he said.

I threw the ball back to him. I was going to drop the questions, but something else was bothering me. "Why did you tell her to ask her mother?"

Gav's next throw rocketed over my head. He never missed his target. That was my warning. We threw the rest of our passes in silence, and then I left for practice.

Part of me wanted to ask Natalie when I saw her next, but the funny thing was, I didn't think she knew any more than I did. I would've asked Jane what she thought, but the looming state and regional championships were all she could seem to think about, especially since I'd missed that meet in South Carolina because of a stomach bug, and especially since my practices weren't going well.

"You need to point your toes," Coach Jane said. "And you need to stop looking down, or you're going to lose points for that, too." We were on our way home from my workout. "And for heaven's sake, you've got to push through on your rotation, or you'll keep coming up short and never stick your landing."

Jane loved to talk like she was one of my coaches, even though she wasn't. She'd never even competed in gymnastics, but that didn't stop her. Coach Andrea was full of praise and encouragement, but when it came to Jane, there was always something I was doing wrong and she always had something to say about it.

"If you can't get it right, you'll never win. You might as well give up."

No matter what, I'd never be good enough. Our car rides

were always filled with her criticisms and attempted motivational speeches. I made sure to turn my head when I rolled my eyes. I stared out the window, searching for the white house with the sign for the psychic. We passed it on every trip to and from practice, and I kept hoping to catch a glimpse of the person inside. What did a psychic look like? I wondered. Did this one read palms or use a crystal ball, and could my hands foretell anything if they were covered in calluses?

"Discipline is doing what you don't want to do when you don't want to do it," Coach Jane said, interrupting my thoughts. I'd heard that one a hundred times.

These days it was taking more and more discipline for me to get excited about gymnastics. I had so much on my mind besides handsprings and roundoffs, but this was no time for distractions. And there was no time for me to get my homework done, but Jane didn't want to hear about that, either.

GAVIN

"Everything all right?" Dad asked, coming outside after Randi left. "Looked like you and Randi were havin' a disagreement about somethin'."

"Everything's fine," I said.

Things weren't fine. We were having a disagreement 'cause of him. If my old man hada been smarter about things, maybe it coulda been different for us, but you can't expect that from a high school dropout, so him and Mom got stuck sending every extra cent they made to some lying rich guy—and that was all thanks to Mrs. Kurtsman. I couldn't believe her no-good daughter went around acting like she didn't know anything about it. She was just like her mother—no conscience.

Dad held his hands up, and I threw him a pass. " 'Cause if anything's wrong and you want to talk about it, I'm here to listen," he said.

The whole thing made me so angry that I couldn't talk about it. Randi didn't like that, but she got the hint after a while.

"Everything's fine," I said again.

Dad waved his finger to the left, and I went running in that direction. He hit me with a perfect pass when I was in full stride.

"Nice throw," I said. I had to get a lot better before I could pass like that. I wondered what Dad woulda done in high school if he hadn't had to quit.

"I've gotta get goin' to my next job," he said. "Keep practicin' and keep an eye on your sister."

"Okay. I will."

School rolled on, but if you took away recess and Woods reading aloud, there wasn't anything I liked about it. I say that 'cause the other day it was announced that there'd be no more birthday parties. Someone had gone and decided that our celebrations took up too much valuable teaching time when we had the CSAs to prepare for. Poor Scott was madder than a linebacker on steroids when he heard that.

"No way!" he cried. "That's not fair!"

The kid loved those silly parties, so I kinda felt bad for him, but Woods showed little sympathy.

"Mr. Mason, I'm sorry this decision is so upsetting to you, but you're going to have to deal with it," she said. "Your temper tantrums aren't going to help anything, so tuck in your lips and sit up straight. You heard me tell Mr. Joseph that life isn't always fair, and that means it isn't always easy, either. You've got to roll with the punches and do the best you can."

"I'd like to punch whoever came up with this idea," he said.

"That's enough," Woods snapped. She was practicing tough love again. I was slowly beginning to realize that my teacher woulda made one heckuva football coach. It was during silent reading when she called Randi up to her desk to give her some of that same tough love, and I was sitting close enough that I heard all of it.

"Miss Cunningham, I'm wondering if there's a reason why your homework has been only partially complete the last few days?"

Randi shook her head. She was staring at the floor and picking at her calluses. I couldn't believe she didn't have her homework done. If her scholarship-crazy mother ever found out about that, she'd go ballistic.

"I assume those calluses aren't from splitting firewood," Woods said.

Randi slipped her hands behind her back.

"How often do you have gymnastics, Miss Cunningham?"

"Six days a week," Randi said.

"And how long are the practices?"

"Three hours . . . longer if my mom wants me to work extra." Randi's voice dropped.

"And it takes you how long to get to your gym?"

"About an hour," Randi whispered.

Woods sighed. "That's a lot to balance, Miss Cunningham."

Randi nodded.

"But it's still not an excuse when it comes to school," Woods said.

"I know," Randi croaked.

"It's important that you do your homework so you have practice with these types of questions and problems. Concepts will build from there. I don't want to see you fall behind. You understand?"

Randi nodded again.

"Good. I expect your homework will be done from now on, then. You can go back to your seat."

I didn't look away fast enough. Woods saw that I was listening. That old woman didn't miss much. I was about to find out she'd caught on to me, too.

"Mr. Davids, please come here," she said.

I walked up to her desk, not knowing what to expect. Was she gonna yell at me for eavesdropping?

"Have a seat," she said.

I sat in the chair she had positioned next to her desk for these special conferences.

"I trust by now you've seen that I wasn't born last night, Mr. Davids. I might be old, but I don't miss much."

It was my turn to do the nodding now.

Woods leaned forward and in a hushed voice said, "You're a smart young man, Mr. Davids, but I've noticed the struggles you have with reading."

I don't want to talk about this, I thought.

"I took the liberty of looking in your file. Apparently you don't qualify for extra services."

"I don't qualify 'cause I'm not quite dumb enough."

"Excuse me?" Woods said.

"The lady that gave me those special tests way back when, that's what she told me. I'm not quite dumb enough to get extra help."

"What a horrible thing to tell a child! Who was that?!"

Woods had everyone staring at us now, thanks to her outburst, but she gave them her glare and they all looked away. "That lady doesn't work here anymore," I said, keeping my voice low.

"I should hope not. If she did, she'd be hearing from me, I can promise you that," Woods said.

That made me smile.

"I'm sorry that happened, Mr. Davids. Trust me, trouble reading or spelling doesn't make someone dumb—and neither does not graduating from high school, for that matter."

I was done smiling.

"How would you feel about redoing those tests?"

"No."

"I was planning to ask your father—"

"No," I said again. "I'm not taking any tests."

"Okay, no tests. We'll work on this together, then. Just you and me. But you're going to work. Got it?"

Woods was serious. What did she mean, we'd work on it together? I wasn't sure, but I nodded.

"Good old-fashioned hard work can solve many problems in life, Mr. Davids. But you also need to have the right attitude. You've got to believe. After what that nimrod test lady told you, I'm sure it hasn't been easy believing in your ability, but you can do this. You hear me?"

I nodded again, even though I wasn't supposed to be any good at reading, not coming from my family. But Woods had other ideas about that.

"Good," she said. "For starters, you need more practice. The more you throw that football, the better your accuracy and strength become. Reading is no different, Mr. Davids. The more you do it, the better you'll get. The difference is you enjoy football, so practice is fun. Reading, on the other hand, is a challenge, so you need to be serious about wanting to improve. You've got to be committed, Mr. Davids. But don't worry. I have a few tricks to help you along the way."

"Okay," I croaked.

"And, Mr. Davids, one more thing. I've seen the sketches you have in your journal. Not only do they show how smart you are, but they're very good. I told you before, you have talent. Don't be afraid to pursue it."

I swallowed and nodded. This moment with Woods was what they call a game changer. Things would never be the same again.

NATALIE KURTSMAN
ASPIRING LAWYER
Kurtsman Law Offices

BRIEF #12
October: Black Eye

This notion of the Recruits that Scott had in his head was a problem. Thinking he and Gavin were teammates and buddies at the library, he did something incredibly foolish at recess.

"Can I play?" he asked the football boys.

"Yeah, sure!" Trevor said, acting all excited, like this was a great idea. He wrapped his arm around Scott and led him onto the field. "You can be on your buddy Gavin's team." I moved closer. There was trouble brewing.

I'm intelligent—that goes without saying—but I couldn't make heads or tails of what the boys were doing. The individual starting with the ball (the one called the pitcher, I believe)—which, by the way, was always Gavin for his team and Trevor for the other—would yell go, and then the rest of the boys would take off running every which way. The pitcher would scan the field and then throw the football. If someone caught it, there'd be more running, but I couldn't figure out who was going where—and from what I gathered, neither could Scott. He ran back and forth across the field, waving his arms and squawking like a crazed seagull. All the same, he seemed to be enjoying himself, despite the fact that Gavin hadn't thrown the ball to him—not even once.

Gavin was the last person I wanted to defend, but I must confess, he wasn't trying to be mean; he reserved that for me. He was actually doing Scott a favor by not throwing to him. Trevor, on the other hand, had a different idea. He'd let this go on long enough. When it was his turn to be pitcher again, he stood tall, gripping the football, surveying the field, and the moment Scott looked back, he let it fly. That pass was nowhere near one of Trevor's teammates. It was meant for the kid who couldn't catch. The football drilled Scott in the face—in his eye, to be exact. His arms flailed and his knees buckled. He stumbled about on wobbly legs, bent over, holding his face in his hands. His squawking became that of a dying seagull.

Laughter filled the air, mixed with seagull sound effects from the boys, who thought this was hysterical. "Nice hands, All State!" someone yelled.

I ran onto the field. "Scott, are you okay?" I asked, gently placing my hand on his back.

"My eye hurts," he moaned.

"Sorry, bro!" Trevor shouted. I turned and glared at him. "What? I didn't mean it. I thought he'd catch it."

If I believed for one second that I could actually do it, I would've picked up that grimy football and chucked it at Trevor's face. Yes, that would've been wrong of me, and it's likely it would've only made matters worse, but it would've made me feel better.

"C'mon," I whispered to Scott. "I'll take you to the nurse. You need an ice pack."

I glanced back and saw Trevor slapping five with Mark and some of the other boys. I saw Gavin standing as still as a statue, and then I saw Randi approaching the football.

"Hey, Trevor," she yelled. She didn't bend down to pick up the ball. Instead, she booted it, and the moment Trevor turned around, that thing hit him square in the not-so-funny-spot. It was a home run.

"Field goal!" Randi yelled.

Trevor fell to the ground. He looked rather pale.

"Nice hands, All State!" I yelled.

Randi ran over and joined Scott and me. Gavin watched us leaving the field, but he never moved.

"You might have a black eye," Randi said, "but at least you didn't get any blood on your clothes. Your mother probably wouldn't be very happy if you showed up with another pair of ruined pants."

Scott laughed. Randi and I looked at each other, but we didn't smile. Instead, she stuck her hand out, so I shook it.

"I thought you'd give me five," she said, "but a handshake works, too."

"Oh," I said.

We smiled that time.

Trevor

Woodchuck asked me to step into the hall.

"Mr. Joseph, I heard about recess this afternoon. You do realize Mr. Mason has a black eye?"

"It was an accident," I said.

"I see. Of course."

She let me keep talking. "I got confused about who was on my team." I was searching for excuses again. "It was an honest mistake."

"Interesting that you've mentioned that word 'mistake' again," Woodchuck said. "I don't believe you, so I think you'll spend tomorrow's recess researching mistakes."

I hated this old woman. Hated her.

"Was there anything you wanted to say?" she asked.

I gritted my teeth and shook my head.

"Mr. Joseph, I'm pleased to see you aren't going to argue with me about your consequences. Perhaps you're learning something about responsibility. You may go back in and take your seat."

I didn't need to research mistakes. I knew all about them. Brian had been telling me my whole life that I was a mistake. The mailman dropped me off at the wrong house. Santa left me under the wrong tree. Mom and Dad were given the wrong kid. If I had come with a receipt, they would've returned me. Brian's ten years older than me. My parents never even wanted another baby, and then I showed up.

That's why when Woodchuck told me to write about my goals and what I wanted to be when I was grown up, my paper was blank. It didn't matter what I wanted. The only thing I'd ever be was a mistake.

SCOTT

"What happened to your eye?" Mom asked the instant she saw me.

"I hurt it playing football with my friends. I missed the throw and the ball hit me in the face. But don't worry, Mom. It looks worse than it is."

"Oh, really? How many fingers am I holding up?"

"Four," I said. "Now stop."

"I'm four!" Mickey yelled from the backseat.

"No, you're three," I reminded him.

"Scott boo-boo."

"It's okay, Mickey."

My little brother was quiet after that, but as soon as we got to Grandpa's, he jumped in the front seat with me and touched my eye. He needed to see for himself. After he was satisfied, he hopped out of the car and ran inside.

Mom didn't let us watch much TV at home, but she let Mickey watch his shows at Grandpa's because it kept him out of her hair while she was making dinner. Grandpa didn't care because it kept Mickey from touching his things—and Grandpa didn't want his stuff monkeyed with because he had everything just so. Mom and I never said anything because we didn't want to get Grandpa upset, but the truth was he had so much junk in his house that he couldn't remember what he did and didn't have and he didn't have a clue where stuff was anymore—but I had a plan to help. The last book I read in the library was called *The Memory String,* and it gave me an idea. When I got done making Grandpa's memory string, he'd finally be able to throw out all the garbage that had built up in his house and still remember Grandma.

Mom went into the living room to say hi and check on Grandpa before she got started making his dinner. This was her routine, and this was my chance. I had to move quick, because I knew Mom wouldn't spend that much time chatting with Grandpa and I didn't want her to know what I was up to. I also didn't dare risk Grandpa finding out. He would've been ready to hang me if he discovered I was taking his things.

First, I stuffed my backpack with the usual pile of his junk mail. When I was done with that, I raced to the bathroom. On the back of the toilet Grandpa had a dish of seashells. Really, it was Grandma's dish. She had collected the shells from their trips to the beach. Grandma loved the beach, especially the ocean, so these were perfect for Grandpa's memory string. I sifted through the dish and picked out a few of the ones with holes so I could slide them onto Grandpa's string. In that book I read, the little girl only had buttons on her memory string, but I planned on making Grandpa's a little different. I stuffed the shells in my pocket and then went out to the living room.

I sat on the ottoman in front of Grandpa's chair and moved

the TV tray in between us. "You're white today," I said. "You move first."

Grandpa reached down and slid his pawn forward two squares. This was our afternoon routine. Mom thought it was great. Playing chess helped to exercise our brains, and it kept us quiet while she was getting dinner together. I was killing two birds with one stone—that's how helpful I can be.

"You're at a real disadvantage, playing with only one eye today," Grandpa said. "Maybe I should play with my eyes closed."

He was teasing me, because I'd never beaten him. "Funny," I said.

He chuckled. That was good—Mom said it was good for Grandpa to laugh.

"How was your walk today?" I asked.

"Hah?"

"How was your walk?" I repeated.

"Same as always, I suppose." He moved his knight.

"How come you do it every day if it's always the same?"

"It's something your grandmother and I used to do together. Just got in the habit, I suppose."

"Mom says the walking is good for you because the mind and body work together. She says your walking helps keep your mind sharp, same as our chess matches do."

"Your mother's a smart lady." He slid his rook into position. "You want to know what else is good for me?"

"What?" I said.

"Your stories. They keep my heart young. Tell me more about those friends of yours."

Maybe Grandpa liked my stories, but I think what he liked

most was having someone to talk to. It was a lot for Mom to do this every day, but it was important. When we weren't there, Grandpa spent his time sitting in that same chair of his, staring out the window and talking to himself. His memory string was going to help him remember Grandma, but I still needed to find a way to help him with his loneliness. I wouldn't give up. I'd figure something out.

7

A GRAND IDEA

Trevor

As promised, Woodchuck kept me in for recess. She had me sit at the computer and search "inventions by mistake."

"That one," she said, pointing to the link she wanted me to choose.

I clicked on it and the page opened.

"Mistakes, Mr. Joseph. Sometimes they can turn out to be good things—when we learn from them, that is. Read through this website and give me a report on what you find."

Woodchuck waddled back to her desk, and I pretended to get to work. No way she'd be able to tell if I went to a different website. The old lady's eyes weren't that good. She was the one making a mistake by leaving me alone. I was going to skim through her stupid site so that I could give her a few words for my report, and then I was changing it to ESPN.

That was my plan, but once I started reading about this stuff, I got interested. I wanted to stay mad and bored with her dumb assignment, but this was kinda cool. I never knew we had so many things in our world that came from mistakes.

Did you know potato chips were a mistake? George Crum was the chef when some pain-in-the-neck customer kept sending his plate of fried potatoes back, complaining and asking for them to be thinner and fried longer. The jerk kept it up. It sounded like something I'd do to be a wise guy, but when I read this story, it didn't sound so funny. George Crum didn't find it funny, either. He got so mad that he sliced the potatoes super thin and fried them to a curly crisp and *voilà*—the customer asked for more, and the potato chip was born. How cool is that?

When I got done with that story, I moved on to the next one, about penicillin. I'd taken that stuff before when I was sick. A long time ago this scientist, Alexander Fleming, left a stack of dirty petri dishes by his workstation. Supposedly he was in a hurry to leave on vacation. I wondered if he had a hot date, but probably not if he was some dorky scientist. It turns out, when this dude returned days later and began cleaning up his mess, he noticed that one of the petri dishes had colonies of staph bacteria everywhere except near a spot of mold that had started growing in that same dish. He discovered that the mold stopped the bacteria and, from that, penicillin—one of the most widely used antibiotics—was born. Who would've thunk it?

"Find anything interesting, Mr. Joseph?"

I jumped. Man, Woodchuck had the sneak attack down pat.

"I must walk on silent feet," she said, "or else you were so engrossed in what you were reading that you didn't hear me coming." She raised her eyebrow.

I didn't say anything. I wasn't about to tell her I thought this stuff was cool.

"Interesting how things don't always turn out as one might expect, isn't it, Mr. Joseph? The same is true for people. The world is full of individuals who've achieved despite the odds, but there are also those who've wasted their talents and opportunities. You're at the age when you need to begin asking yourself which you're going to be, Mr. Joseph. A waster or an achiever? Because in the end it's up to you. It doesn't matter what anyone else has to say."

I stayed quiet.

"Tell you what, Mr. Joseph, why don't we hold off on that preliminary report of yours"—she pointed at the few words I had written—"until you've had time to do more thorough research and can provide a more detailed summation."

"You're telling me I've got to miss more recess?"

"No. Not unless you earn that consequence for some future transgression, of course."

"So does that mean I'll do more of this work during class?"

"Perhaps. Would you be okay with that?"

"Sure. Fine. If I have to, I mean." I didn't want to sound excited, but I was definitely cool with that.

"Good," Woodchuck said. "You can return to your desk now. Your classmates should be coming in from recess any minute."

A waster or an achiever?

GAVIN

When we got to the library this afternoon, first thing Scott said was "This room is lonely, like my grandpa. We should have a party and invite a bunch of little kids so the room has company. My grandpa likes it when he has company."

This wasn't one of Scott's brilliant stupid ideas. This one actually made some sense.

"What a wonderful idea!" Magenta cheered. "A party! It'll be like our grand reopening. Okay, team, let's do it."

"So what's that mean for today?" I asked, slowing her down a bit and moving us past that team talk.

"Well, it means we've got a party to plan, but I was also wondering if one of you could add something more to that area over there."

She pointed to the reading nook. Several beautiful pictures of book covers and storybook characters had been painted on our new yellow walls.

"Gavin's really good at drawing," Randi said. "He should be the one to add something."

I shrugged. "I wouldn't know what."

"How about a picture of your favorite book?" Magenta suggested.

"I don't have one," I said. I don't know any children's books, is what I really meant.

"Do *The Very Hungry Caterpillar*," Scott said. "Every kid knows that one."

I didn't, but I didn't say so.

"That's another wonderful idea," Magenta agreed. I wanted to tell her Scott never ran out of wonderful ideas, but I bit my tongue. "Girls, why don't you find a spot and start making plans for our party, and I'll get Gavin set up with his *Hungry Caterpillar* project." She didn't say anything to Scott, 'cause he already had his nose buried in a different book. Must be she figured it was best to leave him there. That was a wonderful idea.

I sat down and read *The Very Hungry Caterpillar*. It took me a little bit to get through it, but I didn't feel dumb looking at it, 'cause I had to in order to do my drawing. I could see why Scott picked this book. That caterpillar liked sweets about as much as he did. It was a good story, a perfect example of things needing to get ugly before getting better.

Mrs. Magenta had given me a bunch of different brushes and markers. I grabbed a black Sharpie and got started drawing my caterpillar. After getting it outlined, I began adding color to his fat body and happy face. About that time, Magenta came over to check on my progress.

"Randi was right," she said. "You're an excellent artist, Gavin."

"Thank you."

She stood there watching me for a minute. "I looked in the system and couldn't find your name," she said, "so I went ahead and added your information and got you a library card. Now you can check out books whenever you'd like. I hope that was okay."

"Thanks," I said to be polite. I knew I'd probably never use that card.

"In fact, I've already checked something out for you," she continued. "I hope that was okay, too."

"Really?" I stopped coloring and turned around.

"Yes. I noticed you always have that football with you, so I wanted to give you this story. It's called *Crash,* written by Jerry Spinelli." She handed it to me. "This is the audiobook. Instead of reading the story, you can listen to it."

"I didn't know they did that with books."

"Oh yes. And they're wonderful. It was your teacher's idea."

"You mean, Mrs. Woods?"

"Yes. She put a note in my mailbox at school asking me to find you an audiobook."

"She gave you a note? She didn't just ask you?"

"It's complicated."

"Oh."

"Don't worry about that. I know you'll enjoy the story. One of the main characters loves football, just like you."

"Thanks," I said again. But this time I wasn't just being polite.

She smiled. "I'll let you get back to work now."

Boy, Woods was sure holding up her end of the bargain. She was meeting with me every day about my reading. We'd gone over how to track the words, and she'd gone out of her way to get me large-print copies of what we were reading in class, and now she was trying to help me with these audio-books. Maybe I only nodded when she asked if I understood that I was gonna have to work at this, but to Woods that musta been as good as my word. I had to do my part now.

"Mrs. Magenta," I called, stopping her before she got too far away.

She turned around. "Yes?"

"Can I get a copy of *Crash* to follow along in while listening to it?"

"Yes, of course," she said.

"And can I also check out this one?" I held up *The Very Hungry Caterpillar*. "I'd like to read it to my little sister."

"Absolutely," she said, taking the book from me.

"Thanks," I said again. Then I went back to coloring.

Even though she was my pain-in-the-butt sister, I was kinda excited to read that caterpillar story to her. It'd be more prac-tice for me, but I also knew Meggie was gonna like it. Maybe she didn't have to miss out on bedtime stories like I had.

Randi

What're you supposed to do when somebody asks you a question? You can ignore them, if you're a snob. I'm not. Talking to her didn't mean I liked her. We were just chitchatting while making plans for the grand reopening of the children's room. We were just passing the time.

"Why don't you play football with the boys at recess?" Natalie asked me. "You're better than most of them. I've seen the way you pass the ball with Gavin."

"Coach Jane doesn't want me to," I said. "She doesn't want me to get hurt, because I've got gymnastics that I need to be ready for. I've got a big Halloween competition coming up."

"That makes sense."

"Yeah." I sighed.

Natalie looked at me in a way that made me feel like she was seeing through me. "Good luck at that game," she said.

I chuckled at the way she called my meet a game, but I didn't correct her. "Thanks," I said. "I think I'll go check on Gavin now to see how he's coming along with his drawing." Natalie and I already had a craft planned, and we were just about done making our flyer on the computer. We just had to save and print.

"Okay," she said. "No problem."

I knew I wasn't supposed to like Natalie, because Gavin didn't, but I was finding that difficult. She really wasn't that bad. Maybe if she had told me it wasn't okay, or that I couldn't take a break, or that I wasn't doing a good job of helping, then I could've found a reason to dislike her, but that wasn't the case. The girl was nice. I'd just never gotten to know her before.

"Gav, that looks great!" I said. I wasn't surprised. He didn't like to show his drawings, but I'd seen some before. I knew he was good.

"Howdoya like working with what's-her-face?" he said.

What was I supposed to say? I couldn't tell him it wasn't that bad. "I'm just ignoring her."

"Good idea. Whatever you do, don't trust her."

I wanted to ask why, but I held it in. I changed the subject. "Who did these other pictures?" I stepped closer to the wall. "They're really good."

"I don't know," he said.

"The colors are so vibrant. Is that someone's name?" I pointed to the spot I was talking about.

Gavin glanced over at it and shrugged. "Maybe."

"Artists put their name next to their work," Mrs. Magenta said, spooking us with her reminder. We hadn't realized she was standing there. "I'm sorry. I didn't mean to startle you," she added.

I looked at Mrs. Magenta and then back at the name on the wall. It was hard to read because of the way it was written, but suddenly I knew what it said. "Mrs. Magenta, are these your paintings?"

She nodded and gave us a sheepish smile.

"Wow! They're amazing!" I said.

"Thank you."

"Randi's right. They're incredible," Gavin agreed. "You should be selling your stuff."

"I dreamed of doing that once, but I'm afraid I'm not good enough."

"Says who?" Gavin asked.

"Yeah, it all depends on who's judging," I said. "And believe me, I know a thing or two about judges."

"Well, you two have certainly made my day with your enthusiastic reviews of my work," Mrs. Magenta said.

"You should try again," I told her.

"You should try again," Gavin repeated.

"I never tried a first time," she said.

"Why?" Gav and I asked together.

"Oh, it's complicated." She sighed. "But I'm glad my work gets to be next to yours, Gavin. Your caterpillar is fantastic. You've got talent. You should pursue it."

"I don't know," Gav mumbled.

"Mrs. Woods told him the same thing," I said.

"Really?" Mrs. Magenta said. I couldn't tell if she was shocked or pleased to hear that. She was quiet for a moment, then said, "Don't forget to put your name next to your caterpillar."

And with that, she turned and walked away. Gav and I looked at each other.

"Wonder what that was all about," he said.

"Me too. And that isn't the only thing I've been wondering about lately."

And with that, I walked away.

NATALIE KURTSMAN
ASPIRING LAWYER
Kurtsman Law Offices

BRIEF #13
October: A Cat Sighting

It had been a productive afternoon at the library. Randi and I created a flyer to advertise our party, and we posted a blurb about it on the library website. In addition, we found a Thanksgiving craft (paper-plate turkeys) to do with the children and we made plans for snack, all while also enjoying some conversation—and it wasn't the meaningless gossip that I'd predicted. On the contrary, it was nice—and telling. Randi was dealing with pressure in gymnastics from Coach Jane, and I had the sneaking suspicion it was getting to be too much for her. I was able to make this deduction because of my superb lawyer skills and knack for deciphering body language, but it would take more time and observation before I knew how bad the pressure on her was.

Aside from our work together, Gavin had added a remarkable drawing to the reading nook—as much as it pains me to admit that—and Scott had stayed out of trouble and out of the way. For our efforts, Mrs. Magenta rewarded us with brownies. All was well until we exited the building.

"Hey, look!" Scott exclaimed. Bits of brownie fell out of his mouth. He pointed toward the bushes, where he'd spotted a gray kitten. Unable to contain his excitement, he scurried closer and knelt down. "Here, kitty, kitty," he sang. "C'mon, I won't hurt you. I've got a piece of brownie for you." He held out his hand.

Trevor nudged Mark and pointed at Scott. Mark smirked and nodded. Those two couldn't let an opportunity like this pass by.

"I think I'll name you Smoky," Scott told the kitty. "Come here, Smoky."

"Hey, Mark. What do you say we use little Smoky as our football?" Trevor said, walking up behind Scott.

"Betcha I can cat-punt farther than you," Mark replied.

"No! Leave Smoky alone!" Scott cried. He tried to block their way, but they just shoved him aside. "Run, Smoky! Get away!" Scott yelled.

Trevor and Mark jumped in front of the cat, their knees bent and hands raised, ready to spring the second it moved. Slowly Trevor circled behind Smoky while Mark held his position.

"Now!" Trevor yelled.

They dove for the cat, but Smoky was gone. He shot through Mark's legs and disappeared around the side of the building like a streak of lightning. Those two buffoons didn't stand a chance against Scott's kitty.

"Nice catch," Trevor said to Mark.

"Shut up."

"Guess Smoky's too fast for you guys," Scott said, sounding like a proud owner. "Better keep training."

140

He should've kept his mouth shut. Trevor walked over and leaned in his face. "I'll get your slimy cat. You can count on it," he promised. He snatched the brownie from Scott's hand and stuffed it into his own mouth. Mark burst out laughing, and then so did Trevor. I stood there, still missing the humor in all of it, as the two of them sauntered off.

"Don't worry," I told Scott. "They'll never catch Smoky. That kitty is elusive."

"Oh, I'm not worried," he said. "They're not going to catch him, because I'm going to rescue him first."

SCOTT

When we got back from the library, I remembered I had something to show Mrs. Magenta. I would've shown her sooner, but I'd lost my work and had to redo it.

"Mrs. Magenta, I know where to sit." She gave me a confused look. "I know where to sit at King Arthur's table."

"Really?"

I pulled the wrinkled paper out of my backpack and smoothed it flat on her desk. "If there's seven knights at the table, you want to sit in chair seven, but if there's ten knights, you should sit in chair five." I showed her a bunch of my calculations. "It's a pattern," I said. "Once you know the pattern, you can figure out where to sit no matter how many knights are at the table. If there are thirty knights, you want to sit in chair twenty-nine. See?" I explained my formula to her.

"Scott Mason, I'm impressed. That brain of yours is good at solving problems."

"Mrs. Magenta, I don't think King Arthur should kill the knights who sit in the wrong chairs, because then the new king won't have any people left in his kingdom. He should keep them alive so they can have a party and then the new king won't be lonely and everyone will be happy."

Mrs. Magenta smiled at me. "Scott, that was my favorite part of your solution. You have such a big heart."

"This was a lot of fun. It was hard, but I really liked it. When can we do another problem like this?"

Mrs. Magenta's face went from happy to sad, and I didn't understand.

"Later," she said.

"How much later?"

She sighed. "Not until after the CSAs, I'm afraid. I've been told to stop taking up class time with these challenges and to focus more on CSA work."

My shoulders dropped. "That stinks."

"I'm sorry, Scott. Please don't leave upset. Today was great. I'm so excited for our party."

"The children's room won't be lonely anymore," I said.

"No, it won't. And that's thanks to your great brain and big heart again."

"Bye, Mrs. Magenta. Thank you."

"Bye, Scott. I'll see you tomorrow. And thank *you*."

I did like Mrs. Magenta said and didn't leave upset. That was because my best idea of the day wasn't the one about our library party, but the one I'd come up with so my grandpa didn't have to be lonely anymore.

GAVIN

I told Meggie I had a surprise for her, but she didn't believe me.

"You're lying."

I shook my head.

"What is it?"

"You have to wait until bedtime," I told her.

"That's because you're lying."

"You'll see," I said.

Later that night I took *The Very Hungry Caterpillar* and walked into her room.

"Surprise!" she yelled, throwing her balled-up dirty socks at me. She hit me square in the numbers. My little sister could make a solid quarterback.

"That's what I get for bringing you a present?"

"What is it? What is it?" she asked, bouncing on her bed.

I sat down next to her. "I thought I'd read you a book," I said.

Meggie's face beamed. "Really? I get a bedtime story?"

"Really," I said.

I opened the pages and introduced Meggie to the hungry caterpillar. Even though sounding out words doesn't come easy for me, once I know them, I'm pretty good at bringing them to life. It's like when I'm outside and throwing the football to all my pretend teammates and scrambling away from the imaginary defenses. The whole while I'm doing that, I'm screaming and yelling like the play-by-play broadcasters. Mom says you'd think there was a stadium of people in our backyard, the way I carry on. I read *The Very Hungry Caterpillar* with my same excited voices. When I finished, I closed the book and looked up. Mom was standing in the doorway, smiling. My old man was there with his arm around her. He squeezed her tight when she started wiping her eyes.

"Read it again, Gavvy," Meggie said.

I opened the cover and my little sister snuggled close to me. Mom and Dad listened for a while longer, and then they left us alone. I read the book five times that night. When I was done, I tucked Meggie in and turned out her lights.

"Gavvy," she said, stopping me before I made it out of her room.

"Yeah?"

"Will you read it to me for bedtime again tomorrow night?"

"Okay," I said.

I walked to my room, feeling like the best big brother in the whole wide world, and it was because of a hungry caterpillar. I put my pajamas on, and then I took the audiobook and paperback copy of *Crash* that Mrs. Magenta had given me and decided to give it a shot.

That was the first night in a long, long time that I fell asleep to a story.

Randi

Straight leg. Point your toes. Spin.

I wobbled.

The Halloween Gymnastics Spooktacular was that weekend. I was supposed to be at my best, but I wasn't. Now was not the time for flawed steps. These were basic techniques on the beam. What was my problem?

"C'mon, Randi. You've got this," encouraged Coach Andrea.

Split jump. Now!

I wobbled again. Bad. I was bent in half, waving my arms to regain balance and keep from falling. Jane's glare was burning a hole in me, and I didn't need to look at her to feel it. Most of the moms didn't even watch practice, just spent the hours gossiping. Not Coach Jane. She sat outside that large window we had on one wall of the gym, scrutinizing my every move.

Focus. You can do this. Back arch. Reach. Straight leg. Point.

My feet landed on the beam but not centered. I tried to straighten, but I lost it this time. I fell. That would've been a huge deduction. With a mistake like that I could kiss any medal goodbye. "It's okay, Randi. Hop up there and do it again." Coach Andrea tried to keep me positive, but I could hear Jane yelling in my head. Our parents were kept out of the gym to eliminate distractions, but that wall didn't stop Jane from getting to me—and the worst was yet to come. There was no place for me to hide during our car ride home.

"I don't even know why I try," Jane started. "This weekend is supposed to be a warm-up meet. You'll be lucky if you win that, never mind Regionals. You won't even make it that far. You were terrible tonight. What's wrong with you?"

I flinched at her words, but I didn't say anything. I just stared out my window, searching for the psychic's white house.

"Have you forgotten how to stay on the beam? Maybe I just need to stop caring so much. Accept the fact that you'll never get a scholarship. At least I tried."

I was getting used to the put-downs, but it still hurts to hear your mother say those things about you. Coach Andrea never hesitated to tell me when I'd done something well, and Mrs. Magenta always had nice things to say about our work in the library, but positive reinforcement or complimenting was not something Jane knew how to do. I had to remind myself that she only wanted the best for me and that was why she was pushing me. She didn't really mean those awful things she said. I tried not to let it bother me, but it wasn't easy. If you want to know the truth, I was getting sick of it.

I took a quick shower and went to bed as soon as we got home. I didn't even bother with my math homework. What did it matter?

A GRAND REOPENING

NATALIE KURTSMAN
ASPIRING LAWYER
Kurtsman Law Offices

BRIEF #14
November: An Empty—but Smelly—Backpack

Today marked our final trip to the public library. We would be starting on a new project following winter break. What? I had no clue. I suspected that Mrs. Magenta also had no clue. Planning ahead wasn't exactly part of the free-spirit DNA, but she had proven herself a very capable teacher, and I happened to like her—despite her wardrobe. After all, it was thanks to her program that I actually felt like I was doing something important. (I had yet to accomplish anything that qualified as brave, but there was still time.)

I should've known Scott was up to something when he arrived at the art room with an empty backpack. He had crammed his daily pile of papers into our class recycling bin that morning, but I hadn't realized his bag was otherwise empty until now. All his usual garbage and grossness were missing. Well, except for the smell; that rotten odor lingered.

Now, a lawyer needs to be good at analyzing people's

routines and habits. That's simple detective work. When a person veers from his normal tendencies, that's almost always a key piece of information. What you do with that information is critical. That's the next step.

I'll admit, I should've questioned him. I intended to later, but his pack reeked. For the record: I wasn't being lazy. I was procrastinating.

GAVIN

"Gavvy, can you bring home more stories?" Meggie had been asking me that ever since I read her *The Very Hungry Caterpillar*.

"I'll try," I promised.

I wanted more Meggie books, and I wanted another audiobook, too. I finished the one Magenta had given me, and she was right. *Crash* was a terrific story, and that person doing the reading had a voice that took me away, just like Woods.

I loved all the football stuff there was in *Crash*, but it didn't take long before I saw there was more to it than that. There were characters in that story who reminded me of me and Scott and Trevor and Mark, just like there were in some of those other ones Woods had read to us. I was hoping for more audiobooks like that, 'cause I was gonna start using them in school during our silent reading time now. Woods came up with that idea. All this stuff she was doing was helping me. I was getting better at reading, even she said so. And I was holding up my end of the bargain by working hard.

"Where is everyone?" Scott asked when we got to the

children's room and found it empty. "This place is still lonely." He sounded upset.

"Not for long," Magenta said. "Our little friends should be arriving in ten minutes, so we need to get ready. Natalie, can you and Randi organize the Community Room? After story time that's where the children will be doing their craft project and having snack."

"Snack?" Scott repeated.

"Yes," Magenta said.

He didn't waste another second. The kid took off to see what there was.

"We'd better go with him before there's another spill," Randi said.

"We'll take care of everything, Mrs. Magenta. Don't worry," Kurtsman said.

I watched her and Randi hurry after Scott, but I stayed back. "Mrs. Magenta, where do I put these things?" I asked, showing her the items I was returning.

"Oh, I'll take them," she said. "How was the audiobook?"

"It was great!"

"I'm glad you enjoyed it. We need to get you more. Mrs. Woods left another note in my box asking me to help you again."

I didn't say anything, but I sure was wondering why those two had to pass notes and couldn't talk. I followed Magenta to a different area, where there was a wall of audiobooks, but I had no idea which to pick. I didn't know any of these stories. I stared at all the titles. There were so many.

"Would you like me to help you choose a few?" Magenta asked.

"A few?"

"Yes. You need more than one. And how about your sister? I saw that you also returned *The Very Hungry Caterpillar.* Did she like it?"

"She loved it. I read it to her so many times that I didn't even need to look at the words anymore."

Magenta laughed. "I'm going to grab you a library bag we can fill up. I'll be right back."

When we got done, I had a pile of Eric Carle books—that's the same guy who wrote *The Very Hungry Caterpillar*—a few of Magenta's favorites, some Henry and Mudge books that she thought Meggie would like, and three other audiobooks with the paperback copies to follow along in. I couldn't wait to show Meggie. Reading little-kid books in school always made me feel dumb, but sharing these stories with her didn't. I felt something else.

Mrs. Magenta checked all the items out and put them in some canvas library bag covered in butterflies. Then we went to see how things were going in the Community Room. I didn't want the bag—I looked ridiculous carrying it—but I thanked Magenta, 'cause I didn't want to hurt her feelings or make it seem like I didn't appreciate her help.

Little did I know that when we got close to the Community Room, it was my feelings that would get hurt—and I'm no wimp.

Randi

It was just Natalie and me in the Community Room. Scott had disappeared, and Gavin and Mrs. Magenta hadn't joined us yet.

"Not much of a party with only two of the Recruits here," Natalie said.

"No, I guess it's not," I agreed.

"I'm not so sure everyone thinks of us as a team anyway."

I glanced at her. Was she just referring to Gavin? What about me? I hadn't put my name under the rug, either.

"How did everything go at the Halloween competition?" she asked.

"Fine," I lied. Truthfully, it had been a disaster. I fell off the beam, then fell again during my bars routine, which was supposed to be my best event. I ended up losing to girls I'd beaten before. Jane had an argument with Coach Andrea and still wasn't talking to me.

"That's great," Natalie said. "When's the next one?"

"Whenever Coach Jane decides," I said.

"Oh." She looked down and continued organizing the craft materials.

My best friend hadn't even asked me about the meet, but the girl I wasn't supposed to like just did. That made me hate gymnastics even more, but Natalie was only trying to be nice, and here I was being short with her. I felt bad. My problems weren't her fault.

"The state championships are at the end of the school year," I said. "And if that goes well, then there's the regional championships."

"Wow, state and regional. Good luck."

I looked up and she gave me a soft smile. It was one of those looks that said sorry, like she knew things with gymnastics were anything but fine. For the second time I had the feeling Natalie could see through me. "I can't believe Gav's still out there looking at books," I said, changing the subject.

"Maybe Mrs. Magenta's prepping him to do the read-aloud. He seems to like that."

"No, Gav's never wanted anything to do with books, and he definitely isn't going to read aloud."

"A distaste for reading is typical with boys," Natalie said, "Scott being the exception. But that boy's the exception for most things."

"No, it's different for Gavin. He doesn't hate books just because he's a boy. He wishes he could read better, but for some reason the letters run around on the page when he looks at them. Reading and books just make him feel dumb. He plays it off like it's no big deal, but it bothers him. Please don't tell him I told you all this. He doesn't like to talk about it."

"Don't worry. Something tells me Mrs. Woods is on top of

Gavin, but even so, I think you know I won't be talking to him," Natalie said.

I tried not to laugh, but she was right about that.

"And by the way," she continued, "I never got to tell you, but great kick at recess. You made poor Trevor a farmer."

"Huh? What do you mean?"

She chuckled. "You gave him two ache-ers."

I burst out laughing. It was such a cheesy joke, but to hear it coming out of Natalie's mouth was surprising and funny.

"That kick was definitely a slam dunk," she said.

I started laughing even harder. I had to admit, I liked Natalie. I laughed and laughed, and when I finally calmed down enough to wipe my tears, I looked up and saw Gavin standing outside the doorway—but he wasn't laughing.

GAVIN

All the wind was knocked out of me the second I saw Randi laughing her butt off with snobby Natalie Kurtsman. It was worse than taking a helmet in the gut. I felt like I'd been yanked from the game and thrown on the bench.

"You know what, Mrs. Magenta? I'm gonna use the bathroom first. I'll join you in a bit." That was the best lie I could come up with to get me out of there.

"If you think you want any cookies, you better hurry up. Scott doesn't tend to leave things like that sitting around for very long."

"Okay," I said, even though I knew I wasn't coming back. I wasn't in the mood to be around anybody. I would tell Magenta I wasn't feeling good—and that was the truth.

SCOTT

There was something I had to do. I waited until Randi and Natalie were busy, and then I slipped out of the building and walked around the side.

"Smoky," I called. "Smoky."

Nothing.

"Smoky. Here, kitty, kitty."

I held my breath and stood so still Mrs. Woods would've been proud of me. The only moving I did was shivering, because it was starting to get colder. I looked and listened and waited. Then I waited some more.

"Mew," came his cry. *"Mew."*

I found Smoky hiding behind the book bin, near the trash barrel. I got down on my knees. I didn't want to scare him. Slowly I slid my backpack off my shoulders. I unzipped it and pulled out the hot dog I had sitting on the bottom. I broke off a little tiny piece and tossed it closer to him.

"It's for you," I said. "Take it."

Smoky looked at me, trying to decide if he should trust

me or not. Carefully he crept from his hiding place, curious about what I'd just given him. With his ears pricked high and every single one of his ribs showing, he walked out and nibbled the hot dog. I broke off several more tiny pieces and sprinkled them on the ground. With his tail swishing, Smoky started scarfing them down faster than I did my cookies.

"Slow down," I said. "You don't have to eat so fast. I'm not going to take the goodies away."

I broke up the rest of the hot dog and dropped the pieces inside my backpack. I had Smoky thinking with his stomach and not his brain now. He came over and stuck his head all the way inside, searching for his yummy treats. I shoved his butt in and zipped him up.

"Scott, what're you doing out here?"

I jumped. "You scared me!"

"Sorry," Natalie said. "But what're you doing?"

"Nothing."

"You need to come in. This party was your idea, and besides, it's cold outside."

My backpack moved.

"Scott, do you have that cat in there?!"

"No."

Smoky wasn't cooperating. He started freaking out and sent my backpack skipping and rolling across the ground.

"Scott!"

"*Shh!* Please don't tell," I begged. "I'm going to give him a home. I'm helping him, I promise."

"You need to unzip the top. Give the poor cat some air and light. He must be petrified."

"No, he likes it in there," I said. "He likes the warmth." I opened it a sliver to make Natalie happy. "See."

We peeked inside. Smoky yowled and hissed. He appreciated the hot dog, but he wasn't so happy about being in my backpack.

"Don't worry," I told him. "I'm going to give you a nice home."

"Whatever you do, don't let Trevor and Mark find out you've got that cat in there," Natalie said. She stuck her face over my backpack. "You hear that, Smoky?" she warned him. "Be quiet."

Natalie Kurtsman
ASPIRING LAWYER
Kurtsman Law Offices

```
BRIEF #15
November: Smoky
```

I tried to get Scott to stash his backpack under the bushes or behind the book bin, but he refused to leave Smoky unattended. This left only one option, which was to smuggle the cat inside with us.

We rejoined Randi in the Community Room. Mrs. Magenta had just finished reading a few Thanksgiving stories to the kids and was ushering them in for their craft and snack. Gavin was nowhere to be found, but I didn't ask.

Scott slid his backpack under the table and got started helping. He was as excited as the little kids about making paper-plate turkeys. It didn't take long before he had paste all over his hands, but that was because all the kids liked him best—probably because he was a bigger version of themselves. They thought it was great when he showed them how he could lick the paste off his fingers. It was our good fortune that the littles were a noisy bunch, because that seemed to persuade Smoky to lie low.

All in all, it was a most successful afternoon. The children had a great time, and so did we.

"The library felt like a new place today," Mrs. Magenta commented after we had things cleaned up. "Happy and alive. This was a great idea, Scott."

His smile was so big after she said that, it spread to my face.

"This was fun," Randi said. "And, Mrs. Magenta, you are amazing at reading aloud. The kids loved *A Turkey for Thanksgiving.*"

"Thank you, Randi. It's because I had the best teacher."

"Who?" we asked.

"My mother."

Scott's bag jerked under the table, and I knew that was our cue to get moving. Thankfully, Mrs. Magenta left so she could round up the other groups. I shooed Scott out the door before Smoky decided he had something to say. Randi and I finished picking up, and then we went and waited outside with Scott.

The moment Trevor and Mark exited the library, they began searching high and low. They checked under the bushes, behind the book bin, and around the corner. Now I was glad Scott had insisted on keeping Smoky imprisoned in his backpack. Trevor and Mark were determined, but they weren't going to find what they were looking for, not as long as Scott kept walking and Smoky stayed quiet.

When we were a good distance down the sidewalk, I glanced back and saw those two bozos still standing outside the library, scratching their heads. Then they shoved each other and came running, apparently calling it quits on their kitty search. They ran past Randi and me and stopped next to Gavin and Scott. Little did they know, they were closer to Smoky now than they'd ever been.

"Whoa, Gavin! What's with the old-lady bag, dude?" Mark said.

"You checked out books!" Trevor cried. "What a loser."

"You can't even read!" Mark said.

"They must be alphabet books," Trevor joked.

Those two idiots thought they were so funny. When Gavin didn't respond, Trevor shoved him. "What's wrong, bro? You're supposed to say something back. You know we're just messing with ya."

"Yeah, you're no fun anymore," Mark said.

I was picking up on Gavin's cues, even if they weren't. He wasn't playing. They'd hit a sensitive spot, and then they took it too far. They got what they were asking for. Maybe Gavin didn't say anything back, but he certainly shoved back. He sent Trevor flying sideways.

It's a basic reflex to grab on to something, anything, when you're falling. Trevor latched on to the nearest thing he could find, which was Scott—his backpack, to be exact.

GAVIN

I was so mad I lost my head and shoved Trevor. On the football field every official's yellow penalty flag woulda been flying, moving my team back fifteen yards for unsportsmanlike conduct, but here on the sidewalk the result was something different.

Trevor went flying into Scott, and the next thing you know, he had ahold of Scott's backpack.

"Let go!" Scott cried.

"Hey, Mark! I think we've found old Smoky!"

Trevor wasn't letting go. He unzipped the top of Scott's bag and stuck his arm in like he was gonna pull that cat out. Trevor tried a lot of dumb things, but this was at the top of the list. Old Smoky came to life when he saw that hand reaching inside. He yowled like a tiger, not an innocent little kitty. Trevor jumped and shrieked louder than a prissy schoolgirl wearing a skirt. He was lucky that cat didn't tear his hand off. He was left bloodied, with bite and scratch marks all up and down his arm.

Scott spun around. "I told you to let go. I always have my backpack booby-trapped."

Mark couldn't stop laughing at Trevor. "You wimp!"

"I dare you to stick your hand in his bag," Trevor said. "Or better yet, how about I stuff your face in there?"

I pulled Scott along. We kept walking and left those morons arguing by themselves. When we got a little ways down the road, I reached out and we slapped five.

SCOTT

I climbed in our car and put my backpack on the floor in front of me, in between my knees. "Hi, Mom."

"Hi, kiddo. All set?"

"Yup."

We got going but didn't make it very far before Smoky started growing restless. I'd had him trapped long enough. I shifted in my seat to make it look like it was me moving my backpack, but then my kitty had another one of his freak-outs. My bag yanked and jerked every which way, and then it began making noise.

"What was that?" Mom said.

"What got?" Mickey yelled from the back. "See! See!"

All of a sudden Smoky let out a wild yowl.

"Scott, do you have a cat in there?!" Mom yelled.

"See! See!" Mickey cried.

I unzipped the top of my backpack, and Smoky stuck his head out.

"Where did you get that thing?!" Mom shrieked. Our car

swerved and a horn blasted. Mom snapped back to attention and gripped the steering wheel.

"This is Smoky," I said. "I found him outside the library. He needs a home, so I'm going to give him to Grandpa."

"See!" Mickey shouted.

"You'll see him when we get to Grandpa's," I said. "I can't take him out right now."

"No, you most certainly won't take him out right now," Mom said. "That thing could have fleas and diseases and who knows what."

"No, he doesn't," I said. "I checked him. He's going to be great company for Grandpa and make him less lonely."

"That cat is going to give me something else I need to take care of. I've got half a mind to pull over and make you let him out right now."

"No!" Mickey yelled.

Smoky meowed and Mom huffed.

"I'll help you take care of him," I said. "A cat isn't as much work as a dog. You'll see." I scratched Smoky's ears, and soon our car filled with the music of his purring. Mom glanced over at us and shook her head.

As soon as we pulled into Grandpa's driveway and parked, my little brother weaseled out of his car seat and climbed into the front. "Hi, Smoky," he said. He touched Smoky's whiskers and squealed.

"Listen, you two," Mom said. "I don't know what your grandfather is going to say about this cat. He might not want it in his house. If that's the case, then Smoky will have to go. Understand?"

"Yes," we said.

We climbed out of the car and, as usual, Mickey took off running inside. I thought he was rushing to get to his TV shows, but instead he was all excited to tell Grandpa we had a surprise for him. "Gampa present! Present!"

"Huh?"

"Don't tell him, Mickey!" I yelled from the kitchen. "It's my surprise!"

I hurried into the living room and kneeled down. Mom was right behind me. "I brought you a present today, Grandpa."

"A present? It's not Christmas yet, and I told you I don't want any presents."

I unzipped my backpack, and Smoky stepped out and stretched.

"A cat?" Grandpa said, sitting up straight. He wasn't yelling. That was a good sign. "Where in the devil did you get that creature?"

"His name is Smoky," I said. "I got him at the library."

"Did you say Smoky?"

"Yup, him is Smoky," Mickey said.

"Well, how about that. Your grandmother had a cat when we first met, and it had the same name. Looked a lot like this one, too. We never got another one, because she didn't think Smoky could ever be replaced. She loved that darn cat. And now here I am with Smoky again."

Mom sighed. I looked up at her and smiled.

"Good kitty," Mickey said, petting his back. Smoky rubbed against Mickey, and then he jumped into Grandpa's lap. He was much friendlier out of my backpack than in it.

"Well, hello, fella," Grandpa said, scratching him behind the ears.

"He likes you," I said. Grandpa ran his hand along Smoky's back, and then the kitty curled up in his lap and started purring.

"If he wants, he can stay," Grandpa said. "I'll need to get a litter box and some food."

"I'll take care of all that," Mom said. "You're sure you want him to stay?"

"Why not?" Grandpa said. "We'll enjoy each other's company."

I couldn't hide my smile. My idea worked!

"Don't say it," Mom said, pointing her finger at me.

"Told you so." I couldn't resist.

"I said don't say it."

"Him told you so," Mickey repeated.

"Ugh!" Mom groaned. "That's it. I'm going to start dinner." She pretended to be fed up with us, but I heard her chuckling as she walked away.

I slid the chessboard between Grandpa (and Smoky) and me, and we settled in for our daily match. I was so happy, Grandpa could've checkmated me on his first move and I wouldn't have cared.

Before leaving that afternoon, I made a trip to the bathroom, but I took the scenic route and stopped by Grandpa's bedroom first. I found an old ring and necklace that had been Grandma's and stuffed those in my pockets. Grandpa's memory string was coming along. I still didn't know how or when I was going to give it to him, but I'd eventually figure that out. I was on a roll with ideas. By bringing Smoky here, I'd just saved Grandpa's life and didn't even know it.

Trevor

I got up this morning ready to even the score with Gavin. That crap he pulled when he shoved me, that wasn't cool. Talk about mistakes. Library Boy had made a big one. He's just lucky I got sidetracked when I grabbed on to Scott's backpack. I swear, if I could've wrestled that cat free from his bag, I would've ripped all the whiskers out of its face. Gavin and Scott didn't stick around after that, and that was smart, but I wasn't done with them. I was taking care of business today. That was my plan, until I found out school was canceled because of a broken water main. That meant I was home for the day with my brother.

Brian was "in charge." That's how it was every day after school until Mom and Dad got home from work. That's how it had been all summer, and I hated it. Can you believe my parents actually paid my brother for this crap? I didn't need babysitting. I could take care of myself. But this was Mom and Dad's way of helping my stupid brother get enough money together so he could finally move out of the house. I couldn't wait for that day to come.

"Yo, Trevor!"

That was idiot Chris yelling my name. He and Garrett were playing video games in Brian's room. They were my brother's best goons. They hung out at our house all the time, mooching off us.

"Yo, Trevor!"

What did he want now?

"Yo, Trevor! Don't make me come and find you."

I wanted to keep ignoring him, but Chris was a jerk—and he could be mean.

"What?" I said, stepping into the doorway.

"What, sir?" he corrected me. That's what he thought I should say. Fat chance.

"Yes, ma'am," I said, pushing his buttons.

"I'm thirsty. Get me a soda."

"Me too," my stupid brother added. "And grab one for Garrett."

Chris flashed me his wicked smile, and I went to fetch their order. It was a lose-lose situation. I didn't want to wait on them, but not getting it would've been a bad idea. Not getting it would've hurt.

"Here are your stupid sodas," I said, putting the drinks on my brother's dresser.

I tried to hurry away, because I didn't want to be around when they opened them, but Chris wasn't done with me yet. "Bring it over here," he said. "Can't you see I'm busy?"

Yeah, busy, all right. Busy sitting on his fat rear. I picked up one of the cans and stuck it in his face.

"Open it," he said.

There was no getting out of it now. I pulled back on the tab, and the soda exploded. It sprayed everywhere. I dropped the can and turned to run, but before I could get away, Chris grabbed my arm and pulled me into a headlock. He had his forearm wrapped around my neck, so when he squeezed, I couldn't breathe and I started seeing stars. That's what happens right before you get choked out. That arm wrapped around your neck pinches off your carotid artery and stops the blood from carrying oxygen to your brain. When there isn't enough oxygen reaching your brain, your world becomes dark and muffled, you start seeing stars, and then you're out. I didn't go out this time, though. Instead, Chris took a pair of Brian's dirty underwear and rubbed them in my face. He was trying to stuff them in my mouth when I heard someone yelling, "Let him go!"

It was Mark. He never bothered to knock or ring the doorbell anymore, because he came over almost every day. Mark was an only child, so he got bored at home by himself. He'd picked the right time to show up today.

"Let him *goooooooo*," Chris mimicked in a singsong girly voice. He shoved me into Mark, and I started laughing. "It's your own fault," he told me. "You weren't nice with the sodas."

I kept laughing at Chris, and he started turning red in the face.

"Get out of here, you sissies!" he yelled.

I left before he grabbed me again—and before any of them saw I had tears in my eyes. I went into my bedroom and pumped out another set of bicep curls. Brian never used the weights after he got them, but I was using them. I was going to get even with those jerks one day. When I finished my last rep, I handed the dumbbells to Mark.

"It'll be better when we have practice every day after school," he said.

I nodded and he started his set. We didn't say anything more. It wasn't fun to talk about getting beat up. We never talked about it.

Randi

It wasn't often that Jane and I left practice early. As a matter of fact, it had never happened before. Missing practice was the last thing Coach Jane wanted after my disastrous showing at the Halloween Gymnastics Spooktacular. So already she wasn't in the best of moods. She had hoped to schedule her parent-teacher conference in the morning, before school, but Mrs. Woods was unable to make that work.

"I can't believe that old woman is so busy that she can't find time to meet early in the day," Jane complained. We were in the car, racing to get back to Lake View Middle. Jane had taken the last time slot of the night, but we were still going to be cutting it close.

"I don't know why you feel like you need to have a conference anyway," I said. "I'm getting all As. There's nothing to talk about."

"I just do. It's part of being a good parent."

And so is yelling at your daughter when she doesn't win? I thought.

"Besides, I like to hear your teachers brag about you," she said.

Instead of smiling, I felt my body stiffen. Something told me Mrs. Woods wasn't going to be doing any bragging. My first marking period report card may have had all As, but my current math grade was anything but an A. I had missed several homework assignments and gotten a 72 on my last test. That was the lowest grade I'd ever earned in my whole life. If Mrs. Woods mentioned that to Jane, I'd be hearing about it for the rest of eternity.

I was hoping for another broken water pipe or a flat tire or anything to make us miss our appointment, but none of that was my destiny. Instead, it was smooth sailing, and we made it to school a few minutes early. I sat next to Jane in the chairs Mrs. Woods had put in the hall for the people waiting.

The conference ahead of us was just finishing up. I heard them saying their thank-yous. I couldn't tell who it was, but I knew it wasn't Gavin's parents, because they never attended these sorts of things. I was glad it wasn't Gav, because he was mad at me and I couldn't handle another person's anger right now. Jane's was enough, and she was about to get even angrier once she discovered I wasn't only falling off the bars but off high honors, too.

The classroom door opened, and Natalie stepped out with her parents. We glanced at each other. Natalie gave me a small wave, and I did the same back—Gavin wasn't there to see me.

"Good evening, Ms. Cunningham. It's nice to meet you. I'm Pearl Woods."

"Please, call me Jane," Mom said, shaking my teacher's hand.

I saw the look on Natalie's face. She'd just discovered Coach Jane's secret identity.

"Hello, Randi," Mrs. Woods said.

I smiled but I didn't shake her hand. My hands were all sweaty and gross from where I'd been picking at my calluses. I went to sit back down, but Mrs. Woods stopped me.

"Randi, I'd like you to come in with your mother," she said. "I think it's important for my students to hear what I have to say."

I gulped. Then I turned around and gave Mrs. Woods another one of my forced smiles. Could she see how nervous I was? Had I known what was coming, I would've made up an excuse and hidden in the bathroom. I wasn't prepared—and neither was Coach Jane.

We followed Mrs. Woods into the classroom and sat across from her at our front table. Jane didn't waste any time.

"Mrs. Woods, before you begin, and before I forget, I wanted to ask you about the CSAs that the kids will be taking this spring. I understand the scores are really more of a grade for the school, but are they used for anything else?"

"The scores will be used to help us form groups for seventh grade," Mrs. Woods explained. "They're not the only thing we look at, but they're something we consider."

"In other words, Randi's scores will determine whether she gets placed in the advanced group or not?" Jane asked for clarification.

"It's one piece in the equation, yes," Mrs. Woods said.

"Randi needs to be in the top group."

"You must be pleased about her top-effort grades, then."

"Yes," Jane said. "I always tell her, as long as she's giving her best effort and working her hardest, I'll be happy."

That was a lie.

"Even if she's not in the top group?" Mrs. Woods asked.

Jane didn't respond. Mrs. Woods was on to her.

"It's funny you bring up tests, Ms. Cunningham."

I tried to swallow, but my throat had gone dry.

"Did you happen to see Randi's last math test?"

"I see all her papers."

"So you're aware she got a 72 on last week's test?"

"What?!"

"Must be you missed that one somehow," Mrs. Woods said, glancing my way.

Was my teacher trying to ruin my life? Jane turned and glared at me. Once she had me alone, I'd be getting a major earful.

"We're starting to deal with more challenging material in all subject areas, and we're moving fast," Mrs. Woods continued. "It's the only way we can have the children ready for those tests you're concerned about." She smiled at Jane, but Jane didn't smile back. "I suspect Randi would be fine if she just had a little more time for her homework and studying. Maybe one less day of gymnastics, or shorter practices, would help," Mrs. Woods suggested.

"I'm afraid that's not an option," Coach Jane said. "Randi has some very important meets coming up, high-level competitions, and she must prepare for them. She needs to do well, because her last one didn't go as we had hoped."

"But no matter the result, you'll be happy as long as she does her best, isn't that right, Ms. Cunningham?"

"Yes, of course," Jane said through gritted teeth. "And since she's my daughter, I know that her best means she'll win. Randi's performance at these competitions could help her earn a college scholarship, Mrs. Woods."

"Ms. Cunningham, let's be realistic. No college coach is going to look at Randi's sixth-grade results. The pressure you're putting on her is not healthy, nor is it good for your relationship."

"Excuse me?!" Jane snapped. If she were a dog, all her hair would've been standing on end. She looked ready to bite my teacher. "Mrs. Woods, are you really going to talk to me about parenting, because your job is to be the teacher, and from what I see by Randi's lack of production, it looks like you're failing in that role. So please do not try to talk to me about my parenting."

"Ms. Cunningham, I've experienced much in my lifetime, and I'm simply trying to help by sharing some of what I've learned along the way. I know you want the best for your daughter out of love, but the pressure you're putting on her is going to burn her out and ruin your relationship."

Jane turned to me. "Randi, please go wait in the hall. I need to talk to Mrs. Woods in private. And close the door behind you."

The closed door did little to drown out the yelling and shouting that Jane was doing. I sat in the chair with my knees pulled close to my chest. Mrs. Woods was right about the pressure I was feeling, but I'd never been able to tell that to Coach Jane. My teacher wasn't trying to throw me under any bus. She was trying to protect me—but wasn't that a mother's job?

"Randi?"

I wiped my eyes and looked up. Natalie was standing there.

"I forgot my notebook in my locker," she said. "I came back to get it." She held it up to show me.

I sniffed and nodded, and then the classroom door flung open and Jane stormed out. "Let's go!" she said. "Our conference is over."

I sprang from my seat and followed her stomping feet down the hall, my eyes cast on the floor. I glanced back when we turned the corner, and I saw Mrs. Woods and Natalie watching me with pained expressions. I wanted to tell them not to waste their time feeling sorry for me. It wasn't going to make any difference. I used to think that if rocks could change, so could people—but not anymore. Jane was harder than any rock.

9

THE HOLIDAYS

GAVIN

I loved Mom's tacos, but the best thing she made was Thanksgiving dinner. She whipped up this glaze for the turkey and a corn dish that was amazing. The only thing I wasn't crazy about at Thanksgiving was when my old man made us go around the table saying what we were thankful for. He didn't want me and Meggie to be spoiled kids, feeling bad about what we didn't have, 'cause in his view we had what was most important.

"I'll go first," Mom said. "I'm so thankful for my beautiful children and the man who came to fix a leaky toilet."

Dad reached over and took Mom's hand. "And I'm thankful for the woman who was cleanin' the house with the leaky toilet and for our remarkable children."

"How about you, *mija*? What are you thankful for?" Mom asked Meggie.

"I'm thankful for Gavvy reading to me," she said.

Mom and Dad smiled at me.

"I'm thankful for my family, our health, and our house," I said. I gave a canned response, 'cause the truth was, I wasn't feeling real thankful, not with the way things had been going with Randi and Kurtsman. And nothing got better when I went back to school after Thanksgiving.

The first thing that happened was our school big shots up and decided they needed to take something else away from us. Guess they weren't in the giving spirit, even with Christmas being right around the corner. This time they announced there'd be no more reading aloud in any of our classrooms. Woods was told to stop. Those extra minutes were to be used for more CSA prep now.

"Is the Grinch on that school board?" Scott yelled. "This is the worst decision ever! You better break that rule, Mrs. Woods. We love when you read to us."

Woods didn't say anything. You could see that this news hurt her, too.

It was one thing for those morons to come up with a stupid idea, but a stupid idea that took away one of the few parts of school that I liked stunk worse than throwing a pick-six. In case you don't know, that's an interception that gets returned for a touchdown. It's the worst thing that can happen to a quarterback. Scott was right: this was a terrible decision. But it still wasn't the worst of what happened.

When I walked into the caf and spotted Randi sitting with Kurtsman that first time, I almost got sick. They sat together every day now. I hadn't thought Randi would ever stoop to Kurtsman's level, but I was wrong. She threw away our friendship for that snobby girl.

I'd lost my best friend. How much uglier could things possibly get? The answer to that question turned out to be a lot.

Randi

Jane had a freak-out after her conference with Mrs. Woods and banned me from going to Gavin's house. "That boy is not helping you to reach your potential. You will not turn out to be some lowlife, like his parents."

That was what she said. She had to blame someone for my shortcomings. I hoped she didn't mean it and that she only said those things because she was upset, but she didn't take it back. Apologizing wasn't exactly Jane's strong point.

She never said sorry, but she also wasn't saying much else. We always had a quiet holiday season, because it was just the two of us, but it was quiet for more reasons than that this year. Jane had resumed the silent treatment. There was never any telling how long it would last, but I could handle it. More concerning was the fact that she wasn't the only one not talking to me.

I would never tell Gav what Jane had said, but I wished I could tell him why I wasn't coming over anymore. That just wasn't going to happen, though. The only chance I had to talk to Gav was at lunch—and there was the problem. The day after we returned from Thanksgiving break, Natalie and Scott sat with me in the cafeteria. It happened fast, and out of the clear blue.

"Hey, teammate. Can we join you?" Scott asked, taking me by surprise, as he was so good at doing. I looked up from my lunch. Natalie was by his side. I was sitting alone, waiting for Gav to join me. What was I supposed to say? I'm not a mean person.

"Sure. Okay," I said.

When Gav spotted me sitting with them—at our table—that was the last straw. We didn't have a fight or any sort of blowup. That wasn't necessary. Gav wanted nothing to do with the Recruits—and now he wanted nothing to do with me.

It was that simple. Gav stopped talking to me, and Scott and Natalie started sitting with me. That's how Gavin dealt with things, but it didn't keep me from knowing what he was thinking and feeling—we'd been best friends for a long time. The only thing I still didn't understand was his hatred for Natalie. I was happy to have Scott and Natalie with me—but I missed my best friend.

"How's math going?" Natalie asked. I swallowed the bite of apple I had in my mouth and looked over at her. I knew she wasn't really asking about math. I shrugged.

"I can give you a hand with your math," Scott said. I shouldn't have been surprised. Scott was always wanting to help.

"That's nice of you," I said, "but I don't know when we'd find the time."

"Right now."

I looked over at Natalie again. She shrugged.

"Are you sure?" I said.

"Yeah. Go and get it."

I never ate much at lunch anyway because of the special diet Jane had me following, which was supposed to keep me lean and strong. Unfortunately, it also left me hungry, but since I was done eating, I went and got my homework.

Scott tried his best to explain fraction rules and what those letters showing up in math problems meant, and I tried my best to understand what he was telling me, but his brain was wired different than mine and I just wasn't getting it.

I sighed. "We have to go soon," I said. Our lunch period was almost over. "I don't know if I'll ever get this done, but thanks for your help."

"Just give it here," Scott said, taking the paper from me.

I let him take it. When he said he'd give me a hand, I didn't realize that meant his hand would end up doing all the work for me. Letting him do it wasn't going to help me learn the material. I should have said no. But it was just one homework assignment. And it was going to help me keep Jane happy.

SCOTT

School had turned into the most boring thing in the universe. We weren't even allowed to have classroom holiday parties— and we always had classroom holiday parties!

"Ladies and gentlemen, I've been told we need to take a practice CSA this morning," Mrs. Woods announced.

"No!" I yelled.

"Mr. Mason, need I remind you that life isn't always fair? These aren't my decisions, but this is what we have to do."

"If I was Santa Claus, I'd be leaving zero presents and lots of coal for whoever is making these awful decisions."

Mrs. Woods didn't tell me that was a bad idea. She passed out our tests, and we didn't say anything else, but I did do a lot of hot breathing.

It's a good thing I still had my recess and Mrs. Magenta's program, because without those two things I would've been ready to quit school. Mrs. Magenta always had something exciting planned for us. Even with the little bit of time we had left before winter break, we were going to make the most of it. She wasn't slowing down.

"Welcome, my harmonious bunch. The winter months can be lonely for the elderly, and the holiday season even lonelier." She was right about that. Grandpa was always sad around Christmas. "So we're going to put our warm hearts together and bring melodies to the Senior Center."

"What do you mean, melodies?" Trevor asked.

"We'll be caroling," Mrs. Magenta clarified.

"You mean singing?" Mark said.

"Yes."

"Can we sing Ozzy Osbourne?" Trevor asked.

"Yeah," Mark agreed. "'Crazy Train.' *All aboooard. Hahahaha! Ay Ay Ay Ay.*"

"Thanks for that rendition, Mark, but I'm not sure that's the best choice for this occasion," Mrs. Magenta said. "I'm happy to listen to any other suggestions you might have later, but first we need to get started preparing. We'll spend today making ornaments and decorations to bring with us, and then we'll practice our songs."

"Mrs. Magenta, I'd like to suggest at least one Hanukkah song and a few menorah crafts," Natalie said. "We need to be mindful and respectful of other religions and beliefs."

"What's your religion?" Trevor poked. "Brownnosing?"

"Shut up!" Natalie snapped.

"That's enough," Mrs. Magenta said. "That happens to be a wonderful idea, Natalie. Can you take care of that for us?"

"Yes."

"Fantastic. Thank you."

"Brownnoser," Trevor grumbled

Mrs. Magenta went on to demonstrate and explain making stained-glass ornaments using tissue paper. The ornaments glittered when Christmas lights were behind them. They were very pretty.

Gavin made a football, and I made one of those turkeys like we did at the public library. I was good at making those now. I didn't get that much paste on my hands, either, so I didn't feel sick to my stomach after licking my fingers clean this time. Trevor and Mark said their ornaments were stockings, but they sort of looked more like dirty socks. The craft project was fun. I was excited to put mine on the tree at the Senior Center so all the old people could see it.

After we finished our decorations, Mrs. Magenta got us organized as a choir and handed each of us a folder with the sheet music and words for a bunch of songs. We practiced singing all of them. Mrs. Magenta said she really liked the extra-high note I hit during "five golden rings," but that only happened because that was when Trevor gave me a wet willie.

We did all the normal carols and hymns and one extra, which was my favorite, "Grandma Got Run Over by a Reindeer." Even though my grandma wasn't around anymore, Grandpa and I still liked that song. I was excited to sing it for a bunch of old people at the Senior Center. I knew they'd like it, too.

NATALIE KURTSMAN
ASPIRING LAWYER
Kurtsman Law Offices

BRIEF #16
December: Caroling

Mrs. Magenta was like a bird with its wings clipped during the school day. When we got to explore with our hands and minds and problem-solve, she soared, but now that she had to keep us doing math and answering questions, she was no longer able to fly.

Thankfully, school administration had not interfered with the after-school program. Mrs. Magenta was an altogether different person on the days when it met, full of life and happiness. Sure, she was eccentric, but her energy was contagious—and I loved it.

I was eager for today's excursion to the senior center. The only drawback was the fact that we had to ride a school bus to get there.

"Awesome!" Scott cheered. "I love the bus!"

I couldn't fathom getting excited about riding one of

those filthy yellow rectangles on wheels. As I expected, the thing was disgusting. It looked gross, smelled gross, and felt gross—but none of that registered with Scott. He ran up the steps and headed straight to the back, plopping beside Gavin in the second-to-last seat.

The boy amazed me. He sat with Randi and me during lunch, and then thought nothing of sitting with Gavin on the bus. He was clueless about the tension and animosity that existed between the Recruits. I actually envied him at times like these.

Mrs. Magenta settled in the front, and I found my spot next to Randi in the middle of the bus. Before sitting down, I caught sight of Trevor and Mark in the last seat—which is where they belonged, but that also meant they were directly behind Scott. It didn't take long for the trouble to begin.

"Can you stop kicking my seat?" I heard Scott ask.

Then I heard him ask again.

And again.

Gavin never uttered a word. He was in one of his foul moods, and I had a strong suspicion it was because of me—or, more specifically, because I'd become friends with Randi and was sitting with her now. I never intended to steal her away from him, but that's how things had played out. In my defense, I wasn't keeping him from hanging out with us. That was his choice.

"Please stop kicking my seat," Scott requested.

Things were escalating back there, but luckily we arrived at the senior center before it got too bad.

"Hi, Nancy. We made it," Mrs. Magenta said, greeting the woman who was waiting for us at the door.

"Hi, Olivia," the woman said. "We're ready for you. Everyone's very excited."

"Great," Mrs. Magenta said. "This is Mrs. Ruggelli," she told us, introducing the woman. "She's the director here. She'll show you the way."

Olivia? Nancy? Obviously they knew each other.

"Welcome," Mrs. Ruggelli said. "Follow me."

She led us to the community hall, a large space where we found a crowd of old people sitting at tables, waiting for us. Trevor and Mark weren't only the biggest jerks in the world but the biggest wimps, too. They were petrified. Of singing or of the old people, I don't know. So what did they do? They made jokes, because somehow that was supposed to be funny.

"Hey, Mark, which of these old geezers do you bet poops himself first?" Trevor whispered.

"Got my money on the drooling lady over there," Mark replied.

"That's hysterical," I said. "Real mature. I bet the old-timers are saying the same things about the two wimps standing up here."

It took Trevor and Mark a minute before the lightbulb came on and they realized I was referring to them, but by then we had started our first carol, "Hark! The Herald Angels Sing."

We performed ten songs for the senior center that afternoon. The crowd favorite was our last one, "Grandma Got Run Over by a Reindeer," which Scott belted. Afterward we hung our ornaments on their tree. I spotted a menorah off to the side, so I knew my decoration was right at home. To be honest, I thought mine looked the best, but it was Gavin's football that I saw some old man touching as we were leaving.

The holiday spirit stayed with us, and we continued singing on the bus ride back. For once my classmates weren't bellowing that obnoxious tune about bottles on a wall; I'd suffered through that on numerous field trips before. More important, our singing also occupied Trevor and Mark, so they managed to leave Scott alone—this time.

Trevor

So what if Mark and I made a few jokes about those old farts. It's not like they could hear us. The only reason I did it was because I was nervous as all heck standing up there in front of them. But stupid girl had to open her trap and get all goody-two-shoes on us. Boy, that rubbed me the wrong way.

People laugh for all kinds of reasons. They laugh when something's funny or when it's silly or even when it's stupid. Pretty much everyone does that. But did you know some people even laugh when they get hurt or when they're embarrassed or scared? I've seen it. I've done it. It's a trick I pull with my brother and his goons all the time. I never want to show them weakness, I never want them to think they're getting the best of me, so I laugh at them— no matter what.

Last year, after I got fitted for shoulder pads at the start of football season, Brian wanted to show me how awesome they were and how I wouldn't feel anything when I got hit.

He was trying to make it so I wouldn't be scared to tackle, which is something a lot of new kids are afraid of when they start football. Not me. I wasn't afraid. But Brian needed to put on a show for his goons. He took this aluminum bat he had lying in his closet and hit me on the shoulder with it. I didn't flinch.

"See that?" he said. "You didn't feel a thing, did you?"

"Not a thing," I said, hoping he was done.

He lifted the bat and brought it down on my other shoulder. "See? Nothing."

"Give me that bat," Chris said. "You're not doing it right if you want little Trevie to know he's safe in those pads." He stepped back and gripped the handle like a baseball player. "Keep your hands at your side," he ordered.

I wanted to run, but my legs wouldn't go. I didn't feel anything when he connected with the pads over my chest, but the momentum of his swing kept going after hitting me, and the bat flew up and caught me right in the teeth.

I jumped back and grabbed my mouth. "Ah! The pads aren't covering my face, you idiot!"

"Yo, I didn't mean it, Trevie. You moved," Chris said, blaming me. "It's your fault."

The problem was, I hadn't moved. I spit blood and felt around the inside of my mouth with my tongue. I smiled at them, and then they really started cracking up.

"Whoa, you look like a beaver," Chris said.

My front teeth were broken in half. I went ahead and laughed with them even though nothing was funny. Nothing was ever funny when it came to Brian and his goons.

I gave Mom some made-up story when she got home, and she called the dentist and scheduled an appointment for the next morning. My teeth were fixed, and Mom and Dad still had no idea about what had really happened. Brian and his goons thought that was funny, too.

Randi

It was Christmas Eve. No school. No gymnastics. No anything. Just Jane and me at home. The silent treatment was over. This was the one time of the year when the two of us were close to what I really wanted.

"Let's have chili for dinner tonight," Jane said. "It's cold out and I want something warm."

"Sounds good."

"Want to help me make it?"

"Okay." The kitchen was the only room in our house where the wall between us sometimes came down.

"I'll get things simmering on the stove while you start dicing the vegetables," she said. Jane hummed along to the dinner party music she had playing. It was old jazzy stuff, but I liked it. I liked how it made her happy. "Think you could do your floor routine to a song like this?" she asked.

No, please don't ruin things by bringing up gymnastics. I shrugged.

"Randi, you need to dice the peppers smaller. I don't want big chunks in my chili. Pay attention to what—"

I stiffened, waiting for more, but that was it. Jane stopped midsentence and turned back to the stove.

I finished with the peppers, scooped them onto the cutting board along with the onions, and carried them to the pot. "Vegetables are ready," I said.

"You can dump them in." Her eyes were red, and I wasn't sure if that was from the onion, the seasonings, or something else.

Our chili finished cooking to the sounds of Jane's jazz music, but we'd grown quiet—and this wasn't more silent treatment. Dinner was very tasty, and it warmed us up, but there was still a coldness in our house that it hadn't fixed. I hoped tomorrow would take care of that.

Before bed I wrapped Jane's present. I didn't have the time to do my own shopping, so I gave Natalie some money and she picked up a new cookbook for me. Jane was going to like it. Natalie also gave me a small gift. I felt bad because I didn't have one for her, but she said that was okay. I felt even worse because this was the first Christmas when Gav and I didn't exchange gifts. I missed my best friend.

Christmas was better. Jane and I had breakfast together, watched the parade, and went to the movies to catch the season's big opening-day release. We didn't exchange gifts until after dinner, but I liked that, because it made our special day last longer.

Jane loved her cookbook. Then it was my turn. After I opened several small gifts, Jane gave me the one she was most excited about. I tore open the package. It was a new leotard.

"I thought this might help motivate you and get you psyched for Regionals," Jane said.

"Thanks."

I hated it. Our special day was over.

10

AFTER BREAK

GAVIN

It was our first day back from Christmas break, and school went from bad to worse. It was like we'd come out after half-time and Mr. Allen pulled a trick play right off the bat. He called a special assembly in the gymatorium.

"I hope everyone enjoyed a relaxing and fun-filled holiday break," he began. "Now it's time for us to get back to work. It may seem like a long way off, but our CSAs are right around the corner. They'll be happening before you know it. I've gathered you here today because I'm excited to announce that we've been able to secure additional help to better prepare you for the big tests."

"Boo!" someone behind me shouted. That someone was Trevor. "Boo!" he yelled again.

Mr. Allen stopped and searched the bleachers, looking for the person who'd dared to do that, but none of us were giving Trevor up, not when we were on his side. It was pretty obvious from Mr. Allen's face that he didn't find this very funny. He kept glaring at us as he continued with his grand announcement. "I'd like to introduce Mr. Moore, Mr. Proctor, and Miss

199

Cohan," he said. "This trio of experts will be administering regular practice tests in each of your classrooms over the next several weeks. The best part is, we'll get immediate results, which will help your teachers know what to work on between now and the real thing."

Mr. Allen made it sound like preseason scrimmages before the opening game when we'd analyze the film and work on our weaknesses during practice. The only difference was, I wasn't pumped about these practice tests like I woulda been about a scrimmage—and neither were any of the kids sitting around me. I didn't see any teachers looking all that thrilled, either. Mr. Allen's exciting news belonged in the toilet with the rest of the terrible ideas our school big shots had already sprung on us this year.

SCOTT

We came back from break, and Mr. Allen dumped these mean people in our classrooms who told us we couldn't read the good books that we wanted to read anymore. All because we had to do more of those awful tests (whose pages stunk worse than dead skunk, by the way), and then came the unimaginable—No More Recess! Instead of getting a chance to burn off some energy, we had to spend our extra time with Mr. Test Man, completing practice tests that were full of nothing but boring passages about nothing that interested me, and the questions Mr. Allen's test experts wanted me to answer at the end of those boring passages were even boringer. It was horrible.

"Here you go, Mr. Test Man. Here's your dumb test," I said. "Merry belated Christmas."

Mr. Test Man didn't like my attitude. I didn't care, because I didn't like him. It was his fault they took away my recess. He was especially upset when he saw that I had filled in my answer bubbles in a Christmas tree pattern. He took my paper and left the room.

A few minutes later Mr. Allen was at our door. He called me into the hall.

"Scott, nothing about this is funny!" he yelled, shaking my Christmas tree in the air. Why was he yelling? Mr. Allen never yelled. "Do you understand me?"

"Mr. Allen, these practice tests are boring and easy. And so are the CSAs. You don't have to get so upset."

"Yes, I do," he growled. "I need you to ace the CSAs. I need everyone to ace them."

I'd never seen him like this. He was turning red mad. "Will you let us have recess again when they're over?" I asked him.

"If you do what you're supposed to from now on, you can have extra recess," he said.

"And what about Mrs. Woods being able to read to us? We want that back, too."

"Yes, and Mrs. Woods can resume reading aloud. But first things first. You need to ace your test."

I smiled. "Deal."

There was a light at the end of this Complex Student Abuse tunnel, and I was bursting at the seams to tell Natalie and Randi the news when we got to lunch. "Guess what?" I said. "If we do what we're supposed to on the CSAs, then Mr. Allen will be giving us recess back and Mrs. Woods will be able to read to us again. I know because Mr. Allen made a deal with me."

"And what exactly are we supposed to do on the tests?" Natalie asked.

"Ace them," I said. I took Randi's math sheet and raced through the problems. I got her homework done faster than ever today. Good news always gives me energy.

NATALIE KURTSMAN
ASPIRING LAWYER
Kurtsman Law Offices

BRIEF #17
January: Test Experts and Bus Rides

It was a relief when Mrs. Magenta announced our new community service project. She actually had a plan and wasn't going to wing it, as I'd feared. Must be our winter break had done her good. Unfortunately, the same could not be said for Mr. Allen or many of his teachers. Rather than returning fully recharged, they looked exhausted. Something at Lake View Middle School was weighing them down—and I had reason to believe it had everything to do with our looming CSAs.

For starters, I'd noticed more whispering among the faculty when passing them in the hallway, and they weren't telling jokes—even their words sounded tired.

"It doesn't matter what I do, they're never going to pass," I overheard one teacher saying to another. "I thought it was bad last year, when I had kids crying and throwing up because the test was too hard, but all this hoopla is making it even worse."

The second teacher let out a heavy sigh. "I know," she said. "I feel so bad for the kids."

This was telling, but a truly scary warning came the next day, when one of our teachers left school in an ambulance after an apparent panic attack. One would think such an event would've clued our administrators in that things were getting out of control, but that was not the case. I don't know all the details surrounding the incident, so I shouldn't say any more; I'd only be contributing to the rumor mill.

There are two things I can report, however. First, Mr. Allen's trio of test experts were not helping our situation. To begin with, they desperately needed lessons on how to dress. The one called Moore looked like a clown in his high-water slacks and long, shiny black shoes; he spent today walking around with toilet paper stuck to his heel, while the Proctor guy had white powder on his tie and a shirt that refused to stay tucked in over his doughnut belly. The lone woman, Miss Cohan, always seemed to have her slip showing and lipstick painted on her front teeth. The only thing missing from their outfits was KICK ME signs.

Fortunately, the second item I can report was a bright spot for us. Mrs. Magenta had a wonderful new idea. "Caroling was such a positive experience for all, I've decided to continue with trips to the senior center for our next service project," she announced. "We're going to bring the old people some company and sunshine with your smiles."

I thought this sounded delightful, until I remembered that our commute there and back required riding the bus.

Once again Scott bolted up the steps and headed straight to the rear, plopping beside Gavin in the second-to-last seat, and once again Trevor and Mark were sitting directly behind them. Clearly Scott hadn't learned anything from our first trip. It didn't take long.

"Can you stop kicking my seat?" I heard him asking.

Right on cue. *Here we go again,* I thought.

"Hey! Give it back!" he cried.

What now? I glanced over my shoulder.

"Give it back!" he cried again.

"What?" Trevor said, playing dumb.

"Gimme my hat!" Scott yelled.

From her place up front, Mrs. Magenta was unaware of what was happening, but our bus driver saw everything in his mirror. "Turn around and sit down!" he roared.

I suddenly remembered this man from my previous field trips. Bus Driver Ted had a zero tolerance policy for people standing while his vehicle was in motion. He slammed on the brakes, and our gross-mobile lurched, which successfully jarred every last one of us and sent Scott flying backward. He would've landed in the aisle if Gavin hadn't caught him. Bus Driver Ted meant business. We got the message; he was an effective communicator.

Scott planted it. There wasn't anything I could do to help him at the moment, but I was determined to see him get his hat back before the end of the day.

Randi

Mrs. Ruggelli led us into the community hall, where the old people were gathered. They were quiet and staring at us, and we were quiet and staring at them. Singing carols to them had been one thing, but today it felt like we were two gymnastics teams sizing each other up before competition.

"Find yourselves an empty seat," Mrs. Ruggelli said, gesturing toward the tables. "My friends are eager to meet you."

That was it? We were just supposed to go and sit with some random old person and strike up a conversation? A row of stone-faced judges perched behind the scorer's table at my gymnastics meets weren't as scary as these strangers. All I can say is, it was a good thing we had Scott. He knew just how to break the tension.

"Are those frosted cookies?!" he cried, pointing to a table on the far side of the room. "With *sprinkles*?!"

Must be Mrs. Magenta forgot to give Mrs. Ruggelli the heads-up about Scott and goodies. He didn't even wait for an answer. Like a tracking missile locked in on its target, he shot over there while the rest of us stood motionless. No one said a word. No one tried stopping him. We didn't even know if the cookies were for us, or for later, or what! For the old-timers, I imagine watching Scott was a bit like watching one of those ancient silent movies. They were enjoying this. The stillness that filled the community hall reminded me of the quiet that falls before a gymnast's big move—and we had no idea Scott's big move was yet to come.

"What're you guys waiting for?!" he cried. He wasn't fazed by all of our staring faces or the dead silence. His sole concern was the pile of treats he had balanced on his plate. "They're heart-shaped cookies for Valentine's Day! And there's even juice!" he exclaimed, lifting his cup high for all to see.

Too bad what Scott didn't see was the step down in front of him. He must've forgotten about it being there as a result of his cookie craze. The only thing on his mind was getting to a table so he could gobble up his goodies—but he never made it. Thanks to that forgotten step, his foot didn't land where he expected.

Scott's plate went flying. His juice went flying. He went flying. He skidded nose-first across the floor, sprawled out on his belly, his arms stretched out above his head. It was another perfect ten for another spectacular tumbling routine. The once-silent community hall erupted in laughter.

"Smooth move, Slick!" Mark yelled.

Every crooked back in the place suddenly went straight as the room of old folks perked up to get a better look at their movie star.

"Are you all right, honey?" the old woman closest to Scott asked. She sprang from her chair like someone half her age.

I bet these seniors hadn't experienced excitement like this in years.

Scott got to his feet. He was fine, but his clothes were not. He had red fruit juice all over his pants and shirt.

"My clothes!" he cried. "My mom's going to be so upset!"

I believed him. This was the second outfit he'd ruined.

"Don't worry, sweetie. I can get that out for you," a plump old lady said.

"Give your clothes to Eleanor, lad. She can get anything out," an old man advised.

"Yup, give 'em to Eleanor," a second old man agreed.

I'm almost positive the old folks didn't mean that very second, but Scott wasn't wasting any time. He ripped his shirt and pants off—right then and there! I'd never seen an almost-naked boy before, and after seeing Scott, I can tell you I'm in no hurry to see another one. What a sight he was, standing there in his Batman underwear. The old folks were laughing their wrinkles off. We're lucky no one had a heart attack. But Scott still wasn't fazed. It wasn't the frosted cookies that had his laser focus now but his stained clothes. I was impressed. I wished I could focus like that, have everything around me— especially Jane—disappear as I stared down the bars.

Eleanor waddled over and took the heap from Scott's arms. "Follow me, sweetie. We'll get these washed out and see if we can't find something more for you to put on in the meantime. Don't want you stuck parading around in your skivvies."

"Way to go, Captain Underpants!" Trevor yelled.

I laughed. We all laughed. How could you not?

Scott grabbed a handful of his frosted cookies off the floor and left the room behind Eleanor. Nobody was better at winning over a crowd than Scott. Unfortunately, it seemed we were always laughing at him and not with him. I didn't think he cared, and I'd never cared either, but things were different now. He wasn't just the kid who did my math homework. He was my friend.

GAVIN

I didn't expect this to be fun, but I didn't count on it being scary, either. Singing to the senior citizens was bad, but asking us to go and sit with them was something different. I was staring at more old people than I'd ever been around—enough for a full football team. I scouted my prospects.

I spotted two different bald guys with long arms who could play tight end for me. And the old man with unsteady hands, his buddy with the trembling jaw, and the two round women with nodding heads—they were perfect for the offensive line. The specialist positions would be filled out by the old-timers with reliable limbs and white hair, no hair, and messy hair. The old man and woman who kept drooling were made for the defensive line, where you needed to be nasty and not care about getting dirty. The gentleman with the newspaper could be my stat man. I'd play quarterback. The only thing left to find was our coach.

It might not sound like it, but this was an intimidating bunch. Only Scott knew how to handle this all-star team of old folks. He got everyone laughing with his ridiculous cookie fumble and follow-up strip show. Talk about breaking the ice. After that the old-timers didn't seem so scary. I glanced around the room for a place to sit, and that was when I noticed the old man off to the side. He wasn't paying attention to us. He was too busy with his paper and pencil. I tucked my lucky football under my arm and moved closer to see what he was doing. He had X's and squares and circles all over his paper, but his X's were lined up and in order, and then he started drawing arrows.

"They call him Coach," Magenta said, stepping beside me.

"Is he drawing up football plays?" I asked her. " 'Cause it sure looks like it."

"I don't know. Let's ask him."

Magenta placed a hand on my back, and we inched closer. "Hi, Coach," she said.

The old man looked up with a blank face. Magenta stood there for a few seconds, waiting for him to say or do something, but his expression never changed. "This is Gavin," she finally said. He grunted and went back to his paper. Magenta nudged me. "Go on," she whispered.

"Excuse me," I said. "Is that a double reverse you're drawing up?"

"A double reverse with the option to pass," he said. "Big game this weekend. Thomson is a tough squad, but we'll get them with this play."

"How does it work?" I asked.

The old man explained his play to me. Then Magenta gave me a chair, and I sat there while he went through his notebook showing me one scheme after another, telling me how his team was gonna attack Thomson High and how a football game was a lot like a chess match—you always wanted to be one move ahead of your opponent. The man was a genius. I'd never had anyone talk football with me like this. Dad tried, but he didn't always know what he was talking about—not like this old guy.

"How do you know so much about the game?" I finally got up the nerve to ask him.

Coach looked up from his playbook and glared at me like it was the first time he'd ever seen me. "Who're you?!" he yelled, slamming his notebook shut. "Are you a spy for Thomson High? You get away from me! Help!"

I jumped out of my chair and backed away. I'd never even heard of Thomson High. What was wrong with this guy? Was he crazy? Why was he yelling at me?

"It's okay, Coach," Magenta said, rushing over to us. Director Ruggelli was with her. "This is Gavin," Magenta reminded him. "He's your visitor today. You've been talking football plays with him for the past thirty minutes."

"I don't know anyone named Gavin!" Coach barked.

"I think it's time for you to take a rest," Ruggelli said. "Let's get you back to your room. Does that sound good?"

I stood there and watched her lead Coach away. I was still shaking. The old man had scared me bad.

"You didn't do anything wrong, Gavin," Magenta said, placing her hand on my shoulder. "Coach gets confused. He's slowly losing his mind." She sounded sad and tired, telling me that. "Please don't be scared of him. I haven't seen him so happy talking football in a long time. I hope you'll chat with him again when we visit next."

I shrugged.

"I should've told you ahead of time. I'm sorry."

"It's okay," I said.

I didn't want her feeling bad. I'd been in football heaven before the old man flipped out. I was still thinking about all the plays he'd shown me when Scott suddenly reappeared and made us forget everything. The next stunt of his took the cake.

Natalie Kurtsman
ASPIRING LAWYER
Kurtsman Law Offices

```
BRIEF #18
January: Agnes and Eddie
```

It was thanks to Scott's show-stopping performance—which there will never be words to adequately describe—that things in the senior center finally began to loosen up. I took Randi's hand and had her follow me to a table where two cute old ladies sat. They had their hair pulled back in clips like little girls, even though they were all gray and wrinkled.

"Hello, I'm Natalie and this is my friend Randi," I said, properly introducing us. That was the first time I had called Randi my friend, and it felt natural. It felt . . . good.

"Hi," said the one wearing the purple clip. "I'm Agnes and this is my friend Edna, but you can call her Eddie."

"Mind if we sit down with you?" I asked.

"Sit down and tell us about those boys!" Eddie ordered. "You've got some cute ones over there. Which ones are chasing you?"

"Ugh! Never mind her," Agnes said.

"Or should I ask which ones are you chasing?" Eddie teased, looking my way.

Me? Chasing a boy? Puh-lease! Randi and I looked at each other and smiled. Who were the mature ones here?

We sat down and spent the next half hour playing a game of Sorry! with our new friends. Agnes and Eddie needed help turning over the cards and sliding their pieces around the board, but Randi and I didn't care. In between moves, Eddie continued to give us a hard time about boys and Agnes would huff and scold her; it was both funny and fun. We did a lot of laughing, but everything came to an abrupt stop the moment we heard the commotion.

Out of nowhere the old man Gavin was visiting started yelling. Mrs. Magenta and Mrs. Ruggelli were over there in an instant to help rectify the situation. It didn't last very long, but it was enough to put things back to the way they were in the beginning, with people barely breathing and silence so thick you could cut it with a knife. But never fear, we still had Scott, and he'd chosen to return when we needed him most.

The boy never ceased to amaze me. Just when I thought he couldn't possibly do anything more shocking than what he'd already managed, he proved me wrong. Apparently, stripping down to his Underoos wasn't enough, because he came back wearing a lime-green nightgown with silver snaps down the front, decorated with pink and peach flowers. It had to be something from Eleanor's closet. The boy certainly didn't do himself any favors.

"Check it out!" Trevor cried. "Captain Underpants has turned into Key Lime Flower Pie."

Trevor's remark was met by a chorus of laughs, from young and old. I shook my head. What else could I do?

"Well, that boy sure is different," Agnes commented.

"Different is okay," I said, defending my friend.

"Yes, it is," Agnes agreed. "I never said it wasn't. He's the boy Eddie and I would be chasing if we were you."

"You've got that right," Eddie said. "Knew that as soon as I saw his underwear."

Now Randi and I were cracking up with everyone else. Fortunately for Scott, he was spared much ridicule and laughter thanks to good timing and Mrs. Magenta.

"I'm sorry to say, but we must get ready to leave now," Mrs. Magenta announced. "Please take a minute to clean up and say goodbye, and then you should make your way out to the bus."

The old people smiled and waved and thanked us for coming. They were the happiest bunch around, like a house of little kids on Christmas morning. It warmed my heart.

Agnes and Eddie told Randi and me to come back soon. "And stay out of trouble," Agnes said.

"Yeah, don't do anything we wouldn't do," Eddie added, and winked.

"Okay," I said. I grabbed Randi's hand and pulled her along. We needed to get to the bus.

"Do you think those old women know us better than we know us?" Randi asked me as we were leaving.

"What're you talking about?"

"You know, like maybe they can see what's coming."

"There are no such things as fortune-tellers," I said.

Staying out of trouble had never been a problem for me.

SCOTT

I was happy when Mrs. Magenta told us we had to sit in the same seats on the way back. That was a great idea, because it meant I got to sit next to Gavin again, and Trevor and Mark were behind us, but so were Natalie and Randi. They were in the last seat on the opposite side of the aisle. They must've made it back there before Mrs. Magenta announced same seats, because that wasn't where they sat on the way over.

"Yo, Gavin, what did you do to make that old fart so mad?" Mark asked. He was standing and peering over the back of our seat.

"Shut up," Gavin said.

"You're lucky he didn't kick your—"

"I said shut up," Gavin growled.

"Easy, killer," Trevor said. "We're just kidding with ya." Now *he* was standing and peering over the back of our seat, too. He looked at me. "You better give him a hug, Key Lime Flower Pie. A hug from you will make him feel all better."

"You better sit down," I told them.

"You gonna make us?" Trevor challenged.

Don't say I didn't warn them. I'd learned my lesson on the way over. Hitting the brakes fast and quick when you weren't expecting it was Mr. Bus Driver's signature move. When he did it this time, Mark and Trevor's throats rammed into the top of our seat. Their tongues shot so far out of their mouths, they looked like gagging lizards.

"Sit down!" Mr. Bus Driver roared.

Trevor and Mark weren't always good at listening, but they sat down for our driver from the Black Lagoon. I glanced back and saw them rubbing their necks. Then I glanced up front and saw Mr. Bus Driver looking in his rearview mirror and smirking. Thanks to his signature move, Trevor and Mark left us alone and didn't dare stand up for the rest of the ride.

"I know how you can help that old man," I told Gavin.

"Oh yeah? And how's that?"

I explained to Gavin how memories were the most important thing an old person had. That memories were their treasures. I told him the old man at the senior center needed help remembering his and keeping them straight. Then I told him all about the memory string and how it worked and how one could help his friend. Gavin didn't say much about my idea, but I knew it was a good one. I didn't tell him I was making a string for Grandpa. That was top-secret.

When we got back to school, everyone jumped up and started pushing to get off the bus, but not me. If you put your hands on the tops of the seats, one on each side of the aisle, you can lift yourself up off the ground and swing your legs. It's tons of fun. I was happy I was wearing Eleanor's nightgown, because my legs were free and I was able to really swing them hard. I was flying fast and high when I heard the ruckus be-hind me.

"What the—"

"Watch out!"

I turned around just in time to see Mark topple onto Trevor. Somehow Trevor's sneaker got tied to the leg of his bus seat.

"Ha ha ha!" I laughed, and pointed. "Have a nice trip. See you next fall."

"Get going," Gavin hissed, pushing me forward. "Don't egg them on."

Natalie and Randi stepped over the Mark-and-Trevor pile and came down the aisle behind us.

"What happened?" I asked them as soon as we got off the bus.

"We don't know," Natalie said, handing me my hat.

"Hey, thanks."

She nudged me along, but we didn't get away fast enough. Trevor and Mark had managed to get themselves untangled and came bounding after us. Trevor marched right up to Nata-lie. "You think you're funny?" he said.

"No, I think it's time you and Mark stopped being bullies," she said, not giving an inch.

Why were they acting like this? I didn't like it.

"We're not bullies," Trevor countered. "We're just joking around with our friends. Having some fun. You're the bully, tying my shoelace to the seat like that."

"Yeah," Mark agreed. "You're the bully."

That was the first time I ever saw Natalie not know what to say. "Stop it!" I yelled. "Stop it. I don't like it when my friends fight."

"Scott's right," Randi said, getting in between them. "Every-one just cool it." She got Trevor and Mark to take a step back, and then she pulled Natalie away. Gavin was already storming off in the other direction. I stood there.

"Hey, Scott," Trevor said. "You know Mark and me were just having fun with ya, right? We were going to give you your hat back. We're not bullies."

"I know," I said, "but neither is Natalie."

"Cool. See you tomorrow," Trevor said.

"See you tomorrow."

I put my hat on and beelined it for the art room. I grabbed my stuff and told Mrs. Magenta thank you, then hurried back outside. Mom was curious and Mickey was excited when I got in the car with my bag of wet clothes and my new outfit.

"Scott girl!" Mickey hollered. "Funny girl!"

Mom gave me her raised-eyebrow look.

"Why girl? Why Scott girl?"

"Yes, please enlighten us so your brother can stop yelling," Mom said.

I told them the story. When I got done, Mickey wanted to know if I had any more cookies. Mom only shook her head and smiled.

"Eleanor got the juice out of my pants and shirt," I said.

"That's good. I'll dry your things at Grandpa's so you can put them back on. You don't want to get Eleanor's nightgown all dirty."

That was smart thinking. Sometimes Mom could come up with good ideas, like me.

"What in the Sam Hill are you wearing?!" Grandpa cried when I walked in. It didn't take long for him to snap out of his trance today.

"Scott girl! Funny girl!"

Grandpa's and Mickey's yelling scared the bejeepers out of Smoky. The cat jumped from Grandpa's lap and ran for cover.

"My after-school group went to the senior center today," I told Grandpa. "I tripped and spilled juice all over my clothes, so Eleanor washed them for me and gave me this to wear in the meantime."

"They must have some good-looking gals over there if they're parading around in those sorts of outfits."

"Dad!" Mom said.

"You'd like it there, Grandpa. Everyone is really nice."

"That might be so, but Smoky and I have our place right here. I'll leave the wild-women chasing to you young fellas. Just be sure to tell me about it."

"Dad!" Mom cried again. "You're too much. I'll leave you two alone to talk your foolishness."

"Good," Grandpa said. "This here is man talk."

Mom huffed and marched off with my bag of wet clothes, but I knew she was smiling.

I pulled the chess table over, and Grandpa and I settled in for our afternoon match. Either I was getting better or Grandpa was still thinking about wild women, because after a few minutes I had the upper hand, and I'd never beaten him before.

"Scott, your clothes are ready," Mom called from the other room.

I was about to checkmate Grandpa for the first time ever. I reached out to make my killer move, but before I got the chance, Smoky made his. Out of nowhere he jumped onto our board, knocking pieces everywhere.

"No!" I cried.

"Don't you dare tell me no!" Mom yelled. "Get in here now!"

"Good boy," Grandpa whispered, patting Smoky on the head.

I pointed at the cat. "You owe me one," I told him. Then I turned and went to get my clothes before Mom got really upset.

After changing, I took time to find something for Grandpa's memory string. I decided to take two of my favorite pictures of Grandma and Grandpa. I slid them into my backpack with my usual stack of junk mail. No, picture frames couldn't go on my string, but I'd decided Grandpa might as well have a memory box to go with his string of objects.

I wouldn't know how terrific that idea was until later.

Trevor

I got right in Natalie's face, and she tried giving me some line about bullying. Like that was going to work on me. I told her she was the bully, and that shut her up fast. Miss Perfect suddenly realized she wasn't so perfect after all. The truth can hurt. Who did she think she was, throwing bullying in my face? She didn't know about that stuff like I did. Nobody did. She wasn't going to make me feel bad or feel sorry for anyone. The heck with that. Nobody was feeling sorry for me. People like Natalie had no idea.

Once someone gave her a noogie that made her skull hurt and her hair fall out, she could talk to me about bullying. After she got nailed with charley horses that turned into big purple bruises up and down her arms and legs, she could talk to me. When she suffered through a wedgie that left her picking at her crack for a week, she could talk to me. But not until then. And these things weren't even that bad, not compared to choke-outs and some of the other garbage I'd been through. But even I hadn't seen the worst of it. Not yet. That didn't happen until a couple days after this fight with Natalie went down. It got real bad.

We had this new four-player video game, so my brother and his goons let me play with them. Sometimes they were cool like that. But then my brother announced, "I'm going to sit on the throne."

Brian didn't just call the toilet his throne. He really treated it that way, and by that I mean he could sit there for over an hour. When he left, I started sifting through our old games to see if there was something different the three of us could play while we waited for him to return. I wasn't paying attention to Chris or Garrett, and that was my mistake. All of a sudden I realized how quiet it was. I thought they had ditched me, but when I turned around, I saw how wrong I was. They grabbed me. I was able to put up a decent fight, but I still had more bicep curls to go before I could outwrestle two of them. Chris pinned me down, and Garrett took my brother's athletic tape and went to work. First, one strip across my mouth so I couldn't scream. Next, they wrapped my wrists together behind my back. Then it was my ankles. And last, just to be funny, they stuck tape on my eyebrows.

Satisfied, Chris and Garrett sat down and started playing video games again. I wasn't getting free, not this time. Not until they got bored and let me go or someone saved me.

"Hey, Trev. Get me a soda," Chris said. He looked at me and laughed. I closed my eyes so I didn't have to see him. I closed my eyes to keep my tears inside.

I was stuck like that until we heard the toilet flush. Then Chris ripped the tape off my eyebrows and mouth. As soon as my wrists and ankles were freed, I jumped to my feet and shoved him into his chair. I stood over him, fists clenched at my side.

"Easy, killer," he said, holding his hands up. "We're just messing with ya. Having some fun. You know that. Don't get all huffy mad."

My chest heaved. I was seeing red. I didn't care if he was bigger than me.

"What's going on?" Brian asked, returning from his bathroom kingdom.

I stormed out of there, knocking into my loser brother on my way out.

"Hey! Watch it!" he said.

I didn't stop. I hurried to my room and collapsed on my bed. I buried my face in my pillow and cried. I couldn't help it this time. I cried and cried.

"You okay?" It was Mark. "Trev?"

I rubbed my eyes dry and got up. "I'm fine," I said. I grabbed the dumbbells and started my set.

"You okay?" he asked me again. "What happened?"

"I said I was fine." I shoved the dumbbells at him.

He started his set but kept looking at me.

"Why do you come over every afternoon?" I said.

He stopped lifting. The weights hung at his side. "What do you mean? Because you're my friend."

"Yeah, but you know these guys are here, and sometimes they pick on you, too. And you still come back. Why? If I could get away, I would."

"I'm bored at home by myself." His gaze dropped to the floor. He couldn't look at me and say this next part. "But I also come to make sure you're okay."

Normally I would've punched him in the arm and told him not to be all sappy, but I didn't do that this time. It felt good to hear him say that. It felt good to know I wasn't all alone and that he had my back. I took the dumbbells from him and started my next set.

"I can't wait till next year, when we have practice every day after school and we don't have to deal with these idiots anymore."

"Yeah," Mark said. "Me too."

But he wasn't looking at me when he said that, either.

11

A GAME-CHANGING PLAN

NATALIE KURTSMAN
ASPIRING LAWYER
Kurtsman Law Offices

BRIEF #19
February: Not Meant for Our Ears

I was having a difficult time thinking about anything but Trevor and Mark's absurd accusation. Was I a bully? The question wouldn't leave me alone. Here I was, supposed to be focused on Mr. Proctor's all-important practice test, but I was struggling to concentrate. The CSAs were a breeze—I could be half asleep and still ace them—but this particular section was giving me a headache. I was reading about survival of the fittest and couldn't help but wonder if there were bullies in the animal kingdom. Seriously, wasn't I merely protecting one of the members of my pack? Did that make me a bully?

I set my pencil down. Then I leaned back, closed my eyes, and massaged my temples. After this brief pause I sat up and looked around. Apparently I wasn't the only one who'd had enough of this test, because Mrs. Woods was nowhere to be found. Since Mr. Proctor was here, policing his exam, she must've seen this as her opportunity to step out and take a break.

Poor Mrs. Woods had been battling laryngitis for weeks. It was getting better now, but she was still using a wireless microphone in our classroom. From a fashion standpoint, the microphone was not that cumbersome or gaudy. Mrs. Woods simply slipped it around her neck and wore it as a pendant. The device was synched to our classroom speakers, and once her weak voice was projected through the sound system, we were able to hear her—even when she was elsewhere in the building.

"Good afternoon, Mrs. Woods. Is your class at specials?"

That was Mr. Allen's voice, which could only mean one thing: Mrs. Woods had forgotten to turn her microphone off.

"No, Mr. Allen, as a matter of fact my students are busy taking another one of those ridiculous practice tests," Mrs. Woods snapped. "I hope you realize this CSA business is doing more harm than good."

Instantly I sat up straight, as did my classmates. After picking his jaw up off the floor, Mr. Proctor came to. "Don't listen to that," he ordered. "Eyes on your tests."

I give him credit for trying, but he didn't stand a chance.

"This is the way of the world nowadays, Mrs. Woods."

"That may be so, Mr. Allen, but that doesn't mean it's right."

Whoa! Mrs. Woods had better be careful. Insubordination was grounds for termination.

"Mrs. Woods, you were hired to be a teacher, and I expect you will do your job."

"I *was* doing my job until you people made all these changes and stuck those test goobers in my classroom. Being a teacher used to mean much more than producing test-taking robots."

At this juncture Mr. Proctor was standing on a chair, fiddling with one of our speakers, desperately trying to disconnect it. I'm quite certain he didn't appreciate being called a test goober, though that description fit him much better than his shirt did. His belly was showing now.

"The tests themselves are not all bad, Mr. Allen, but what we've become as a school because of these tests is despicable. We're not keeping our students' best interests in mind or at heart. And the pressure you're putting on everyone—students and teachers alike—it's enough to make someone hate what they once loved. Trust me when I tell you, these children hate school, Mr. Allen, and that is our biggest failure. If you can't enjoy what you're doing, you'll never want to work hard at it."

I watched Randi's body deflate when those words were spoken. Her mother needed to hear this speech as much as Mr. Allen, if not more.

"Mrs. Woods, if you want things back to the way they were, then I suggest you get your students ready to perform on the CSAs. Plain and simple. I don't like this test craze any more than you do, but our only chance to change it is with results. Results speak."

We waited for more, but that was the end of it. Mr. Proctor was still fumbling with the speaker when Mrs. Woods came storming back into our classroom. Spotting him on that chair, she immediately put two and two together.

"You can leave now, Mr. Test Goober," Scott said. "Our teacher has returned."

"Mr. Mason, please do not disrespect our guest. I shouldn't have said that, and I'm sorry you heard it.

"Mr. Proctor, please accept my apology."

Mr. Proctor gathered his things and left without a word. He didn't even bother to collect our practice tests.

I braced myself, because the moment our door closed, I expected Mrs. Woods to read us the riot act. She had to be enraged after her argument with Mr. Allen, but that didn't faze you-know-who in the least. Seriously, where would we have been at times like these without Scott?

"It's okay, Mrs. Woods. I make lots of mistakes, but your mistakes don't have to define you. Even though I goof up, I'm still going to do something that helps people someday."

"Thank you for that advice, Mr. Mason."

"My mom says what's important is that you learn from your mistakes." Scott wasn't done yet. "I hope you've learned your lesson, Mrs. Woods. The last thing you want to do is forget and leave that microphone on when you go to the bathroom, especially if you've ever got a case of the rolling thunder farts like my dad gets."

Mrs. Woods broke out in laughter—not even she could hold it together after Scott said that. The rest of us joined her. Scott had us in stitches. Indeed, everything that happened with that practice test was outrageously funny in the end, but none of us would've been laughing had we known what was about to occur with the real tests.

Randi

Jane was no longer sitting outside the window scrutinizing my workouts from start to finish. The first time I glanced over and saw she was missing, I began hyperventilating. Where was she? I panicked. Was she in the gym, ready to yell at me because I needed to tighten my routine? I looked all around, but Jane was nowhere to be found. I checked the window again, but she still wasn't there. Slowly I regained control of my breathing and resumed my exercises. I didn't see Jane all night.

This was how my practices had been going recently, and I was having my best workouts. But things got even weirder. One night after practice, when I came out of the locker room and walked into the lobby area, I spotted Jane talking to Coach Andrea. I felt my body go weak. Was she pushing Coach Andrea again, demanding answers for why I wasn't doing better?

"I needed to do this a long time ago," I heard Jane say.

"You're sure?" Coach Andrea asked.

"Yes. Take her off the list," Jane replied.

"Okay." Coach Andrea nodded. "It's going—"

The second they saw me coming, their conversation ended. Coach Andrea gave me a small smile, and then Jane turned and walked out of the building. I followed her to the car. I had the eerie feeling I'd just seen and heard something I wasn't supposed to see or hear, kind of like what happened in school with that conversation between Mrs. Woods and Mr. Allen. But where was Scott to say something and make it all better?

Jane and I rode in silence, but an hour is a long time to keep asking yourself the same question over and over. It bubbled up inside me to the point that I couldn't stand it anymore. I didn't need Scott. I finally broke and said something. "What list did you take me off?" I asked.

"The list of gymnasts competing in the St. Patrick's festival," Jane said.

How was I supposed to respond? That was not what I was expecting her to say. I didn't know what to think. After bombing at the Halloween event, I needed to win the St. Patrick's Gymnastics Festival, not skip it.

"It's time for you to have a little break, Randi. You need to recharge your battery so you're ready for States. We're going to ease up so you can focus on school and get caught up in math. So you can nail those CSAs."

I was so confused. Was this about me and what was best for me, or getting me ready for States and top classes and scholarships? It was too little too late. I didn't need any extra time for math. My math was already done. Scott finished it for me during lunch. He did it for me every day. He always tried his best to explain it, and I always nodded like I understood, but really I didn't get any of what he was saying. I just let him do the work for me. That wasn't my plan when this started, but that's what it had become. Without his help, there was no way I was going to correctly answer all those questions on the CSAs. I'd hold my own, but I wasn't going to ace them like Jane was hoping. I wished I could make it right, but there was no turning back now.

I showered when we got home, and then I pretended to do my homework. Jane never checked on me. I wasn't sure if this was more of the silent treatment or us just being bad at talking to each other.

The silence continued the next morning, but breakfast waiting on the table for me definitely said something. I just wasn't sure what.

GAVIN

Woods was right when she told Mr. Allen we hated school. We hated it for a lot of different reasons, but everyone agreed that all that test garbage they kept making us read was awful. Most of the time it was about places and stuff I'd never even heard of before, and that just made it harder and dumber. I was psyched when Woods gave Mr. Allen a piece of her mind and sent Proctor packing. That was a good day. And after all that went down, Scott asked Woods to read to us and she did. What a treat that was. But now it was back to the grind.

"I'm not leading a bunch of rebels in mutiny," Woods said. "We'll do what we're supposed to, and it'll all be over soon. March is almost here."

Not soon enough, I thought.

Even though everything about school stunk, I was still working hard on my reading at home. Woods got me the audiobook of *Shiloh* so I could reread it, and I also had all those books from the library.

It was a few nights before our next trip to the senior center when Meggie wanted to try a new story for bedtime. She pulled a softcover out of my trusty library bag that musta been one of those favorites Magenta had snuck in there. This one had a long name, *Wilfrid Gordon McDonald Partridge*. There were so many "d's" in the title that I was all mixed up before I even got started. But Meggie didn't care. She wanted me to read it. So I did my best, and wouldn't you know it, that story was about a boy with that long, tricky name trying to help some old lady in an old person's home to find her memories.

When I got done, Meggie said what she always says. "Read it again, Gavvy." And I did. I read it a whole bunch of times. And each time I got better at reading it, but I also started thinking more and more about what Scott had told me on the bus. Yeah, Scott was a nut, crazy enough to wear an old-lady nightgown, and he couldn't catch or throw a football to save his life, but he also mighta been right about this one. Maybe?

I still didn't know what to think of the old man they called Coach, but I decided to try to help him. I loved talking football with him, but that junk he pulled where he started freaking out and yelling at me wasn't funny. If he did that again, he could forget about me and his memories.

We found the all-star team of old folks sitting in the community hall, waiting for us just like always. Director Ruggelli didn't give Scott a chance to mess up today, though. She started shooing us along, encouraging us to find a place to sit so we could get busy playing our games and doing puzzles. I looked but I didn't see Coach anywhere.

Magenta pulled me aside. "He must be in his room," she

said. She knew who I was looking for. "C'mon. Let's go see if we can find him."

I followed her down the hall and around the corner. A good quarterback is focused on his play but pays attention to the shifting defense, too. I wasn't that good yet. I was too busy worrying about me and my plan and what was gonna happen with Coach to bother paying attention to anything else—and there was plenty for me to be noticing.

Magenta was right. We found Coach in his room, bent over his desk. It wasn't X's and O's today, though. He was busy doing a paint-by-number. Meggie did those things.

"Hi, Coach," Magenta said. "Painting today, I see?" She rubbed his back.

"Who's that?" Coach said, pointing but not looking at me.

I squeezed my lucky football.

"That's Gavin," Magenta reminded him. "He's from my school. You met him the last time he was here. You had fun talking football with him. He's back to visit with you again."

"Is he going to read to me?" Coach asked.

"I don't know. You'll have to ask him."

"I'm not very good at reading," I said. "The letters move around on me instead of sitting still like offensive linemen."

"That's okay," Coach said. "You keep working at it like you do those football plays and you'll get it mastered. With good old-fashioned hard work you can accomplish most anything. You're already getting better at it."

How could he know that?

Magenta smiled. "Come and get me if you need anything," she whispered. "I'll be in the Hall."

I nodded, but the second she left the room I wanted to yell for her. Can you still be a football player if you're a chicken?

"You keep the nose of that football covered, Valentine," Coach ordered. He was looking right at me now. "And keep your elbow tight to your side. I don't want to see you fumbling."

He definitely had me confused with someone else, but that was okay. I liked the way he was talking to me. He was coaching me. I'd never had a coach before.

I nodded.

"It might not be football season, but you practice good habits now and you'll be ready in the fall. What position are you going out for?"

"Quarterback," I said.

"You've gotta be a leader to play that position, Valentine. Are you a leader?"

I shrugged.

"We're gonna have to work on that," Coach said. "A leader can't be wishy-washy. You've got to be confident."

"I can do it," I said, looking him in the eye.

"That's better. There's hope for you yet, Gavin. I've got a way of knowing these things."

All of a sudden he remembered my name. Did he understand who he was talking to? Did he know what he was talking about when he said I could be a leader?

"You like art, Valentine?"

"I like drawing," I said, "but I don't like showing people my stuff."

"Confidence, Valentine. Confidence."

I nodded.

"My daughter's a beautiful artist," Coach said. "Got a few of her paintings hanging right over there."

"They're nice," I said, barely giving them a glance. I wanted to talk football, not art.

"I used to do these paint-by-numbers with her when she was little. I knew back then that she was talented, and she loved it, but she never liked sharing. Always afraid of what people might say. Her mother wanted her to succeed so bad that she made her scared of failure. It was out of love, but you can't be that way, Valentine! You've got to put yourself out there if you ever want to taste victory. You've got to go for it."

"Did your daughter go for it?"

"Not with art, even though that was her passion. Her mother's worrying filled her with self-doubt, so she took a safer path—the one her mother wanted—and it ruined their relationship."

"I'm sorry," I said.

Coach looked at me again. "It's never too late, Valentine. There's still time on the clock."

I didn't know what to think. I was feeling more confused than Coach. I didn't even know if his story was real. If it was, I hoped his wife and daughter made up before his time ran out, but I didn't come prepared to help him with those memories. I had other stuff with me.

"I brought you a few things," I said. "I can't leave the football, 'cause it's my only one and I need it to practice, but you can keep this." I handed him a whistle.

Coach put it around his neck and picked up the ball. He got to his feet and started pacing about the room.

"See that poem over there, Valentine?"
He pointed.

"Yes."

"Read it. And read it out loud so I can hear the words."

"But I told you, I'm not good at reading."

"And I told you with hard work you'll get it mastered. You've got to believe in yourself, especially as quarterback, so get working. Read it to me."

I began, and then Coach joined in with me. He didn't even have to look at the words, 'cause his memory was working. He had this memorized like I did *The Very Hungry Caterpillar*.

THE GUY IN THE GLASS
—DALE WIMBROW

When you get what you want in your struggle for pelf,
And the world makes you King for a day,
Then go to the mirror and look at yourself,
And see what that guy has to say.

For it isn't your Father, or Mother or Wife,
Whose judgement upon you must pass;
The feller whose verdict counts most in your life,
Is the guy staring back from the glass.

He's the feller to please, never mind all the rest,
For he's with you clear up to the end,
And you've passed your most dangerous, difficult test,
If the guy in the glass is your friend.

You may be like Jack Horner and "chisel" a plum,
And think you're a wonderful guy;
But the man in the glass says you're only a bum
If you can't look him straight in the eye.

You may fool the whole world down your pathway of years,
And get pats on the back as you pass,
But your final reward will be heartache and tears
If you've cheated the guy in the glass.

"You hear that, men?!" Coach yelled. I swear he was seeing his team huddled together in the locker room. "What's it mean to you, Valentine?"

"We've got to lay it on the line, sir. Play our hearts out and give it our all. So we can look the guy in the glass in the eye when it's all said and done—no matter the outcome."

"That's right!" Coach yelled. "If you can do that, then Thomson High doesn't stand a chance. Now get out there and follow your leader to victory!" He blasted his whistle.

My heart was racing a million miles an hour. I was ready to sprint onto the gridiron. I woulda given anything to play for Coach. He was the best.

"Looks like you boys are having fun," Magenta said.

And just like that, our locker room vanished. Coach sat down and returned to his paint-by-numbers.

Magenta walked over to his side and rubbed his back again. When she looked at me, she saw my disappointment. "I'm afraid it's time to go," she said. "I'm sorry."

I nodded. "See ya later, Coach."

"Practice tomorrow, Valentine. Three o'clock sharp."

"Yes, sir."

"Bye, Coach," Magenta said.

The old man didn't say anything. He was lost in his painting now.

Me and Magenta left and made our way down the hall. "Today went well?" she asked.

"Great," I said. "He musta been an amazing coach."

"He was."

"Do you know anything about his wife and daughter?"

"Why?" Magenta asked, sounding startled by my question.

"He was talking about his daughter's art and how his wife was so scared of her not succeeding with it that his daughter did something else instead, and it ruined her relationship with her mother."

Magenta stopped. "He told you all that?"

"Yeah, why?"

She was silent. She kinda looked stunned, like a player who just had victory taken from him by some last-second miracle play.

"Is all that stuff true that he was saying?" I asked her.

She nodded. "I can't believe he remembered all that. Did he say anything else?"

"Yeah. That there's still time on the clock for them."

She smiled. "Keep the nose of that football covered, Valentine."

"I will," I said. I tucked the ball tight under my arm and jogged out to the bus.

Randi

We loaded into the bus, but before we pulled away from the Senior Center, Mrs. Magenta stood at the front and asked for our attention.

"Okay, caring souls, please listen up." Mrs. Magenta sure was different, but she had a way of making me smile—like Scott. "I hope you're all feeling warm inside despite the cold outside, because you're making a lot of people very happy when you come here. I'm so proud of you."

"Hey, lady, can we get a move on?" Mr. Bus Driver interrupted.

"When I'm finished," Mrs. Magenta said, staring him down. "Don't be rude."

I didn't see that coming. Up till then I didn't realize Mrs. Magenta had a little Mrs. Woods in her.

She turned back to us. "Please listen carefully," she continued. "I have an important announcement. Earlier today I was informed that a change has been made. We will still be gathering for our next after-school meeting, but we will not be making this wonderful trip. Instead, since it is getting close to the CSAs, our administration has decided that all school-related programs, such as ours, will be required to use their next session for additional CSA practice. We will resume visiting our friends at the senior center after the tests."

Trevor didn't need to boo. The bus filled with moans and groans.

"I'm sorry," Mrs. Magenta said. "This was not my decision." She sagged into her seat and seemed to be looking out the window, still upset, and then we pulled away from the curb.

"Don't worry. Things will be all better after the tests," Scott told us. "Mr. Allen and I have a deal."

"Whatever," Gav mumbled, pretending not to care.

"No, really. You'll see," Scott insisted.

"Dude, believe me, I wish you were right, but—" Mark stopped midsentence, but it was too late. He'd already said too much. What did he know that we didn't?

"But what?" Trevor said.

Mark sighed. "My dad says there are a few nuts on the school board who want to make the tests part of the eligibility rules. They think it'll motivate us to do better."

"Whaddaya mean?" Gav said, turning around.

"I mean the school might decide we can't play football in the fall if our test scores aren't good enough. So chances are, me and Trev will be watching the games from the bleachers with you next year."

"What? You didn't tell me that!" Trevor yelled.

"I didn't want to," Mark said, his voice trailing off.

Trevor slumped against the window.

"They can't do that!" Gav exclaimed. He'd been dreaming

about playing forever, and now he was going to lose his chance before it even got here.

"Yes, they can," Mark said. "Look at all the other junk they've already pulled. My father's fighting it, but he doesn't think he's going to win this one. What do you care, anyway? It's not like your mother was going to let you play."

"I was gonna play next year!" Gav yelled. "And my mother's not the reason I've never played before. It's her fault!" He pointed at Natalie.

"Me?!" Natalie cried. "How's it my fault?!"

"Ask your mother," he said. That was the second time Gav had told her that, and I still had no idea what it was all about.

"Really? You get to play?" Mark said. He didn't care one bit about Natalie.

"I was supposed to," Gav said, "but if this thing with the CSAs happens, then I'll never set foot on the field. There's no way I'll get a high-enough grade. I wish there was some way we could ace those dumb things so the school would stop making them such a big deal. It's not like that test even has anything to do with real life."

That sounded like something his father would say. "You're not the only one who needs to ace them," I said. Gav and I hadn't been talking, but he knew what I meant. Suddenly the tests mattered for each of our destinies.

"Mr. Allen is wishing for the same thing," Scott said.

"Who isn't?" Mark replied.

"I'm going to make it happen," Scott announced.

"Yeah, okay," Mark said. "Who're you, our fairy god-mother? Don't forget to wear your cute nightgown when you grant our wishes."

"Shut up, Mark," Trevor snapped. "Scott, can you really do that?"

Trevor had seemed so defeated and out of the conversation, but suddenly he was very interested in what Scott had just said. Why?

"I can do it," Scott answered. "I'll find a way."

He was serious, and we all knew it. We knew he'd hatch some brilliant plan. And even though it would be risky—and wrong—we didn't tell him not to do it. Instead, I think we were all hoping he'd come through for us.

NATALIE KURTSMAN
ASPIRING LAWYER
Kurtsman Law Offices

BRIEF #20
February: Mother's Story

After what transpired on the bus, I should've been concerned about Scott and the potential wrongdoing he had everyone headed toward, but I was only thinking about one thing: asking Mother about Gavin.

The first time Gavin made that rude comment about lawyers, I dismissed it. I never bothered to mention it to Mother. I defended my case by demonstrating that lawyers are great people. But this time Gavin didn't make a broad, unfair generalization about lawyers. Instead, he pointed his finger at me and blamed my mother for his current situation. That was different.

I intended to question Mother the moment I got in the car, but Father was the one to pick me up today. That was out of the ordinary, and when I asked him to explain, he told me my mother was buried in work. "It's been one of those days," he said.

One of those days or not, I needed answers. When we got to the office, I headed straight for the conference room, where Father had told me I'd find her.

"Hi, Natalie. How was your day?" She sounded tired and looked spent. There were papers spread all over the table in front of her.

"It was fine," I said. I recognized that Mother was exhausted, but this couldn't wait. I pressed on with what I came to talk about. "Mother, there is a boy in my class and after-school program who has made more than one unfair and upsetting comment about lawyers. I haven't let it bother me until this afternoon, when he blamed his not playing football on you, which seems completely preposterous. How is that even possible?"

"What's his name?"

"What?"

"The boy. What's his name, Natalie?"

"Gavin Davids," I said. "Why?"

Mother sighed. She removed her glasses and rubbed her eyes and face. "You better sit down, Natalie. I need to tell you a story."

"You mean his claim isn't absurd?!"

"Please sit down and let me explain," Mother said again.

I took a deep breath and sat in the chair opposite her. I placed my folded hands on the table.

Mother slipped her glasses back on. "The story I'm about to tell you took place several years ago," she began.

I nodded.

"It was late one evening, and an old man by the name of Red was without heat. Something had broken in his house. He didn't know what to do, so he called the one guy who he knew would help.

"Temperatures were supposed to drop below zero that night, so the young man getting the phone call never hesitated. There was no way he would ever let Red spend the night in those conditions.

"Making the drive was the hard part. Once there, the young man didn't take long to have everything working again. Red didn't have money to pay, but this was no surprise to the young man; he'd known Red ever since he was a boy, helping his father on the job, and this was how things had always been. Instead of money, Red offered the younger man a beer in appreciation. The younger man didn't actually want the drink, but he took it so Red wouldn't feel bad.

"As fate would have it, on his way home the young man came upon an old lady stranded on the side of the road with a flat tire. Of course the young man stopped and helped—no surprise there. He got the spare on for the old woman, and she was very grateful, thanking him profusely because that was all she could do. She got in her car and he got in his truck. And then the old lady pulled out without looking. She never saw the Mercedes-Benz that came careening around the corner. The car was speeding. It swerved, fishtailed, lost control, and crashed into the man's truck."

Mother stopped.

I leaned forward. "Did anyone get hurt?"

"Not right away."

I scowled. "I don't understand."

"I was here, in my office, when this obviously wealthy gentleman came in looking for an attorney to handle his lawsuit. He had an easy case, Natalie. He'd been driving his Mercedes just after dark when a truck that was parked along-side the road suddenly pulled out in front of him. The truck was missing a taillight, and there was an empty beer bottle found inside on the floor."

"But that's not what really happened," I said.

"I didn't know that. We sued the man in the truck and won easily. He was ordered to pay for all the damages to my cli-ent's car and for all the medical bills related to his injuries, which were ongoing—and no less made-up."

"But that's not right!" I exclaimed. "How could that happen?"

"The man in the truck didn't have a lawyer. He didn't men-tion the old lady when he was given the chance to defend himself."

"Why? Why would he do that?"

"Because he's the good guy in the story, Natalie, except I didn't know that—not for a long time. Remember your twisty-slide day, earlier this year, when I picked you up and you could tell I was upset about something?"

Again I nodded.

"It was on that same day that I happened to run into my old client, in the grocery store of all places. I asked him how he was doing, and he laughed. Then his arrogance got the better of him; he had to brag. The truth came spilling out. He told me exactly what had happened on that fateful night and said something about good guys always finishing last. When he stopped, I felt like I'd been run over by his fancy car. I had to fight the urge to slap him. He walked away, laughing his creepy laugh, and I thought I was going to be sick. I left my cart full of groceries and stumbled outside. I sat in the car, crying, for the next hour."

I felt terrible for Mother, but what she said next floored me.

"Natalie, the good guy in the story was Michael Davids, whom I presume to be Gavin's father."

Those last words sent my world spinning. It was like hearing the judge announce a major verdict not in your favor. Gavin wasn't lying; Mother had ruined everything for his family. It was too much to comprehend. I pushed back from the table and ran out of the room.

I'd never been so disappointed in anything. Justice was supposed to prevail in the courtroom, not corruption.

Trevor

This thing with the CSAs and eligibility couldn't happen. I had to be able to play sports. I didn't care if I had to sit on the bench because of my grades, but I had to be on the team. There was no way I could spend another year going home after school.

Scott had to come through for me. I would've done anything for that kid right then.

SCOTT

I liked helping people. I was good at helping people, but I'd only ever helped one person at a time before. Now I was going to help everybody. Mark. Trevor. Randi. Gavin. Natalie. Mr. Allen. Everybody.

I had to do it. Mr. Allen had wished for it, and all my friends were wishing for it. They needed me. So I was patient and careful, and I came up with a genius plan—my best plan ever. It wasn't hard.

I hated the CSAs. They were dumb, boring, and easy. Because of them we'd lost birthday parties, Mrs. Magenta's fun projects, read-aloud time and free reading, and then our recess.

But all of a sudden, for the very first time in my whole entire life, I was excited for the test. Finding a way to supply the answers without getting caught made the CSAs so much more interesting and challenging—and important. They were no longer Complex Student Abuse. They had become my Communication System for Answers.

I was ready. This was going to be a piece of cake. And the icing on my cake would be getting my recess back and hearing Mrs. Woods read to us again after the dumb tests were finally over, because Mr. Allen and I had a deal.

Randi

All this time I'd been hoping for a psychic to read my future and tell me my destiny, but instead I was sent a wish-giver. Scott was our very own genie. We'd said the magic words on the bus ride home, and now he was prepared to grant us our wishes.

"I've invented the perfect system," he told Natalie and me at lunch. He leaned closer, giddy with excitement. "CSA now stands for my Communication System for Answers."

Natalie's eyes widened and so did mine. Had Scott really come up with a way for us to ace the tests? The bus ride had happened a couple of weeks ago and there was never any talk about it afterward. I guess I just thought it had been one of those times when boys talked a big game but never really did what they said and you never really believed them anyway. Besides, you don't exactly go around pestering somebody for a plan to cheat, so I'd just assumed Scott had given up on the idea. I couldn't blame him. Why should he even do this?

"Scott, have you been working on this system for the last two weeks?" Natalie asked.

"No! I came up with it in no time," he said, proud of himself. "That was easy. The hard part's been waiting to reveal it until we got closer to the test date so no one forgets it."

Nothing Scott did should've surprised me at this point in the year, but this was different. I had more butterflies swarming in my stomach than showed up before any of my gymnastics meets.

"This is my signal for 'A,'" he said, scratching the top of his head.

Again I glanced at Natalie, but she never said a word. What was she thinking? I couldn't read her mind like I could Gavin's. I hadn't known her long enough yet. She never said anything about Scott doing my math, and when I tried asking her if she knew why Gavin had mentioned her mother on the bus, she didn't say much then, either.

"I have absolutely no idea," she said.

"Really?"

"Yes, and I don't feel like talking about it. Rehashing it will only make me upset again."

I wasn't a mind reader, but something told me she suddenly knew more than she was letting on. For being mortal enemies, she and Gav were a lot more alike than they'd ever care to admit. But whatever was going on, it was between them.

"Pay attention," Scott hissed. "I don't have time to keep going over this with you. I've got other people to show."

He drilled us and quizzed us over the next several minutes, and then he got up and walked over to Gavin's table. I wanted Scott's plan to save us all in the worst way, to make all the bad go away, but I wanted it to help Gavin more than anybody else. Even more than me. My old friend deserved a chance.

I turned back to the girl sitting next to me. I had another wish. I wished there was a way for me to have both Gavin and Natalie as my friends, but there wasn't anything our genie could do to make that happen—and that was for reasons I still didn't understand.

NATALIE KURTSMAN
ASPIRING LAWYER
Kurtsman Law Offices

BRIEF #21
February: Scott's Plan

Scott sat down with Randi and me at lunch and unveiled the elaborate cheating scheme that he had masterminded. He fully intended to take the test and secretly share the correct answers with the rest of the class, question by question, using some silent code that he had devised.

This was wrong—I know the difference between right and wrong—but I wasn't going to tell on them. I'm not a tattletale—never have been. Additionally, there was no way I could do that to Randi; she needed this. And so did Gavin, like him or not. After what Mother did to his father, the least I could do was turn a blind eye to this matter. I owed him that much.

In my view, my classmates had good reasons for cheating and I had good reasons for not telling—perhaps the most convincing being the fact that Scott and Randi were my friends.

I'd never had friends before, but I was certain one thing you never did was rat on one—did you? (That was precisely why I never said anything when Scott started doing Randi's math homework.) Besides, the way I saw it, what my classmates were doing was no more wrong than what Lake View Middle was doing. Even Mrs. Woods had declared our school's approach to the CSAs harmful.

This test conspiracy most certainly wasn't anything I was going to participate in, so I simply stayed out of it. The problem was, I couldn't shake one burning question: Was I doing something wrong by allowing this to happen?

I didn't want the answer. That scared me.

Trevor

I was eating lunch with Mark and Gavin when Scott waltzed over and plopped down at our table.

"Pay attention," he said. "We need to do this fast so no one gets suspicious."

"What are you talk—"

"Shh!" he snapped, cutting Mark off. "Watch." He scratched the top of his head. "That's the signal for 'A.'" Next he tugged his earlobe. "That's 'B.'"

He showed us the signal for "C" and "D" and his sneaky way of helping us keep track of what question number we were on. Then he ran through the whole thing again and quizzed us a few times.

"Got it?" he asked.

"Got it," I said.

"Any questions?"

We shook our heads.

"Good." Scott glanced around the cafeteria, making sure he wasn't being watched, and then he started to get up.

"Wait," I said.

He stopped and looked back at me.

"Thanks."

"That's what friends are for," he said. He scurried off to Alex and Corey's table. After that he went and sat with Connor and Adam.

"We can't talk about this with anyone else," Gavin said. "Not now. Not ever. If this gets out—"

"Don't worry. Mum's the word," I said.

"Mum's the word," Mark repeated.

"Good. Let's just hope Kurtsman keeps her big mouth shut," Gavin said.

Natalie had already stuck her neck out for Scott more than once, so there was no way she was going to throw him under the bus now. Anyway, I let Gavin worry about her. I had other things on my mind.

12

GAVIN

Mom had dinner ready. We were just waiting on my old man to get home from his last plumbing call. He did a lot of late-afternoon and early-evening appointments, 'cause it was easier for working people to schedule those times.

"I'm home," he called, coming through the front door. "What's for supper? It smells delicious."

"It's ready," Mom said. "Come to the table."

Dad washed his hands and joined us. "I'll tell you what, puttin' in an honest day's work sure makes you hungry. I'm starvin'."

Why did he have to go and say that dumb word? He loved that dumb word—"honest."

"You might not be born with much, you might not have much, but you can be honest," Meggie said, repeating one of Dad's favorite sayings.

That was when I lost my appetite. "I'm not feeling too great," I said. "May I be excused from the table?"

"*Niño*, are you all right?" Mom asked.

"Yes. I just want to lie down."

"Okay."

As hard as I tried to have Dad's talk go in one ear and out the other, that didn't always work. After hearing someone say something enough times, it sorta gets stuck in your head, whether you like it or not, including that piece of wisdom that Meggie had just spouted off. Deep down I knew my old man was right—even if he was a high school dropout.

The only time my father hadn't been all the way honest was in court. He didn't lie, but he also never mentioned the old lady when he had the chance. That was nice of him, but it made my life miserable. Well, enough was enough. My time had finally come. I'd paid my dues. It was my turn to play football, to have my chance to be a hero and a leader on the field, so it wasn't fair for some dumb test to mess that up. I needed to pass this thing. If I didn't, then I wasn't gonna amount to anything. I'd be a nobody for the rest of my life—like my old man.

Was I gonna do this? You betcha. I was done wrestling with that question. It wasn't something me and Randi would be proud of, but I knew from the look she gave me in school that we were in it together—and that felt good.

I had my mind made up—but I couldn't tell the guy in the glass.

Trevor

I wasn't worried about me. I was willing to do more than cheat on a lousy test to make sure I wasn't stuck with my brother and his goons again next year. It was a no-brainer. But it was a different story for Mark. I'd been worrying about him ever since Scott made it real. Mark was my best friend, but he wasn't like me. If he ever got caught, or if his father found out, it would mean huge trouble.

"Are you really going to do this thing Scott's got planned?" I asked him the day before the test. It was only the two of us at lunch. Gavin hadn't joined us yet.

"Yeah, I'm doing it. What're you even talking about?"

"I know it's different for you with your dad being on the board, that's all. I'd understand if you said you were out."

"Dude, do you think I'm a wimp or something? Of course I'm doing it. We're in this together. You joined Mrs. Magenta's program for me, and now I'm doing this thing with you. We always have each other's back."

That sounded fair, but we both knew I didn't join that

program for him. And Mark was in this because he knew what was at stake for me, and somehow that made me feel even worse.

The other person I couldn't stop worrying about was Scott. The only reason that kid was even doing this was to help us—and for what? We hadn't even been nice to him—at least, I hadn't. I didn't know why, but when I got around Scott, I acted a lot like Chris—and I hated Chris. I definitely wouldn't be excited to help Chris—not with anything. So what did Scott want to help me for? I was the last person he should've been helping—but he was, so I was going to make it up to him. I didn't know how, but I was good at paybacks. I'd figure something out, because I owed him.

Randi

It was the night before the CSAs, and I was sitting in bed, getting ready to turn my light off. Jane walked in. "I just wanted to tell you good luck on the tests tomorrow," she said. "I know you'll ace them."

"Thanks."

She patted my knee. "Good night."

"Good night," I said.

What was that all about? Was she trying to be nice? Why did she have to say that about acing the tests? If she was trying to help me relax, that didn't work. I felt so confused that not even a crystal ball could've helped me sort things out.

When I finally lay back and closed my eyes, I was greeted by the worst night of sleep I'd ever had. Even worse than the night before last year's state championships, when I tossed and turned and saw Jane every time I dozed. She stared at me from the stands, from across the floor, and from behind the judges' table. She was in my dreams again tonight, standing over my desk, waiting for me to bubble in my answer. She stood there twirling her thumbs, running out of patience. I glanced across the room to where Scott was sitting. I got his signal and darkened in answer choice "B." Jane smiled and patted me on the back.

Anything, just as long as I landed in the advanced group. You do whatever it takes to make it to the top. That shouldn't even be a question. You don't even need to think about it. No need for a signal when it comes to that. But I heard one.

The sound of an alarm rang through the dark. It was fuzzy and faraway in my sleepy world, but it grew closer and louder. I rubbed my eyes and sat up in bed. The fogginess in my brain lifted as the wail of the sirens faded. The noise had been real. Was destiny sending me a warning?

SCOTT

I always have a hard time falling asleep on Christmas Eve. I can't wait to see what's under the tree. I know that's not the meaning of Christmas, but there's no way to shake the thought of presents—and frosted cookies!

Tonight was like Christmas Eve all over again, except it was my turn to play Santa Claus. I was the one bringing the big present to class tomorrow. I was going to make a lot of people happy. I was so excited that when I finally fell asleep, I did it with a smile on my face.

Several hours later I was awakened by lights and voices— Mom's shaky one, Dad's worried one, and one I didn't recognize. What was going on?

I crept down the stairs quieter than a mouse on Christmas morning, but not because I was hiding from Santa. I didn't want Mom or Dad to catch me out of bed. I stopped halfway down the steps, where I could peek into the kitchen and hear what was being said. If someone was in trouble, I wanted to help. I didn't see anyone, but I heard plenty.

"Any idea what could've caused it?" Dad asked.

"Your father-in-law said he made some soup before bed," a strange voice answered. "We think he left the stove on. It didn't take much. The house went up fast with all those papers."

I heard Mom sniffling.

"He's lucky he made it out, Mr. Mason," the strange voice continued. "That cat saved his life."

Dad stepped into the light and pulled Mom close. She wrapped her arms around him and buried her face in his chest.

"I'm sorry," the strange voice said as its owner came into view.

Dad nodded. "Thank you."

I watched him shake hands with the fireman, who then left our house. Mom and Dad stayed, hugging in the kitchen, so I snuck down the rest of the steps and tiptoed into the living room. I found Grandpa sitting in a chair and staring out the window, mindlessly petting Smoky, who was curled up and sleeping in his lap. It was the same thing Grandpa always did, but it was different tonight. Tonight he looked lost and sad.

"What're we going to do?" I heard Mom asking Dad. "This is terrible. He's lost everything." She was crying again.

Lost everything. Lost everything. Mom's words repeated in my head.

It was time. I hurried back to my room and collected all of Grandpa's memories. Then I carried his box out to the living room and knelt in front of him. He never moved. He kept staring out the window.

"Grandpa," I said, "you didn't lose everything tonight. I have some of your memories right here. I've been collecting them for you. I got the idea from a book I read."

Slowly he turned and looked at me. I opened the box and lifted out his memory string. Grandpa took it and held it in his hands. I watched his fingers rub the different objects. Then he leaned forward and I watched him touch and hold the rest of the things I had collected. I watched him remembering.

When he sat back, I looked up and saw the tears on his cheeks. I'd never seen my grandpa cry before. Was he upset with me for taking his stuff?

"Scott," Grandpa croaked, "this is the best present anyone has ever given me. I thought I'd lost everything of your grandmother's tonight. Thank you."

My smile stretched ear to ear. I could feel it.

"And this cat," Grandpa said, scratching Smoky's ears. "I need to thank you for him, too. He saved my life. I never would've woken up without him."

My smile grew even bigger.

Dad clapped his strong hand on my shoulder and gave me a squeeze, and Mom hugged me and kissed the top of my head.

"How long have you been standing behind me?" I asked them.

"Long enough," Dad said.

I hadn't messed this one up. Not this time. I tried to do something helpful, and I got it right. I did something special. It was one of the happiest and saddest times in my whole entire life.

When Mom finally took me back upstairs, my eyes closed

before I even fell into bed. I'd never been up so late, but it was okay because I got to sleep in. Getting me to and from Lake View Middle was more than Mom or Dad could think about after the night we'd had, so I stayed home from school the next day. Mom made me. Our whole family stayed home.

NATALIE KURTSMAN
ASPIRING LAWYER
Kurtsman Law Offices

BRIEF #22
March: Moral Dilemma

It was time for the tests—and no Scott. He had everyone counting on him. Where was he? His ingenious plan covered everything but this possibility.

Randi needs help. Gavin needs help. What do I do?

Natalie, don't you know the difference between right and wrong?

GAVIN

Woods had our desks pulled apart. We knew the drill. It was silent when she started passing out the answer booklets. I couldn't stop looking at Scott's empty chair. Every few seconds I'd glance over there. This was unbelievable. My dreams of being the star quarterback were disappearing before I even got a chance. How was I ever gonna pull this off? How was I gonna ace this thing without Scott?

Suddenly something unexpected happened. It happened so fast I didn't even have time to think about it. And I didn't want to. I didn't want to change my mind. I saw the signal and filled in the first bubble. I waited for the next signal. The answers came for every question after that.

Randi

Cunningham's my last name, so I decided it was in my destiny to be cunning. Isn't it funny how you can come up with all sorts of explanations to convince yourself of something that you know isn't true?

I was just cheating a little. It wasn't like I needed anyone's help to pass the test. I had most of the answers right on my own. But passing wasn't good enough for Jane. That wasn't the goal. "I know you'll ace them," she had said. I needed perfect scores on the bars and beam, and I needed a perfect score on the CSAs.

I got Natalie's signal and bubbled in my final answer. That was it. My results would arrive sometime during the summer, and I would be placed in the top group. Mr. Allen and the rest of Lake View Middle would get the good news and start celebrating our success. Jane would sigh in relief—maybe she would say something—and I would start breathing again.

That was the way it was supposed to go.

GAVIN

It didn't go exactly as planned, but it worked, sorta like when a quarterback scrambles out of a broken play and turns nothing into a big gain, maybe even a touchdown. But when it was all said and done, I didn't feel like celebrating with any end zone dancing. I didn't feel like celebrating at all. I felt worse.

I only did it 'cause I had to, and 'cause everyone else was doing it. Trevor and Mark did it. Randi did it. Even Miss Perfect Natalie Kurtsman did it!

Too bad I was smart enough to know that didn't make it right. If they were all smoking and drinking, I wouldn't have joined in. That woulda been easier to handle than this stuff with the CSAs, though.

"You can be honest," my old man liked to say.

I wasn't.

NATALIE KURTSMAN
ASPIRING LAWYER
Kurtsman Law Offices

```
BRIEF #23
March: Guilty
```

I don't want to talk about it.
  I only did what I had to.
  It was Scott's fault.

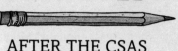

13

AFTER THE CSAS

Trevor

It wasn't supposed to be any big thing for me, but I was angry after we got done. I'd been angry all day. Why did Natalie Kurtsman have to get involved? I never said I'd pay her back. At least Gavin could stop worrying about her telling on us now, but I was worrying more than ever about Scott. Why wasn't he in school? He wouldn't leave us hanging like that on purpose. That wasn't his style. Something must've happened.

I was a mess of feelings, and sometimes when you're all mixed-up like that, it can make you explode. All you need is somebody to push your button, and that was exactly what happened at dinner. It wasn't often that we sat down and ate together as a family, but tonight was Mom's birthday, so we were celebrating with a big order of Chinese food.

"How'd your tests go today?" Mom asked.

"Fine," I said.

"He failed," Brian wisecracked.

"Look who's talking," Dad said.

"What's that supposed to mean?" Brian shot back.

"It means the guy who flunked out of college and is still living at home and doesn't have a decent job should keep his mouth shut."

"That's enough!" Mom snapped, banging her hands on the table. "It's my birthday, and you two will not sit here arguing."

Dad and Brian bit their tongues and shut up. I wished it wasn't Mom's birthday, because if you asked me, Dad needed to kick Brian's butt. He needed to kick his butt all the way out of the house. My brother was a loser. He and his goons worked at some all-night service station and then slept all day until I got home. Brian was freeloading off Mom and Dad and going nowhere.

"At least now that the tests are over, you can start up your program with Mrs. Magenta again," Mom said, returning to her pleasant voice. "You seem to enjoy it."

I nodded.

"What're you and Mark even doing that stupid program for?" Brian wanted to know.

That was all it took. I sprang from my chair. "Are you kidding? Anything's better than spending my afternoons with you and your goons. I can't wait till next year when I have football and basketball practice every day after school and I don't have to see your ugly faces anymore."

I threw my chair aside and stormed off.

"Trevor!" Mom called after me.

Dad and Brian started yelling at each other again.

"Trevor!" Mom cried.

I slammed my bedroom door and cranked my radio. I didn't want to hear any of it. I hated my brother. I hated the CSAs and all these stupid rules. I hated everything.

Mom gave me time to cool off, and then she knocked and came in to check on me. I was lying on my bed, throwing a tennis ball up at the ceiling. She walked over and turned my music down. "Honey, are you okay?" It was quiet in the house now. She sat next to me. "Is everything all right?"

"I'm fine," I said. "Sorry this happened on your birthday."

"Did you want to talk about anything? You really got upset with your brother out there."

"No."

Mom stayed there for a while longer, but she saw she wasn't getting anything more out of me. She sighed, and then she got up and left my room. After not talking about something for as long as I had, you don't open up and spill everything just because your mommy calls you "honey" and brushes the hair out of your face. I wasn't a baby—and I wasn't going to be like my brother or his goons. I could handle things on my own. Maybe I was a mistake, but I was going to be one of those mistakes that turned out to be something good. I'd made my decision about that question Woodchuck had for me. I was going to be an achiever, not a waster.

Randi

What we did on those tests was supposed to take care of things, but instead of breathing easy I felt like I had an elephant on my chest—especially around Jane. I just wanted to forget about the tests, but she ordered pizza so we could celebrate that night—even though we weren't very good at celebrating and we weren't much better at talking. The funny thing was, the silence in between our sentences felt different now. Somewhere along the way that angry feeling that I was used to getting from Jane had tuned into a sad vibe.

"Randi, now that you've aced those tests, would you like to resume gymnastics?" She paused, waiting for my answer, but before I said anything she was quick to add, "If you need more time off, that's fine. Just tell me."

"No. I want to go to practice," I said. I needed something to distract me from the thing that was tearing me up inside. And I wasn't convinced Jane meant it when she said to tell her if I wanted more time off.

"Super," she said. "You've got Mrs. Magenta's program to-morrow, so we'll start back up the day after that."

I nodded. This sounded easy enough, but somehow I knew neither the senior center nor gymnastics were going to make the raw feeling I had in my belly disappear.

GAVIN

Now that the tests were finally behind us, no one was supposed to talk about them. That was the deal, but that didn't last long. By lunch the next day, Mark's mouth was already running.

"Hey, Gavin, guess we took care of those stupid CSAs, huh," he said, plopping his tray down across from me. "No keeping us off the gridiron next year."

"Shut up!" I hissed.

"Sucks it was Natalie who helped us, but better her than fail and no ball in the fall. I still can't believe she did it, but at least we don't have to worry about her big mouth telling on us."

"Will you shut up!" I hissed again, looking around to make sure no adult was listening. "It's not her mouth I'm worried about. If you keep running your trap, we're gonna get nailed, and then we'll be sidelined instead of playing."

"Relax, dude. No one is going to find out. We've got it made in the shade."

That's when I knew we were in trouble. It was only a matter of time. Trevor sat down and I got up.

"Where're you going?" he asked.

"Not hungry," I said. I tossed my lunch in the trash. On my way out of the caf, I glanced at Randi and Natalie. They weren't laughing or celebrating or even talking. They were picking at their sandwiches in silence. Randi didn't need a crystal ball or fortune-teller to see what was coming. This wasn't over. It was a long way from being over.

I headed to the bathroom, but I didn't dare look in the mirror.

SCOTT

It was fun having Grandpa in our house, but there was no way it could stay that way. Dad said if Mom never got a break from Grandpa, she might up and kill him. I loved Grandpa, but I didn't want him to stay, either. If he did, then I'd have to give Grandpa my room and move in with Mickey. Sharing a room with my little brother meant I might be the one to die. We had to find a place for Grandpa, and I knew exactly where.

I was sure Grandpa was going to love the senior center. Mom liked the idea but told Grandpa it was a temporary move. He'd stay there only if he liked it. Mom had me stay home from school a second day so I could go with her when she took Grandpa over there. She said just having me around helped to keep Grandpa's spirits up. I was being helpful without even trying. I was getting good at this.

Mom made Dad take the day off from work so he could stay home with Mickey, because she said there was no way she was dragging my little brother around with all that she had to get done. Dad wasn't happy about it, but Mom was the boss.

It was one busy day. I had no idea how much running around we had to do. First, Mom got Grandpa's paperwork all squared away at the senior center, and then we took him shopping. After losing everything you own in a fire, there's all sorts of stuff you need.

I hated shopping—hated it more than I hated writing! But it wasn't so bad today, because I was helping Grandpa, and it wasn't like I had to try on any clothes. I hated that more than writing, too! Mom grabbed the things she had on her list and threw them in our cart, and Grandpa and I followed her around. I got to drive the cart, which was the only good thing about shopping. I popped a few wheelies when Mom wasn't looking.

When we got done with the business side of things and all that shopping, it was finally time for us to return to the senior center. When we walked in, the place was alive. Mrs. Magenta and my friends were there! I had forgotten they'd be coming today. We didn't normally have community service on Thursdays, but since those school bozos made us use our normal meeting times for test stuff before the CSAs, Mrs. Magenta had rescheduled our program to Thursday for this week.

The test! Oh no! What did they do without me?!

NATALIE KURTSMAN
ASPIRING LAWYER
Kurtsman Law Offices

BRIEF #24
March: Scott's Grandpa

"Where's that boy with the catchy underwear?" Eddie asked. "You're missing him today, aren'tcha?"

That was the same thing I wanted to know. I moved my red piece around the Sorry! board.

"He hasn't been in school the last two days," Randi said.

"That's too bad. I always look forward to seeing him. He brings a little excitement to this place."

"I'll say," Agnes agreed.

Randi and I chuckled. It was the first time we'd even cracked a smile in two days. Perhaps an afternoon with Agnes and Eddie was exactly what we'd needed.

"Who's *that*?" Eddie asked, sitting up straight and nodding toward the door.

Randi and I turned around. A woman and an older man had just come in. The woman looked familiar, but I couldn't place her.

"That's Scott's mother, isn't it?" Randi whispered.

Right on cue, Scott came in next, carrying all sorts of bags and packages.

"That must be his grandfather," I said.

"Do you think that old-timer wears briefs like his grandson?" Eddie asked.

"Stop it," Agnes said, reprimanding her friend. "Must I remind you that you're not as young as you used to be?"

"A fella like that could make me feel young again," Eddie said.

The moment Scott spotted us, he dropped his bags and packages and came rushing over.

"Hi, there, young man. We were just talking about you," Agnes said.

"Where've you been?" I demanded. I didn't mean to sound so accusatory, but it was because of him that I had helped everyone cheat! I had him on the witness stand, and I wanted an explanation.

"My grandpa's house burned down two nights ago, so we've been busy trying to help him."

He blurted out this awful truth in typical Scott style. The pang of guilt that hit me twisted my stomach in knots.

"I'm sorry," Randi said.

"It's okay. I'd been secretly collecting my grandmother's things, so he's still got what's most important. Memories. Grandma's still with him."

"Oh, he's handsome *and* he's a romantic," Eddie squealed. "The best kind."

"Is your grandpa moving in?" Agnes asked.

"Yup, temporarily, but once he meets everyone here, I know he'll want to stay. The only thing is, he can't bring

Smoky, because cats aren't allowed. But Mom said I can keep him. Smoky saved my grandpa's life."

I smiled and my heart hurt.

"Don't worry," Randi said. "Something tells me Eddie won't let your grandpa get too lonely."

Agnes snickered.

"Okay. I gotta go and help now. See you later," Scott said.

"Tell your grandpa if he needs anything to let us know," Agnes said.

"He can come and find me even if he doesn't need anything," Eddie clarified.

Agnes huffed and Randi laughed. I was feeling too guilty to even chuckle.

"I will," Scott said. He skipped off, but he didn't make it very far before coming to an abrupt stop. He spun around and hurried back to Randi and me. "I almost forgot," he whispered. "How did the test go? Is everyone going to be okay?" He was so full of concern, even at a time like this. My stomach knotted again.

Randi and I looked at each other. "Everything worked out fine," she told him.

"Really?"

"Yes. Don't even worry about it."

"Great!" he said. "Now we'll finally get recess back." He skipped off again, this time not stopping.

I couldn't move. I'd tried blaming Scott for what I did, and I now realized there was more wrong with that than what I actually did on those dumb CSAs.

GAVIN

Coach wasn't out and about in the community hall, so me and Magenta went to see if he was in his room again. I was anxious to find him, 'cause I'd brought him something different today.

How do you forget about a memory that keeps haunting you? How do the players who lose the Super Bowl move on? They focus on the next season to help take their mind off the hurt. They keep moving forward. Focusing on the surprise I had for Coach was helping me forget about those tests. Little did I know, I was in for a surprise of my own.

When we got farther down the hall, I started hearing something. It was a voice that I'd recognize anywhere. I glanced at Magenta and could tell she heard it, too. I was confused, but Magenta's expression was something different. We paused outside Coach's door and knocked.

Mrs. Woods stopped reading and looked up from her book. Her face did the same thing as Magenta's.

"Mrs. Woods, what're you doing here?" I said.

"School hasn't let me read aloud, Mr. Davids, so I've been coming here instead. Coach likes it."

"Keep reading!" Coach yelled.

I laughed. "He sounds like us," I said.

Today was the first time Woods had been given the okay to read aloud in class since it had been outlawed. Now that we had those stupid tests out of the way, she picked up *Holes* and started in right where we left off. When she tried stopping, everybody yelled at her to keep going. If you've never had something, then you don't know what you're missing. But if you get used to having something and it gets taken away, that's a different story. We were all so happy to have this part of our day back.

"What're you reading?" I asked her.

"Oh, just a few entries from my journal. Coach likes to hear about the old days."

"Keep reading!" Coach yelled again.

I laughed some more.

"We've got company," Woods informed him.

"I don't know those people. Keep reading!"

"I didn't realize your group was coming this afternoon," Woods said. I couldn't tell if she was sorry or bothered about us showing up.

"We haven't been allowed to visit because of the tests, so we rescheduled for today," Magenta explained. I couldn't tell if she was sorry or bothered about Woods being there. They weren't doing a good job of looking at each other. I guess people who usually talk with notes aren't good at the face-to-face stuff.

"Read!" Coach yelled.

I was ready for Woods to put the old man in his place, but she showed patience that I hadn't seen in the classroom. "Sorry, Coach. It's time for me to go." She patted his arm. "We'll continue this later. You have company."

"Who're they?" he barked.

Coach didn't scare me anymore. I walked over and placed my surprise gift on his table. "I brought this for you," I said. "It's a piece of sod from the fifty-yard line." (Really, it was from my backyard, but I'd played a lot of football on that grass, so I figured it was close enough.)

Coach picked up the shoe box I had placed the sod in and held it under his nose. The old man had all sorts of memory problems, but he knew exactly what he had in his hands. "Were there seagulls on our field, Valentine?"

"Seagulls?"

"Yes, seagulls. It's a sign of good luck when there are seagulls on your field before a big game."

I didn't remember ever seeing seagulls in my backyard, but I didn't tell him that—and this lie didn't bother me. "Lots of seagulls," I said.

"It's going to be a special one on Saturday," Coach said. He took a big whiff of the piece of field in his hand. "I can smell it. Thomson High is in trouble."

Mrs. Woods ruffled her fingers through my hair and left. I was gonna tell her about Coach's other memories, but she disappeared before I got the chance, and Magenta was already long gone. Usually she told me when she was leaving. She musta had something to do.

So me and Coach talked football for the rest of that afternoon. I decided I was gonna bring him to one of my games if

I got to play, but I didn't tell him that, 'cause I didn't want to let him down if things didn't work out. Maybe if there really were seagulls in my backyard, I'da been feeling lucky, but I had more experience with bad luck. A lot could happen between now and then.

SCOTT

My family stuck around and had dinner with Grandpa on his first night in the senior center, but he wasn't much for talking. Grandpa had the same look as when he was lost in thought, staring out his window. He'd been this way ever since the fire. Grandpa was still more sad than he was happy. So after we finished eating, I took him down to the community hall, because it was game night. I thought we could play a game of chess to make him feel better. When we got there, I introduced Grandpa to my friends Eleanor, Eddie, and Agnes.

"Welcome," Eleanor said. "We're happy to have you here."

"Happy," Eddie repeated.

"We're big fans of your grandson," Eleanor said.

"Eleanor's the one who washed my clothes and lent me something to wear," I told Grandpa.

He nodded.

"You let us know if you need anything," Eleanor added.

"Anything at all," Eddie said, batting her eyes.

Agnes whacked her in the arm.

"What?"

I chuckled. Grandpa was going to have his hands full—Eddie hoped with her.

"Who's that?" Grandpa asked, pointing to the table by the window.

"That's Coach," Agnes said. "He sits over there every game night and waits for someone to come along and play him in chess. The poor fella is losing his mind, but he can still play that game like nobody's business."

"Ladies," Grandpa said, nodding. He excused himself and went and sat down across from Coach. Then, without so much as a word, he reached out and moved his white pawn.

I was more happy than sad leaving the senior center that night, and I was hoping Grandpa would start to feel that way soon. It was a good place.

Trevor

Of all the people who deserved to have something bad happen in life, Scott was last on my list. The kid never did anything but try to help. Payback time was here. I got started by giving him a hand with moving his grandpa into the senior center—and that was only the beginning.

When we got back to school that day, I waited until everyone else was gone and then I asked Mrs. Magenta if I could talk to her. She was sitting at her computer. Mark was with me.

"Of course," she said. "What's on your mind?"

"I want to do something for Scott's grandpa," I said. "The guy lost everything he owned in that fire, so I was thinking we could do some sort of clothing or home stuff drive."

Mrs. Magenta stopped typing and looked at me. "Trevor, that is incredibly thoughtful and sweet. Your caring soul is shining. I'm so proud of you."

"Don't hug me," I said.

She chuckled.

"So can we?" I asked.

"Yes. Absolutely."

This project kept Mark and me after school for the next week—an additional bonus. We created a flyer that got sent home, advertising the drive and explaining the cause, and we got signs and boxes organized throughout the school. Woodchuck was right—when the work's important to you, you want to do it. And I'd have more important work to do before the end.

The drive was a mega success. Scott was so happy he didn't know what to say, but that was okay because he didn't need to say anything. I owed him.

SCOTT

Trevor and Mark organized this drive for Grandpa, and my whole school donated to it. Seeing all those boxes full of things was better than seeing presents under the Christmas tree. It made Mom cry.

Things were better after we got Grandpa settled. There was less for Mom to do now, so she wasn't as tired.

"Happy wife, happy life," Dad told me.

Funny how a bad thing can turn into a good thing.

And things were better in school, too. Mrs. Woods was back to reading aloud, and we had recess again!

GAVIN

The last book Woods finished, *Holes,* had curses and kids re-
volting and destiny (which had me missing Randi even more)
and rotten luck all mixed in. I thought that book had everything to do with us, but the next one Woods picked up gave
me the chills.

It was written by some person named Avi, and it was called
Nothing But the Truth. There was only one "b" in that title, but
it still scared the heck out of me. What did Mrs. Woods have
to go and pick that story for? Was every-
body else in my class wondering the same
thing? You coulda heard a pin drop when
she started reading those words.

Natalie Kurtsman
ASPIRING LAWYER
Kurtsman Law Offices

```
BRIEF #25
April: The Fat Lady
```

I had tricked my brain into believing our cheating wasn't bad. Rather, it was necessary. I mean, it was going to make everything better—for a lot of people. Yet, deep down, I knew if I ever landed in court because of this, my only defense would be temporary insanity. My lawyer would have to convince the jury that I was delusional, because there was simply no way cheating wasn't bad.

In the days and weeks following the test, we tried resuming a normal routine at Lake View Middle School, which included Mrs. Woods picking up with her read-alouds and the reinstatement of recess. I was more than happy to have the former back but could've done without the latter. I hadn't missed recess one iota, but the boys were crazy excited to have it in their lives again. Scott ran around the football field in a frenzy. I got Randi to play so she could be his personal protector. I convinced her she wasn't disobeying Coach Jane if she was looking out for Scott more than she was actually playing the game. What I didn't tell Randi was that I was also secretly hoping to see her and Gavin reconnect; the football field provided the best chance for that to happen. I didn't want to lose Randi, but someplace inside of me there was a soft spot growing for Gavin—despite the fact that I didn't like it.

I stood on the side each day, watching, waiting for something bad to happen, but it never did—not out there. On the contrary, many positives took place. To begin with, Trevor and Mark weren't the same big jerks anymore. Something had changed. Believe it or not, those two jokesters had gone ahead and got together with Mrs. Magenta and started a clothing and basic goods drive for Scott's grandpa. The drive was a huge success, but it was the way they started treating Scott on the field that was the biggest surprise: they were actually being cool with him—to put it in Trevor's language. It took a while, but those two had obviously realized that Scott was much more than just a dork. I had to give credit where credit was due. Trevor and Mark did have brains and hearts. I'm not saying they were big, but they were growing.

Eventually, just as I was hoping, Randi and Gavin wound up on the same team, and when that happened, they were unstoppable. Gavin had a way of knowing where Randi was going to be before she even got there. He'd throw the ball to an empty spot on the field, and Randi would arrive to catch it in the nick of time. It seemed like they could read each other's minds. I hoped they were telling each other sorry.

The two of them produced many highlights, but undoubtedly most exciting was the day of Scott's spectacular play. In reality, it was an accident. While running around and waving his arms in the air, Scott inadvertently knocked a pass to the ground. The boys went nuts whooping and cheering. I didn't understand, because I thought the idea was to catch the ball, but they were chanting about defense. Apparently Scott's play was awesome. I was confused. It wasn't like he scored a home run, but what did I care. It was a wonderful scene. I couldn't stop smiling.

This sounds absurd, but recess and this barbaric game of football became the thing I most looked forward to in my school day. Everyone and everything was coming together, and just in time for when we'd need it most, because, unfortunately, the fat lady—please excuse my rudeness—wasn't singing quite yet.

Randi

I felt Gav and me growing closer again with each touch-down pass, and as much as I wanted that, it wasn't making everything better. All I did was worry that our bulletproof plan was still going to backfire and what we had done was going to come out. But I only worried for me. I never thought about Mrs. Woods, or Natalie, or Scott, or my old best friend. Just me.

This was bigger than just me. More than my destiny alone was at stake.

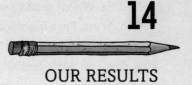

NATALIE KURTSMAN
ASPIRING LAWYER
Kurtsman Law Offices

BRIEF #26
May: Black Suits Arrive

The man and woman wearing black suits arrived on a Monday morning. I knew it wasn't good from the moment they set foot in our classroom, on account of two reasons. First, it was the color of their attire: people dress in black for funerals. Second, it was the way they wore their clothes: whereas Mr. Proctor's notoriously wrinkled shirts had refused to stay tucked over his doughnut belly and Miss Cohan's slips were longer than her skirts—such sloppiness that prevented us from taking them seriously—the man and woman in black were different. These people meant business. They wore their suits like lawyers.

Mr. Allen accompanied our surprise visitors, yet another sign that this was serious. Miss Jenkins, our lunch monitor, and Mrs. Magenta were also with him. So many people in our classroom all at once.

"Is Mrs. Woods getting an award?" Scott asked.

"No, Scott. I'm afraid not," Mr. Allen said. "We need Mrs. Woods to come with us so we can talk to her for a few minutes, that's all. Miss Jenkins will be staying with your class in the meantime."

"Are you with the FBI?" Scott asked the suits.

Their blank faces never changed.

"It's not nice to ignore people, especially when they ask you a question. Didn't your mothers teach you that?" Scott wasn't slowing down. "It's not nice to show up and never say hi, either."

"Scott, that's enough," Mr. Allen snapped. "These people aren't here to socialize." Turning to our teacher, Mr. Allen urged, "Mrs. Woods, please."

Mrs. Woods gathered her belongings and walked toward the door, followed by Mr. Allen and the man in black. I had the feeling she would be gone for longer than a few minutes. What happened next made me catch my breath. Mrs. Magenta reached out and touched Mrs. Woods on the shoulder when she came close. I watched them look at each other for the first time all year, and there was something different in both of their faces. It was a brief moment, and then Mrs. Woods left without saying a word or even passing a glance our way. My eyes welled with tears—and I'm not a crybaby.

The lady with the power slacks and power heels stepped forward. She dressed, walked, and acted like Mother did whenever she had someone on the stand. We were in trouble. It was time to toughen up. I wiped my eyes, and I saw Mrs. Magenta do the same.

"Good morning, ladies and gentlemen. My name is Ms.

Speer," the woman in black began. "I'm here to ask you a few questions about the CSAs you recently completed. We have reason to believe your tests were not administered correctly or—"

"Not more about those tests," Scott blurted. "I thought—"

"Scott," I snapped, cutting him off. "You heard Mr. Allen. That's enough. Be quiet and let Ms. Speer talk." I glared at him in a way that made it clear I wasn't fooling around. He knew I meant business—even without a suit.

"As I was saying," Ms. Speer continued, keeping her eye on Scott now. "We have reason to believe your tests were not administered correctly. There were none of the usual erasure marks on any of your answer sheets. On top of that, you all received perfect scores."

"Whoa! You guys did it without me! That's awesome!" Scott cheered.

"Shhh!" I hissed, warning him.

I watched his face turn from excitement to puzzlement. "But then why are you here?" he asked Ms. Speer.

"Because we find it hard to believe your class could achieve these results without someone supplying the answers—someone like Mrs. Woods, perhaps?"

She was fishing—and Scott took the bait. "You've got it all wrong," he explained. "Mrs. Woods wasn't going to give everyone the answers—I was! But I wasn't here, so—"

"Excuse me?" Ms. Speer interrupted.

"Scott, that's enough," I said, slapping my desktop and rising to my feet. The boy could help others, but he couldn't help himself. He had to be stopped. "You need to remain silent. Everything you say can and will be used against you in a court of law." I turned and faced Ms. Speer. "These are my clients," I said, gesturing to my classmates. "I will be representing them. You can ask me your questions, but you may not speak to anyone else until I've had a chance to meet with them in private. Have I been clear?"

Ms. Speer's eyebrows jumped. "What is your name, young lady?" she asked.

"Ms. Kurtsman," I said, looking her in the eye the way Mother had trained me to do. A good lawyer knows how to make a person on the stand squirm, how to melt a juror with just her gaze.

"Kurtsman? Why do I know that name?"

"My parents are accomplished lawyers. Let's go have a chat, shall we? Counselor to counselor."

My tactic worked. The lady in black saw she wasn't getting anywhere with the rest of my class. Their lips were sealed—even Scott's. She followed me out of the classroom.

Great! But now what?

I had no idea.

GAVIN

Talk about connecting with a book, like teachers were always harping about. The kid in *Nothing But the Truth* gets buried under a lie that snowballs out of his control, and he fails to do the one thing that can help his situation—tell the truth. No one is better off in the end.

Woods finished reading that story to us on a Monday morning, but we never got a chance to talk about it, 'cause in walked Mr. Allen, Magenta, and a couple other people looking for answers—for the truth!

I'm not gonna lie. I was scared. All of us were, except maybe Scott, 'cause he didn't know any better—and Kurtsman. If she was scared, she didn't show it. She went toe-to-toe with that dragon lady in black and lured her away with some fancy lawyer talk. We had one last shot at a Hail Mary pass before time ran out, and Kurtsman was our quarterback. But was she playing for our team or theirs? Was she trying to protect us or save her own skin? I still didn't trust her, but none of that mattered. Sooner or later I'd have to come clean with the guy in the glass.

Randi

At the bigger gymnastics competitions, you can feel the tension in the air, especially when the scores are close. You spend hours sitting on pins and needles. It's nerve-racking and exciting, but as soon as you learn you've lost, the feeling changes. Your body tingles with disappointment as that realization sinks in.

I'd experienced these emotions and sensations many times, but never were they as strong as when the suits showed up and took my teacher. My body tingled all over, but not with disappointment. My worst fears were coming true. What was going to happen when Jane found out? I'd dealt with her after tough losses, but this was going to be way worse. Not only was my transcript going to be ruined, but there'd be a big red flag on it for the rest of my life. I didn't need a psychic or crystal ball to see my future. I could kiss all those great colleges and scholarships goodbye. No one would ever want a cheat—including Jane.

Trevor

After Natalie left with that Ms. Speer woman, I looked over at my collage. My mean old farting teacher sketch was still hanging there. I got out of my seat and walked over and tore that picture and my collage off the wall.

Mrs. Woods was my teacher—and I liked her. She hadn't done anything wrong. We had.

NATALIE KURTSMAN
ASPIRING LAWYER
Kurtsman Law Offices

BRIEF #27
May: Affidavits

> "I swear to tell the truth, the whole truth,
> and nothing but the truth . . ."

This sentence is recited by every person who takes the stand, but that is not the only time or place it matters. It also counts when giving an affidavit. An affidavit is a written statement detailing the history of a certain event. Your statement is a sworn testimony, which means you give it under oath and sign your name to it. There are penalties for giving a false affidavit. For lying. That is called perjury. You can go to jail for perjury.

I should mention that you're never asked to give an affidavit for some wonderful occurrence. You're only asked to give your version of the story when something bad has transpired, when there is an investigation and your testimony is part of that investigation.

I explained all this to my classmates, and then we were

moved to separate locations to prepare our statements. It was time to do the right thing. But what about my friends? What if my story contradicted theirs? I had to believe they would do the right thing as well. This had gone on long enough.

I took all day to compose my affidavit. It began, "This is my sworn testimony. Everything hereafter is the truth, as best as I can remember it. . . ."

There was much to tell leading up to the tests, and I included everything. It was one of the bravest things I've ever done.

SCOTT

Here's how my statement went:

To the Mean People in Black Suits:

Natalie says an affidavit is you telling the truth about what happened. That no matter how scary or painful it is to tell the truth, that's what you've got to do, because if you're caught lying, you will be in big trouble. We're talking trouble with the police and maybe even time in the slammer.

I'll tell you the truth, because I want to help fix the mess I created. And I'll write it all down for you even though I don't write— ever. I hate writing. It's hard. But Mrs. Woods said I'd write when it was important to me, and this is important.

So here's what happened. And it's the truth. If I could swear it on my favorite dead dog's grave, I would (but I can't, because Mom never let me have a dog). So I'll swear it on my grandpa's old house, because that's important in this story. . . .

Trevor

These lawyer people were ready to pin the whole thing on Mrs. Woods unless they got answers. Not long ago I would've thought that was cool. But not now. Things had changed. I wasn't that same kid anymore. I couldn't let this go down. I had to do something. I had to tell them something.

I never mentioned Natalie's name or anyone else's, and I didn't say anything about being a mistake, but I told them why I cheated. I told them all about Brian and his goons. I wrote it all down.

GAVIN

And the truth . . .

Randi

. . . shall set you free.

15

CONSEQUENCES

Randi

Mr. Allen contacted our parents to tell them about our cheating scandal. He told our moms and dads that he'd be holding a meeting in the near future, at which time he would answer questions and share more information. After making those calls, he stopped by our classroom.

"I don't know how all your parents will handle this news," he said. "I want you to be prepared when you get home."

I was definitely not prepared. I was scared. I steadied myself, expecting to find the worst Jane I'd ever seen, but she didn't say one word about it. She never brought it up. Not on that day or any day. This wasn't the silent treatment—we'd been there and done that. If anything, Jane was talking to me more, just not about the big stuff. We were beginning to have conversations during our car rides to and from gymnastics, but we managed to talk without saying anything important.

"How was school?" It was nice to have her asking me that, but I never gave her much for an answer.

"It was good."

"That's nice. I was thinking of making grilled chicken salads for dinner tonight."

"Okay."

"Have a good workout."

"Okay."

We needed to practice talking to each other like I needed to practice gymnastics. This was how things went until the night before Mr. Allen's special meeting. We'd barely gotten back from the gym when I walked into the kitchen to get a drink. Jane had picked up the mail and was reading a letter. She had her back to me, so she didn't know I was there. I stood silently, waiting until she finished. I watched the letter fall to the ground, her hands cover her face, and her body begin to rock and shake in sobs.

"Are you all right?" I rushed over to her.

She threw her arms around me and squeezed.

"Mom?" I barely whispered.

She squeezed harder, and then she let go and ran up the stairs.

I picked the letter up off the floor and looked at it. It was a copy of my affidavit, the one where I wrote about the suffocating pressure I felt at home, and how it was because of Jane that I made an unconscionable decision. Everything I'd ever wanted to say but never had was written in my statement—and Jane had just read it all. I wasn't relieved. I felt dizzy and sick to my stomach.

I threw my letter in the trash and walked back upstairs. Jane was locked in her room. I wanted to knock on her door, but I didn't.

She was still locked in there when I left for school the next day.

GAVIN

They told Woods to take a break while they did their investigating. That made me sick, 'cause she had nothing to do with any of this mess. It didn't look good for her, though, 'cause of that argument she'd had with Mr. Allen. So we got stuck with a sub covering our class, sorta like a backup QB who's thrown in at the end of a game 'cause his team is getting blown away. It's a toss-up who gets sacked more, backup QBs or substitute teachers, but we took it easy on our sub this time around. We were already in enough trouble. How much? We were about to find out.

My old man decided to attend Mr. Allen's special meeting. He'd never gone to a school event of mine before—he was usually working, and this wasn't his sorta thing—but tonight was different. This was a big deal. Even Mrs. Woods showed up, and I wasn't sure she was supposed to be there. I hoped that meant they were done with their investigation and had decided she was innocent.

I sat next to Dad, staring at the cafeteria floor, thinking

that this was probably the first time most of these people had seen my old man, the high school dropout plumber guy sitting in the middle of all these fancy clothes and college degrees. I was relieved when Mr. Allen finally got things started. At least then I knew all those eyes were on him and not us.

"Good evening," Mr. Allen said. "Thank you for coming tonight. Thank you for your patience and understanding while we conducted our investigation and collected information. We had plenty to sort through."

It's hard to listen when your brain won't slow down. I kept replaying it all—the tests, cheating, the suits showing up, my interview, everything—over and over in my head. What I did. What I shoulda done. What I shoulda said. It was all on continuous replay. I was a coach analyzing where his team had gone wrong. If I coulda taken it back, I woulda, but this was real life, not some fairy tale. I heard Mr. Allen when he first started talking, but then I didn't hear another word—not until someone different spoke.

"Mr. Allen," Dad said, rising from his chair. "My name's Mike Davids. I'm Gavin's father. I was hopin' to share a few thoughts."

"The floor is yours," Mr. Allen said.

What in the world was my old man gonna say? Didn't he realize he was surrounded by smarter people than him?

"I agree, our children did somethin' terribly wrong, and for that there needs to be a consequence. But I also believe they did somethin' important. They got us here talkin' about what needs to be talked about. We should all be askin' ourselves who's really at fault in all of this. Do we mean it when we say give us your best and we'll be happy?

"The people behind these all-important CSAs don't ask for effort grades, Mr. Allen. They don't care if everyone is tryin' their best, perseverin', and improvin'. They're only interested in one score, and judgin' any kid or teacher or school on one test score is wrong. Plain and simple. So our kids gave them what they wanted. What we as parents wanted. What you wanted.

"Readin' didn't come easy for me, and it hasn't come easy for Gavin. There are plenty of things I can teach my son, but readin' isn't one of them. I still don't read all that well, and his mother, who isn't from this country, can't read much English, but Gavin hasn't given up."

Why did he have to say that about Mom? What were all these people thinking of her now? So what if she couldn't read much English? I bet Randi woulda taken my mother over her own.

"Gavin's struggled, but he's kept workin'," my old man went on. "And now he's made readin' a part of our house for the first time by sharin' books with his little sister every night. This has happened because of Mrs. Woods and because of Mrs. Magenta's amazin' after-school program—not the CSAs.

"Mr. Allen, I read my son's affidavit, and I can't even begin to tell you how proud I am of him. It takes an honest person and a strong person to admit when he's made a mistake. It's not an easy thing to do, especially when the truth hurts, but our children have spoken, and now we need to listen. I hope the people behind these tests and the rest of us can admit where we've gone wrong, too, and start makin' changes."

My old man finished his piece and sat back down. No one said a word. The cafeteria was silent. He'd given these people something to think about. Then Mrs. Kurtsman got to her feet and started clapping, and soon everyone else joined in. The room filled with applause. I saw Mrs. Woods smiling at her former student, but I didn't see anything after that. I had to wipe my eyes.

My father isn't a nobody. He's a leader. He's the smartest man I know. . . . I hope I can be like him someday.

SCOTT

"I hope your principal can give us some answers tonight," Dad said. We were getting ready for the special meeting. Dad had been upset ever since Mom first told him about Mr. Allen's phone call. "Someone's to blame for this, and I'd like to know who."

I had the answers but I was too scared to tell him and he didn't bother to ask. I wasn't in school to take the CSAs when everyone else did. I took the make-up exams on my own, so Dad didn't think I had anything to do with the cheating. He should've known by now that I was the best at making messes, not avoiding them.

"Good evening, gentlemen," Mrs. Woods said to Dad and me when we walked into the cafeteria.

I smiled. I was glad to see my teacher. Dad nodded.

"I thought you'd like to see this," Mrs. Woods said. She handed my father a stapled packet.

"What's this?" he said.

"Your son's written statement."

"His what?"

"They mailed the others, but I asked Mr. Allen to hang on to Scott's so that I could be the one to give it to you. I know you'll be pleased. I'm very proud of him."

"You wrote this?" Dad asked, turning to me.

I nodded.

When he flipped through the pages, there was no hiding his surprise. Dad's wide eyes and raised eyebrows gave him away. "You wrote all this?!"

"It was important to him," Mrs. Woods said, winking at me. I winked back.

Dad and I found a place to sit, and he began reading. I worried he was going to get upset with me the more he read, because I did all truth-telling in my affidavit like Natalie told me I needed to. But before Dad got done, Mr. Allen started the meeting, and before Mr. Allen finished, Gavin's father stood up and said a bunch of smart stuff that made everyone clap.

That was when Dad leaned closer and wrapped his arm around my shoulders and gave me a firm squeeze. "What you did was wrong, you know that?" he said.

I gulped and nodded.

"But if the world had more hearts like yours in it, we'd be a much better place. I love you, son. I'm proud of you."

I didn't think I could feel any better, but then Mr. Allen finished things off in the best way possible.

"Again, I'd like to thank all of you for coming tonight," he said. "Within the next few weeks I should learn what penalties have been given to Lake View Middle School. I'll share that information as soon as it becomes available.

"As for our students, it is up to me to find an appropriate

consequence, and we all agree that there needs to be a consequence. I've thought long and hard about this and have decided to mandate enrollment in Mrs. Magenta's program starting this summer and continuing throughout the next school year. I realize this might mean canceled trips, vacations, and camps for some of you, and I apologize for that, but this was no small wrongdoing, so that warrants a response that is both meaningful and of significance."

I had to hold my breath to keep from cheering. Others may have been upset, but I wasn't. This meant I got to spend my summer with my friends. Mr. Allen winked at me, and I gave him two thumbs-up and a big smile. He had a deal!

NATALIE KURTSMAN
ASPIRING LAWYER
Kurtsman Law Offices

BRIEF #28
May: What?!

Mother was speed-walking across the parking lot, and I hadn't
a clue why, but I did my best to keep up with her. It reminded
me of that time when I left Scott in the dust on our way to the
office all those months ago. Boy, how things change.

"Mike," Mother called. "Mike!"

Gavin's father stopped and turned around. So did Gavin.
We caught up to them.

"Hi, Gloria," Gavin's father said.

"What you said in there," Mother started, "it was . . . You're
a special man, Mike."

"You're not so bad yourself."

The two of them stepped closer and hugged. What?! Gavin
and I looked at each other, searching for an answer. There
was no glaring or staring, only shock and bewilderment on
our faces. Did we miss something? What just happened? Our

two parents let go and stepped back. I noted the disgusted expression Gavin wore now.

"Good night," Mother said.

"Good night, Gloria."

They went their way and we went ours. It all happened so fast. I was simply dumbfounded. Clearly Mother had more to tell me when we got in the car, so I hoped she was prepared to do some explaining.

GAVIN

All it took was one hug in the parking lot, and I went from thinking my old man was the best to thinking he was an idiot. I climbed in our truck and slammed the door behind me.

"How can you hug that woman after what she did?"

"Because you don't know the whole story," he said, turning the key and starting the engine.

"What do you mean, I don't know the whole story? She's the dirtbag lawyer who pulled all her fancy tricks in court so you got stuck paying all the medical bills and everything else for some rich guy who was really at fault."

Dad eased out of the parking lot and pulled onto the road. "Like I said, you don't know the whole story."

"Then tell me what I don't know. I betcha I still wouldn't be hugging that woman."

"What if I told you that earlier this year, about a week before you came to your mother and me to ask about Mrs. Magenta's after-school program, Gloria Kurtsman tracked me down. She'd had a chance run-in with that rich client of hers, and he couldn't keep his trap shut. He had to brag about how he'd fooled everyone—includin' her. Gloria didn't need to do anythin', but she did. After learnin' the truth, she couldn't sit back and let it go. She said she wished there was a way to take the case back to court and get it reversed, but it'd be impossible to prove the truth after all these years. So she did the best she could. She paid off all the damages and took the money she had earned from the case and gave that to us."

"Mrs. Kurtsman did that?"

"Yup. I tried tellin' her we didn't want the money, but she insisted. She said it was the only way she'd ever feel better about what had happened." Dad slowed and turned onto our road. "How did you think your mother woulda been able to quit her bartendin' job?"

"I didn't know."

"I probably shoulda told you. It's time I start treatin' you like a man."

I was quiet.

"Think you can handle that?" he asked.

"Yes."

"Oh yeah? Why?"

"Because I know being a man has nothing to do with being tough or how much money you make. But it has everything to do with the guy in the glass. You gotta be able to look him in the eye at the end of the day."

Dad pulled in our driveway and parked the truck. "I don't care what those tests say, Gavin. You're a smart kid and a good person."

"I've had the best teacher," I said. And I wasn't talking about Mrs. Woods or anyone else from school.

Trevor

When we got home from Mr. Allen's meeting, Mom and Dad spent time talking alone. They had a lot to discuss after reading my affidavit. It had come in the mail yesterday, but they didn't get around to checking the pile of letters until just before the meeting. I didn't think they'd ever see it, but now the cat was out of the bag. When they got done talking, they came and found me in my room. Mom sat on my bed.

"Trevor, we want you to know things will be different from now on," Dad said. "We didn't know this was happening."

"We're sorry." That was all Mom managed to say, because she burst into tears.

Dad put his arm around her. "We're proud of you, Trev."

Dad and I didn't have much experience with these heartfelt moments, so that's where it ended. He nodded and I nodded, and then he helped Mom stand and leave.

That was the end of their talk with me, but they had a long

sit-down with my brother when he came home from work early the next morning. I know because they were still talking to him when I left for school—and my affidavit was sitting in the middle of the table.

Randi

Jane and I left Mr. Allen's special meeting and drove home, neither one of us saying a word. It takes a while to digest food, but sometimes it can take even longer to digest the truth. I left her alone. I'd had plenty of practice knowing when to do that.

I guess she just needed to sleep on it, because the next morning at breakfast Jane sat down across from me and started talking. "I'm so glad I put you in Mrs. Magenta's program, even though I did it for all the wrong reasons. You needed your friends and a caring teacher around you, because I've been doing a terrible job as your mother."

"It's—"

"No, let me finish," she said, cutting me off. "I'll be forever grateful that Mrs. Woods came into our lives and had the courage to tell me what I didn't want to hear. She was right. I was that person focused only on scores and results. I've been missing out on what's most important . . . even though it's been right in front of my nose. I've been trying to change, but I was too late. The damage was already done. Randi, I'm just as much to blame for what happened with those tests as you are. I'm so sorry, honey."

I swallowed.

Mom reached across the table and took my hand. "Things will be different from now on," she said. "I promise. You're my Destiny, but your destiny can be whatever you want it to be."

16

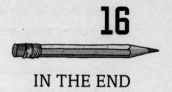

IN THE END

NATALIE KURTSMAN
ASPIRING LAWYER
Kurtsman Law Offices

BRIEF #29
June: The Verdict

A summary of the verdict

We, the defendants, were found guilty of major wrongdoing—twenty-five counts of cheating, to be exact. One for each person in our class. The judge sentenced us to mandatory enrollment in Mrs. Magenta's program starting this summer.

We, the defendants, also had to attend a series of Saturday-morning seminars on the perils of plagiarism and cheating. At the culmination of the seminars, we had to write a paper of reflection, discussing what we learned about what we'd done and about ourselves.

I'm pleased to report that after an extensive interrogation process, Mrs. Woods was found *not* guilty and was allowed to return to our classroom. She was no accomplice of ours (though I did wonder how the woman who missed nothing had missed this).

Lake View Middle School was not let off the hook. The CSAs are not going away. For the next three years our institution will need to follow special testing procedures, which include the implementation of a series of action steps and the presence of several black suits during exam days.

Case Closed.

Not really. Even though this was behind us, that didn't mean it was over. Our story made national news, which I found disheartening. All the good we'd done before this scandal wasn't worthy of even our local newspaper, but our wrongdoing became a major story. Headlines read: CHEATING SINKS STUDENTS AT LAKE VIEW MIDDLE SCHOOL; CHEATING SCANDAL ON ASSESSMENTS; WIN IF YOU CAN, LOSE IF YOU MUST, BUT ALWAYS CHEAT—ESPECIALLY ON THE CSAS. I was quite upset with the media, until I recognized the potential upside. Is it possible that our wrongdoing will prompt other school communities to reevaluate their philosophy and approach to high-stakes testing? Will the words Gavin's father spoke make any difference? I like to hope so. Time will tell.

GAVIN

I had talked to Magenta ahead of time, sorta like a coach talks with his assistants before the big game. There was something I wanted to do, and I needed her help pulling it off.

Today was not one of our normal after-school meetings. Earlier in the week Magenta asked me, Randi, Scott, Kurtsman, Trevor, and Mark if we could stick around this afternoon to give her a hand—all part of my plan. When we got to the art room, she told us she was hoping we could help her tidy up the children's room at the library—it had been a busy place ever since our makeover and party.

"Sure," we said.

"Mrs. Magenta," Kurtsman piped up, "is that your painting?" She pointed to the back of the room, where there was a picture I'd never seen before.

"Yes."

"It's beautiful."

"Thank you, Natalie. I put a lot of time into that piece. I've decided to enter it in an art show this summer."

"You'll win," Scott announced, like it was automatic. "Your stuff belongs in a museum."

Magenta looked at me and Randi, and we smiled. "Good luck," Randi told her.

"Thank you," Magenta said, "for the well wishes and for encouraging me."

Me and Randi smiled some more—and then we looked at each other. There was so much I wanted to tell her, but we skipped right past the talking part and went straight to a hug that said everything that needed saying. We were still good at reading each other's minds. We could talk and fill in the blanks later, when we were passing the football again.

I caught a glimpse of Kurtsman out of the corner of my eye. She was standing on her tippy-toes and silently clapping. The girl isn't that bad.

"We better get going now," Magenta said.

This was my first trip back to the public library since our project there, so besides what I had planned, I was also looking forward to getting some new books. I had my special library bag with me, the one that made me look ridiculous, and I didn't care.

"Gavin, how did you know to bring your stuff with you?" Kurtsman asked. The girl didn't miss anything.

"Whaddaya mean? That's his favorite bag," Trevor joked.

"Dude brings it with him everywhere," Mark added.

I shoved both of them, like buddies do, not like before.

"I mentioned it to him when we were at the senior center last," Magenta said, covering for me. "I thought of it because Coach likes it when Gavin reads to him. I meant to tell the rest of you, but then I got sidetracked and forgot. I'm sorry."

"No worries," Randi said.

That was a perfect lie Magenta came up with, 'cause I was planning on getting a few books to read to Coach. Woods had told Magenta to get me some poems, 'cause Coach liked poems and they'd be good practice for my reading.

"Okay, Recruits," Magenta said when we reached the children's room. "The first area I need cleaned up is the community room."

"What's in there?" Scott asked.

"A mess, but you'll have to go and see. There might also be a surprise."

"Cookies?"

"Maybe."

Scott took off like a bullet, with the rest of our group chasing after him. I stayed behind. Magenta gave me a hand finding some new books. I got a couple different collections of poems for Coach, three new audiobooks and the real books to go along with them, plus a pile of new stories for Meggie, and then Magenta told me she had a picture book that I had to take home to read to my sister. I followed her to the area for "C" last names.

"This one's my favorite," Magenta said, pulling *Miss Rumphius* off the shelf. It didn't have any "b's" or "d's" in the title, so that was a good start.

"What's it about?" I asked her.

"A woman who has a dear relationship with her father and, at his request, makes the world a more beautiful place before she dies."

"How does she do that?"

"She spreads flowers," Magenta said, and smiled. "Miss Rumphius loves flowers, as I do."

She gestured to the wall where me and her had added our artwork. I saw them then. There were flowers hidden in all her pictures. I hadn't noticed that before. She had a small one tucked in a girl's hair, another on a different kid's T-shirt, bunches scattered on a hillside, everywhere and anywhere. They were quiet enough that you could miss them if you weren't paying attention, but they made her pictures special. My favorite was the way she always put a flower in her name. It made it tricky to read, but once you knew that was her trademark, it didn't matter. Her paintings reminded me of others I'd seen, but I couldn't remember where.

"Meggie's gonna love the book," I said. "Thanks."

"You're welcome."

I got all my stuff checked out, and then it was time for the rest of my plan.

"Sorry, Gavin," Kurtsman said. "You took too long. Scott ate all the cookies. He couldn't help himself."

"Did not," Scott said. "Trevor and Mark ate a bunch, too, but I saved you one." He pulled a snickerdoodle out of his pocket and held it out for me.

"It's okay," I said. "I'm all set. You can have it."

He didn't even hesitate. Scott inhaled the cookie and wiped his hands on his shirt. "Fanks," he said, crumbs falling out of his mouth.

We laughed. It felt good to laugh with Randi again. "Any time," I said. "Now follow me." I put my library bag off to the side. Then I grabbed what I needed from the art supplies and walked over to the throw rug.

"Gav, what're you doing?" Randi asked.

I pulled back the rug, revealing Scott's name and our yellow splat. I handed the brush to Randi. I didn't have to say anything. She knelt down and added her name next to Scott's. When she finished, she passed the brush to Trevor. Then it was Mark's turn, and then Kurtsman's. I was last to go. I took the brush.

"Kurtsman," I said. "I was wrong about you. I'm sorry."

She looked me dead in the eye. She was the best at that. "It's okay," she said. "I'm glad things have worked out between us."

"Me too."

We didn't hug or anything like that—one step at a time. I was still a football player, and she was still Natalie Kurtsman. We smiled and shook hands, and then I turned my focus to the yellow splat. With my best artistic touch, I added my name and I printed the words THE RECRUITS along the top. We were a team.

That ugly yellow splat looked much better now.

Randi

Gav made it official when he had us add our names to the yellow splat. Destiny had brought us together. The final pieces began falling into place the next day at recess.

It started out the same as every other football game. Natalie stood on the side. Even after she signed her name, I still couldn't get her to play. Gavin was the quarterback on my team, while Trevor QB'd for the other. Scott ran around like a wild man. Nothing had changed.

It was on our third or fourth possession that Gavin dropped back to pass. I ran a deep post across the field and had all the boys beat. We'd connected on this pass a hundred times in his backyard. It was a sure touchdown, but he didn't throw it to me. Scott was left standing wide open in the middle. Gav tossed a soft spiral to him and everything froze. The wind stopped blowing, the birds stopped singing, and we stopped running. We stood motionless, holding our breaths, pleading with the universe for a miracle. Then the stars aligned and the ball landed in Scott's hands.

"Run!" Gavin yelled.

"Run!" I yelled.

"Run!" Natalie screamed.

Scott ran. That was one thing he'd been good at for a long time. He took off and everyone chased him. He made it to the end zone and tried his best to spike the football, but it bounced off his knee instead. It didn't matter. Every kid playing, whether on his team or not, clamored and jumped around, slapping him on the back. Then Trevor and Mark hoisted him onto their shoulders, and we paraded around the field cheering for our hero. That recess was something I won't ever forget.

"I did it!" Scott yelled.

"You did it!" Natalie shouted. "Home run!"

I love that girl.

The stars stayed aligned for the rest of the day, because later that night I had my best practice of the year. I stumbled on my first dismount, but when I looked over at the window, Mom gave me a smile and two thumbs up. After that I nailed my bars routine and stuck every single one of my landings— and I had fun.

On our way home Mom asked me, "Randi, do you still want to go to States?"

"Are you serious?!"

"Yes. You don't have to go for me."

"Mom, we've been training for this all year. Of course I want to go. I'm not going to back out now. I just had my best practice of the year!"

"Okay," she said. "I just wanted to make sure, because there are some other people who are looking forward to watching you compete."

"Other people? Who?"

"Your friends. Mrs. Kurtsman will be bringing Natalie and Scott and Gavin."

"Really?!"

"Yes. It was Gavin's idea. By the way, you can hang out with that boy as much as you'd like. I was wrong when I said those things about his family, just as I was wrong about a lot of things. You even have my permission to marry him."

"Mom!"

"Just saying."

I couldn't remember the last time Mom and I had laughed together after a gymnastics practice, but that drive home was the best car ride we'd shared in a long time. I forgot all about looking for the white house. I didn't need a psychic or crystal ball anymore. I was in charge of my destiny.

I hoped the stars stayed aligned, but even if States didn't go well, I knew it would still be okay. Mom would be proud of me either way, and my friends would be there for me. Coach Jane was gone.

Mom and I were a couple of new metamorphic rocks. Things had changed, and we had re-formed.

SCOTT

When I hopped in the car after school, the first thing Mom said was "What do you say we get some ice cream?"

"Ice cream!" Mickey yelled in the back. "Ice cream!" He liked his treats as much as me.

"We can swing by the senior center and pick up Grandpa first."

"That's a great idea," I said. Even though Mom didn't need to do everything for Grandpa anymore, we still tried to visit him every afternoon.

When we got to the senior center, Agnes and Eddie were out and about. "You'll find him in Coach's room," Eddie said. "I still haven't figured out how to get him into mine."

Agnes elbowed her friend, and Mickey started laughing. He liked these two old women, and they had taken a liking to him.

"Scott, can you go and find Grandpa while Mickey and I stay here with Agnes and Eddie?" Mom asked.

"It's room 214," Agnes said.

"Okay. Be right back." I turned and ran down the hall.

I didn't have any trouble finding 214. The door was open, so I let myself in. I said hello but no one answered, and that was because Grandpa and Coach were in the midst of another chess match. They had found their equal in each other, so they didn't play only on game night.

"Who's winning?" I said.

"Who're you?" Coach yelled, making me jump.

"That's my grandson," Grandpa answered. "Come here, Scott."

I'd already met Coach, but that's how things worked with him.

"Is he going to read to us?" Coach asked.

"I'm here to get my grandpa," I said, walking over to them. "We're taking him to get ice cream."

"Scott, this is Coach. Coach, this here is my grandson, Scott. Smartest kid I ever met," Grandpa said, introducing us once again.

"Are you going to read to us?" Coach asked.

"No," Grandpa said. "He's here to pick me up. Your wife will be here soon. She'll read to you from her journal."

"What about our game?"

"It's halftime," Grandpa said.

That was smart, because it was the perfect explanation for Coach. He understood.

"It's my friend Gavin who reads to you sometimes," I said. "Not me."

"Valentine's a good reader," Coach said.

"I'll tell him you said that." Gavin had told me how Coach called him that name. "He got a book of poems from the library that he plans to share with you this summer."

"I like poems," Coach said. "That's my favorite one over there." He pointed to the wall behind me.

I turned and looked, but it wasn't the poem that grabbed my attention. "Who's Olivia?" I asked, reading the name that was at the bottom of all those paintings he had hanging.

"My daughter," Coach said. "See how she hides flowers in all her pictures and always puts one in her name."

"Yeah," I said, looking closer.

"She loves flowers," Coach said. "When she was little, we used to love the picture book about a girl who makes the world a better place by spreading lupines."

"*Miss Rumphius*," I said.

"That's right."

"I know that book. It smells good." Grandpa and Coach thought that was funny, but it was true. "Your daughter is an amazing artist," I said.

"I'll tell her you said that."

Grandpa snorted. "C'mon, Scott. Let's go get that ice cream."

"See you later, Coach," I said.

"Thanks for the warning," he replied.

I had to think about that for a second, but Grandpa and Coach were already laughing their heads off. Seeing and hearing those two cracking up together got me laughing with them. It made me happy to see Grandpa happy. And that made me feel even better because I had helped.

"You know something?" Grandpa said after we'd made it down the hall a ways. "This place isn't so bad. I've made some friends, and I've still got Grandma with me. Miss my house and my cat, that's all."

"Mom's working on getting things changed so you can have Smoky here," I said.

"That'd be nice. Gotta have my cat. He saved my life."

"I hope you never lose Grandma like Coach is losing his memories," I said.

"Me too," Grandpa said, rubbing the back of my neck and giving me a squeeze.

Mom and Mickey were waiting for us when we got to the front. "Ice cream!" Mickey yelled. "Ice cream!" He was jumping up and down.

"I'm coming as fast as these old legs will carry me," Grandpa said.

"Ice cream!"

"Bye, boys," Eddie called from the side. "Have fun." She waved at us.

We waved back and walked out the door. Once we got outside, Grandpa said, "I think she's got the hots for me."

"Dad!" Mom cried.

"They've all got the hots for you, Grandpa. Dad says you could have dinner with a different lady each night if you wanted."

"Scott, don't encourage him," Mom said, and laughed.

We got to the car, and I jumped into the backseat with Mickey so Grandpa could ride shotgun. Mom eased out of the parking lot, and we were on our way.

I'll always remember sixth grade. It was the year of my biggest mess-up and my greatest accomplishments. Things were lost (like my permission slip and Grandpa's house), but a lot was gained. We added a cat to the family, I caught my first touchdown pass, Grandpa had friends (and girlfriends), and I had friends (but no girlfriend). I was so excited to start Mrs. Magenta's program again. It was going to be another unforgettable year with the Recruits.

Trevor

The U-Haul was packed. Dad had found my brother an apartment and was moving him out. It was time for Brian to grow up and stand on his own two feet. Dad was done babying him.

I didn't know what to say to my brother, so I stayed away. I stood by my bedroom window and watched my mother hug him and then go wait next to my father. I watched my brother climb into the U-Haul and back out of our driveway.

Brian looked at me right before driving down the road. We saw each other, and then he was gone.

When Mark came over later that day, I told him I was feeling bad about everything that had happened with Brian.

"Trev, you needed to tell. You know that. You did your brother a favor. Besides, I wrote stuff about him and you in my affidavit. I was always scared to tell anyone. I didn't want to make things worse for you. And I didn't want you to get mad at me. But when I had to write my statement, I knew being your friend meant telling. It's not all on you."

"Do you think things will be better now?"

"Here or at school?"

"Both," I said.

"It'll be quiet here, but that won't matter, because we're going to be spending all our time at practice and games."

"The school isn't going to make the tests part of our eligibility, then?"

"Not now," Mark said. "My dad says we got the board to listen and rethink their policies."

"I know making us join Mrs. Magenta's program is supposed to be our punishment, but it's not going to be that bad. I'm kind of looking forward to it."

"Me too," Mark said.

Natalie Kurtsman
Aspiring Lawyer
Kurtsman Law Offices

BRIEF #30
June: Reflection

Would I do it all again? It's hard to say. I wouldn't ever advise cheating, but if I were in the same exact predicament, I have a sneaking suspicion the answer might be yes. Sometimes we do the wrong things for the right reasons. It's not always black-and-white. It's tough when your brain and heart don't seem to agree. But I've found it's easier to change your mind than your heart. You should follow your heart, because a good heart makes a good person, whereas a good brain can still make a bad person. The Recruits all have good hearts—that's what makes us special.

Epilogue

NATALIE KURTSMAN
ASPIRING LAWYER
Kurtsman Law Offices

BRIEF #31
June: A Birthday Surprise

You can choose to have any sort of birthday party, but I would argue the best kind is the one you don't plan. The one you don't know about. The surprise birthday party.

We had it at Randi's house. We arrived early to help with the preparations. Trevor and Mark took care of decorating the place with streamers and signs, while Gavin and I got things set up for our party games. We filled water balloons, hung a piñata, and erected a badminton net. Randi and her mother worked on the food. They baked these monstrous cupcakes covered in extra frosting. Those absolutely needed to be kept hidden, because once Scott saw them, he was going to lose all control.

It's hard to explain how incredibly excited we were. We were giving Scott the party he'd always wanted. We were granting *his* wish this time. We had it all worked out so that his mother would bring him at one o'clock. She was going to make it seem like she needed to stop by to get something from Randi's mother.

As Gavin would say, we executed our game plan and scored a touchdown. Things went off without a hitch. It was textbook. When Scott walked in and we yelled, "Surprise!" his body shook with excitement. It took him a second to gather himself, but once he did, he was jumping up and down and squealing. His mother, on the other hand, was quietly sobbing. Seeing that made my throat tighten.

It wasn't only his arrival that went well, but the entire party. The games, the piñata, the food—all of it. After Scott had stuffed his face with three cupcakes, we decided it was time to give him his gifts. It was at this point in the festivities that we found out we were the ones in for the biggest surprise of all.

Scott ripped the paper away from his first present. "I know you love reading," Gavin said, "so I got you a book. The character in this story, Miss Rumphius, spreads goodness to the rest of the world. It made me think of you."

"Aww," Trevor teased.

"I know this book," Scott said. "It's your friend Coach's favorite, too. He told me when I was over there to get Grandpa. He used to read it with his daughter."

"Wait. What?" Gavin said.

"Coach used to read this book with his daughter when she was little. His daughter loves flowers like Miss Rumphius. She sticks them in all her paintings. He has a couple of her pictures hanging in his room."

Gavin shook his head. "I can't believe it. I can't believe it!"

"Whoa. Relax, bro," Trevor said.

"What is it, Gav?" Randi asked.

He sat back and stared at us. "Guys, Mrs. Magenta is Coach's daughter. And I'm pretty sure Mrs. Woods is his wife."

"What?!" we all exclaimed.

Gavin repeated what he had told us. "Which also means Mrs. Woods is Mrs. Magenta's mother," he added.

I now understood the expression "hit me like a ton of bricks."

Gavin explained everything: from what Mrs. Magenta had said when she first gave him *Miss Rumphius* in the library, to her paintings, to the way she knew so much about Coach and cared for him, to his discovery of Mrs. Woods reading to Coach from her journal so that he might remember. It all made sense, especially when we thought back to the way Mrs. Magenta and Mrs. Woods had behaved this year. Still, it was hard to believe. But when Gavin told us what Coach had said about there still being time on the clock for his wife and daughter, we knew there was something else we wanted to fix—and this time it was something far more important than our test scores. We were thinking of others before ourselves, just as Mrs. Woods had written in our Classroom Doctrine.

Wasn't it interesting how our year together had brought us to this point? Randi would say it was destiny—and I might agree.

ACKNOWLEDGMENTS

My deepest thanks to:

The many players making up the Random House Children's Books team, for bringing *The Perfect Score* to life and for continuing to cheer me on.

Marilyn Burns, for her book *About Teaching Mathematics,* from which Mrs. Magenta's King Arthur problem was adapted.

Rebecca Weston, who believed in this story from its earliest days. Your patience, encouragement, and insights were invaluable to me. It was a pleasure.

Françoise Bui, for helping me reach the finish line.

Leslie Mechanic, for her persistence and care in making the terrific illustrations. Gavin loves them!

My agent, Paul Fedorko, who's always there when I need him.

Beverly Horowitz, who has been with me every step of the way, from the very beginning. I couldn't ask for a better person to be in my corner.

My family. Writing a book is a roller-coaster ride. There are highs and lows. It can go fast and it can go slow. You might even get flipped upside-down and yanked backward. Lucky for me, my family loves roller coasters. Thank you, Emma, Lily, and Anya, for always being ready for more. I wouldn't choose to go on the ride with anyone else. And thank you, Beth, for always making sure I'm okay along the way and especially after the ride is over. I love you all.

Turn the page for a preview of

THE PERFECT SECRET

AUTHOR OF THE MR. TERUPT SERIES

ROB BUYEA

In this sequel to **THE PERFECT SCORE**, the same loveable kids are back, only now they're in seventh grade and in for a year of secrets, discoveries, and kid power!

NATALIE KURTSMAN
ASPIRING LAWYER
Kurtsman Law Offices

BRIEF #1
July: My Goals

Now that school was out, I needed goals for the summer; I'm a goal-oriented person. Here's the good news: I had my first one.

GOALS

- Resolve the strained relationship between
  Mrs. Woods and Mrs. Magenta.

Writing your goals down makes them real. That's something every expert will tell you. It helps you internalize them. Now, I know what you're thinking. This wasn't just *my* goal; it was something all the Recruits wanted. You're right. But it was up to me to lead the way. For one, I'm the smartest. (Just stating the facts.) And for two, the rest of the Recruits had other things to worry about, other endeavors occupying their time.

Randi had Regionals after her stellar state meet, Gavin had football, Scott had his Grandpa, and Trevor and Mark . . . I wasn't certain. Yes, they had changed considerably, but not enough for me to believe that mending relationships had become their top priority. They weren't the next Dr. Phils. So, as you can see, this was up to me. It was my main goal.

Now to the business at hand. I realize you can't make people like each other any more than you can make two people fall in love, but the more you get two people together, the better the chances. Thus, our strategy was born. We had to get Mrs. Woods and Mrs. Magenta together as much as possible, and then, hopefully, they would slowly begin talking. First about the small stuff, ultimately about the big stuff—the hard stuff.

Admittedly, this was a big task. A huge challenge. So huge that all on its own this task could fulfill my requirements for a worthwhile goal. But there was something else that had been on my mind ever since school had ended—before that, actually—and I couldn't seem to shake it. I hadn't decided yet; I hadn't written it down and made it official, but my heart was telling me to go for it.

I wondered, though, *If I do, will I be overstepping my boundaries?*

A PACT IS MADE

NATALIE KURTSMAN
ASPIRING LAWYER
Kurtsman Law Offices

BRIEF #2
Mid-July: Mrs. Magenta's Program Resumes

In years past I didn't see many of the kids from school over the summer, but thanks to Mr. Allen that was not going to be the case this year. In fact, it was the first day of Mrs. Magenta's summer program, so our class from sixth grade was all together again.

It's safe to say we broke more than a few rules when we cheated on the CSAs last spring, but the consequence Mr. Allen handed down wasn't anything I'd consider bad. Rather, the word I would use to describe our consequence would be "constructive."

"Hello, and happy summer to all you caring souls," Mrs. Magenta began.

"Mrs. Magenta, are you—"

"Scott!" I snapped. "Quiet," I hissed through gritted teeth.

"That's all right, Natalie. Am I what, Scott?"

I caught my breath. This was it. Our plan was doomed already, and we hadn't even gotten started. It was my fault. I'd neglected to add a very important goal to my list: Keep Scott quiet!

We'd gone over this at his birthday party. We weren't going to let Mrs. Magenta and Mrs. Woods know that we were onto them. Our attempts at getting them together would be better masked if they thought we didn't know about their relationship or their history, if they believed our actions were innocent as opposed to manipulative. But impulsive Scott was about to let the cat out of the bag already. *Here it comes,* I thought. I could hear him now, *Are you Mrs. Woods's daughter?*

Scott cleared his throat. "Are you"—he looked at me and then back at Mrs. Magenta—"a fan of ice cream?"

I exhaled. Thank goodness.

Mrs. Magenta smiled. "Yes, I love ice cream. A little cookies and cream with peanut butter topping is my favorite."

Eww. I grimaced.

"I like cookie dough best," Scott said.

"That's a good flavor, but now let me ask all of you a question," Mrs. Magenta said. "We will be returning to the Senior Center this afternoon, but I'm wondering if any of you would object to our continuing with trips to visit our old friends for our community service when school starts up again."

No hands were raised. If they had been, I would've been on my feet in an instant, yelling, *Objection!* But none of my colleagues were opposed, and that was good, because getting Mrs. Magenta and Mrs. Woods together was going to be much easier to accomplish at the Senior Center than anywhere else.

"Wonderful," Mrs. Magenta said. "I was hoping not. You see, our work at the Senior Center will never really be done. Our friends there will always welcome our company."

"Maybe we can do something more for them, or for the place, like we did at the public library?" Trevor said.

My eyebrows lifted. *How thoughtful—and sincere. Where is this coming from?* I wondered.

"Do you have any suggestions?" Mrs. Magenta asked.

"No. It's just . . . I've been trying to keep my mind . . . It's just an idea that popped into my head, that's all."

"Well, it's a delightful thought," Mrs. Magenta said. "Let's all think about it while we're there this afternoon and see if we can come up with any projects."

"It's a really good idea, Trevor," Scott said, "like the one you had about collecting stuff for my grandpa after his house burned down."

I was in complete agreement. I'd heard that boys change during adolescence, but ever since the CSAs, Trevor had shown what one might call a complete turnaround. It was actually quite astonishing, but I was not to be distracted. Let me be clear: the best aspect of Trevor's proposal was the fact that it had the potential to give everyone else something to do so I could focus on mending a certain mother-daughter relationship.

"Our bus is here," Mrs. Magenta announced.

I reviewed the day's plan in my head. There were three objectives: (1) observe carefully, especially the two parties involved, and especially when together, (2) collect more information, and (3) get Mrs. Magenta and Mrs. Woods together.

"I'm excited to see Agnes and Eddie," Randi said after we took our seats on the bus.

"Me too," I said. Objective number four: spend time visiting with Agnes and Eddie.

The bus pulled out of the school lot, setting my plan in motion.

GOALS

- Resolve the strained relationship between Mrs. Woods and Mrs. Magenta.
- Keep our plan secret, which requires keeping Scott and the rest of the Recruits quiet—but mainly Scott.

GAVIN

I took my seat on the bus, and Scott slid in next to me. This was it. We were off to the Senior Center. "I hope Coach remembers me," I said.

"He will," Scott promised, making it sound like a no-brainer. "Junior was telling him about Valentine and his tire target last week."

"Who's Junior?"

"I am!" Scott squealed. "Coach gave me a nickname, too!"

I shook my head and laughed. It was just like Scott to get wound up over a nickname. "Well, Junior, even though I wasn't sure if we'd get to visit today, I came prepared." I patted my bag. "I have a special memory surprise for Coach and a couple of different poetry books, in case he wants me to read to him."

"What's the surprise?"

"Can't tell you. You'll have to wait and see." Scott scowled. I also had *Clifford's Manners*, but I didn't bother trying to explain that to him.

A few minutes later our bus stopped outside the front entrance. "We're here!" Scott cried. "Let's go!"

The kid's enthusiasm was contagious. That was one of the things I liked most about him. He had all of us excited. We bounded off the bus.

It had been a while since we'd last visited as a group, but Director Ruggelli was cool and didn't hold us up with any big reintroduction. All she said was, "Welcome back. Your friends are eager to see you."

We followed her into the Community Hall, where we were greeted by lots of smiles and waves. I smiled and waved back, but after a quick glance around the place, I saw that Coach wasn't there. Scott had told me his grandpa and Coach had become best buds and that more than likely we'd find them playing a game of chess in Coach's room, so that was where we headed.

"Told you," Scott whispered when we got there and peeked inside.

"Your grandpa gets to keep Smoky here now?" I asked him after spotting the gray cat on his grandfather's lap.

"Yup. My mom took care of that."

"Nice."

"Ready?" he asked.

I didn't answer. I couldn't help it. I was nervous. *What if Coach doesn't remember me? Is this how Woods and Magenta feel every day?*

"Don't worry," Scott said. "Coach knows who you are. And if he doesn't, we'll remind him."

I swallowed. "Okay. Let's go."

In we went, the brave one—Scott—followed by the

chicken—me. That wasn't how things were supposed to be for a football player, but that was how it was. Scott was our Most Valuable Player.

"Scott!" his grandpa hollered, looking up from his game.

"Hi, Grandpa. Hi, Coach."

"Hello there, Valentine," Grandpa said. "Nice to see you again."

Scott's grandfather knew my real name. Was he just trying to help Coach remember me? I sure appreciated that. "Hello, sir," I said. "It's good to be back." I looked at Coach. "Hey, Coach."

Coach's eyes narrowed on me. Did he remember? I wasn't taking any chances. I put my bag down and reached inside. Once I found what I was looking for, I straightened, took a deep breath, walked over, and handed my surprise to him. Scott's trick of using memory objects to help Coach out mighta been his all-time most brilliant idea.

Coach turned the kicking tee over in his hands. He held it up and studied it. "You've got to be ready for anything, Valentine, and we will be. You can count on that," he promised. He was just beginning to pick up steam. "We're going to catch Thomson High sleeping. We're going to start the game with an onside kick."

Coach got out of his chair and started pacing the room, gesturing with his hands and getting into it as he spoke. "We'll line up normal and then shift left when our kicker moves toward the ball. They won't have time to react. One high bounce, and the ball will be ours!" he shouted. Coach swung his arm low as he got near the chessboard, sending pieces flying across the room.

"Nice one," Grandpa ribbed.

"Ah, be quiet," Coach said. "You were losing anyway. I did you a favor."

"You brought a Clifford book!" Scott cried.

He'd gone in my bag when I wasn't looking. "Never mind," I said, grabbing the book from him. "My sister musta put that in there without me knowing."

"Read it," Coach said, sitting back down in his chair.

"You want him to read Clifford?" Scott asked.

"If Valentine's sister wanted me to hear it, it must be good."

"C'mon, Scott," Grandpa said, walking to the door. "Let's give Valentine and Coach time to visit. I need your help with Smoky's litter box."

After hearing that, I think Scott woulda preferred listening to me read Clifford, but he didn't have a choice. "Okay," he grumbled.

I started reading. It didn't take long before I got to that terrible sentence, and when I did, I stopped. I didn't know what to do.

"What'd you stop for?" Coach barked. "Keep reading."

"I can't."

"Why?"

"The next sentence bothers me."

"Bothers you? Let me hear it."

I swallowed. "'He smiles when he loses,'" I read.

"You don't like that?" Coach asked.

"No," I mumbled. Suddenly it felt silly.

"Me neither!" Coach hollered. "Sportsmanship is important, Valentine, but people today are confused about it. Somewhere along the line that award stopped going to winners, and now it's only ever handed out to the teams that are good at losing. Bunch of baloney, if you ask me."

I loved Coach! I knew he'd hate that sentence.

"I'm not saying sportsmanship doesn't matter, Valentine. It does. You want to be humble in victory and gracious in defeat. But make no mistake about it, if you've worked hard and given your all, then losing hurts. Bad. I hate losing more than I love winning. But, Valentine, it's how we carry ourselves in defeat, how we rise after failure, that tells it all. Because that's when character is revealed."

I needed to think about Coach's words, so I didn't say anything right away, and Coach let me be quiet. He knew I'd say something when I was ready.

"I've been working hard," I said. "My dad helped me hang a tire in our backyard, so now I have a target for practice."

"The good old-fashioned tire, huh? That has helped train many of the great ones. How do you use it?"

I told Coach what I'd been doing, and then he explained a couple of other drills that I could add.

"You know what I like about you, Valentine? You're coachable. You know when to listen. Now grab another book and do some more reading."

Football talk was over, but that was okay 'cause Coach had

given me plenty to think about. I grabbed my Kwame Alexander book. I was rapping out one of his poems when Mrs. Magenta showed up a bit later.

"Hi, boys. How's it going?" she asked. I watched her walk over and place her hand on Coach's shoulder. I held my breath, hoping for Coach to remember her, but he didn't say anything.

"It's going good," I said.

"Well, I'm afraid it's time for us to go. I'll meet you out front." She patted Coach's shoulder and left, but not before I saw the sadness in her eyes.

I packed my things and said goodbye, but Coach didn't say anything. He sat there with a blank face. I wondered where he was, 'cause it sure wasn't there in the room with me. Seeing him glossed-over like that scared me. And it got me thinking. Even though Coach had agreed with me, Randi was right, I was being ridiculous. How could I get all worked up over a silly sentence when Coach was struggling with losing something way more important than any football game? Like I told you, I still had a lot to learn about losing.

Randi

Natalie and I walked over to the table where Agnes and Eddie were seated.

"Hello, ladies," Natalie said. "It's nice to see you again."

"Ha!" Eddie scoffed. "'Ladies'! Did you hear that, Agnes? She called us 'ladies.'"

I'd missed these two. I was already giggling, and I hadn't even sat down yet.

"Must you always be so formal, Miss Natalie?" Agnes asked.

"Natalie's always serious," I said.

"That scowl face of yours is going to give you wrinkles worse than mine," Agnes warned.

"What she needs is a boyfriend," Eddie remarked. "Playing a little kissy face would give her something to smile about, and then those scowl lines would disappear."

"Edna!" Agnes snapped. "For heaven's sake, the girls just got here and you're already starting in on them. Behave yourself, or they won't want to visit anymore."

I didn't say anything, because I didn't want to cross Agnes, but Eddie's naughtiness was one of the things I liked best about visiting. I wouldn't have been surprised to hear Natalie admit the same thing.

"Well," Natalie said. "I don't know much about playing kissy face, but I did bring a new game for us to try. Dominoes."

"Oh, I like that one," Agnes said.

"Whoever loses needs to kiss a boy," Eddie teased.

I tried holding it in, but my laughter escaped.

"Don't encourage her," Agnes said, glaring at me.

I bit the insides of my cheeks, but then Eddie made a face, mocking Agnes, and the laughter came out again. At least this time Natalie was laughing with me. Poor Agnes just shook her head, which made us laugh harder.

We dumped the dominoes onto the table and got them flipped facedown. Then we picked out our bricks and got started. Dominoes is a good game because you can continue visiting and having conversation when it isn't your turn. Eddie and Agnes filled us in on all the gossip at the Senior Center, which took more than a while, and then Natalie told them all about my state meet and upcoming Regionals.

"That's quite the accomplishment, Miss Randi," Agnes said.

"Thank you."

"When I was your age, I was pretty good at hopscotch and jumping rope," Eddie said, "but my favorite thing to play was kissy face."

"Ugh!" Agnes groaned. "You never stop."

I was laughing again, but Natalie wasn't. Not this time. She'd done a lot of talking, but she wasn't listening. Her mind was elsewhere.

"Heavens, child, who or what do you keep looking for?" Agnes asked. She'd noticed how Natalie kept glancing around the hall.

"Cute boys, of course," Eddie couldn't help but blurt out. I was beginning to think loose lips was something she and Scott had something in common.

"Hush!" Agnes scolded. "That's enough." She turned back to Natalie. "How about it, Miss Kurtsman? Who're you searching for?"

Natalie sighed. "Our old teacher, Mrs. Woods," she said.

"You won't see Pearl here now," Agnes said.

"She's never here the same time as her daughter," Eddie added.

Our heads jerked. Natalie and I stared at each other, wide-eyed. "Wait. You know about them and Coach?" Natalie asked.

"We might be old, but we're not off our rockers yet," Eddie said. "We know everything that's going on around this joint. How else are we supposed to run the place?"

"Must be that you girls didn't know," Agnes said. "Otherwise you wouldn't be so surprised."

"We just learned," I said.

"And we need to keep that a secret," Natalie urged. "We can't let them know that we know, so please don't tell."

"You're up to something," Eddie said. "I like it."

"Please don't tell," Natalie pleaded.

"Eddie's right, you're up to something," Agnes said. "I need to know what it is before I make you any promises."

Natalie looked at me again, but all I could do was shrug. What choice did we have? We had to let them in on our plan.

"We intend to fix their broken relationship," Natalie explained.

"When pigs fly," Eddie scoffed.

"What's that supposed to mean?!" Natalie shot back, her voice rising.

"Listen, I know all about getting the boys to love you," Eddie said, "but making those two women like each other again is going to take more than shaking hips and batting eyelashes. You're going to need a miracle."

"Time for us to get going," Mrs. Magenta announced from the front of the room. "Start to wrap things up."

"You girls are playing with fire," Agnes warned. "You shouldn't get involved in their feud. There's more to it than you know."

"We'll tread lightly," Natalie said, "which is why they can't know we're onto them. Will you keep our secret?"

Now Agnes sighed. "I'm not sure I like it . . . but we'll keep your secret—for now."

"And if we see anything that might help you, we'll let you know," Eddie added, leaning forward. "We'll be your insiders, working as your informants. How fun."

"Sometimes you can be such a kid," Agnes said.

"That's what keeps me young. You won't let me get a man, so I've got to do something."

"Ugh!" Agnes groaned and rolled her eyes, but that wasn't enough to get Natalie and me laughing or even cracking a smile now.

We said goodbye and made our way out to the bus. Natalie was feeling discouraged. It was clear this wasn't going to be easy, and we didn't need a crystal ball to see that. But the thing I couldn't shake was what Agnes had said. "There's more to it than you know."

Come to find out, there was more than I knew about a lot of things. Seventh grade was a year of secrets and discoveries.

Seven kids.

Seven voices.

One special teacher

who brings them together.

ROB BUYEA'S beloved

mr. terupt series

Delacorte
Press